THE BIG WAVE

© 2019 Christian Sarti (www.christiansarti.com)

Second Revised Edition February 2019

Bibliographical Information of the Deutsche Nationalbibliothek. This publication is listed in the Deutsche Nationalbibliographie of the Deutsche Nationalbibliothek; detailed bibliographical information can be accessed under http://dnb.d-nb.de

© 2019

Printing, Production and Layout: BoD – Books on Demand
ISBN: 978-3-7494-0992-1

Cover and backside pictures Adobe Stock licenses
"Goddess, Gaia mother earth" © Patrick Hermans
"planet earth in space" © Denis Tabler

THE BIG WAVE

Christian Sarti

Chapter One

The sand was coarse and rough under my naked feet. I could feel it getting warm with the morning sun. After more than ten years I was back on the beach where it all happened.

My flight from Paris had arrived in Chennai very early that day. As I stood there, I finally saw 'The Beach' for what it really was, an ordinary beach in Tamil Nadu, buzzing with life.

Since the big tsunami wave had washed away my life, the inner movie of those events had played in my mind in endless loops.

Brightly painted fishing boats were being pushed into the water by slender, dark-skinned men. The rich musky air of India was thick with morning fires and engine fumes. Sounds from the sea and birds were competing with the noises of human activity.

'I love India. It's such a crazy place,' the thought came like an old reminiscence.

'What am I doing here?'

The fresh morning air carried sounds of hammers on wooden planks. People were repairing boats and building sheds on the upper side of the beach. As I started to walk towards the water, the memories of what had happened more than a decade ago marched back, like an unstoppable army, inexorably taking control of what my eyes were seeing.

The sight of a smiling chai vendor with his pots and heaters sitting on a heap of stones was suddenly overlaid by vivid images of shattered boats, piles of broken wood tangled with lifeless human bodies.

This flow of images threw me back into a hostile parallel reality. I closed my eyes, but it did not shut off the visions. My heart was pounding in my ears, and I could not breathe. Death and destruction were all around. I saw the lifeless eyes of a young girl staring at me through the rubble. The earth shook violently under my feet. I heard horrible roaring sounds, as a dark mountain of water erupted and advanced in a fury.

The monster wave swallowed me into her dark body filled with millions of broken forms, making me one of them. I was wildly tumbled around, as I collided with hard and sharp debris all around me. I desperately tried to surface, but was inexorably drawn deeper into the hellish soup. Then something big collided with my head and I was rescued by nothingness.

The next thing I remember was a sweet smell, voices, people talking.

'This is curious,' I thought, as I had no clue what had just happened nor was I aware of where I was. Then it all

came back in a flash: India! The big tsunami! I blinked my eyes open and saw only a blur of light and colors.

"Where are my children!", I screamed, overwhelmed by raw panic.

As my vision cleared, I saw a dark-haired woman bending over me. She took my hand, and I got another whiff of sweetness. *'Patchouli?'* My mind recognized the scent and found its way back to the reality of the beach.

"Sir, can I help you?" the woman asked.

"I don't know."

"What happened to you?"

"The wave... my family... I can never forgive myself!..." My voice trailed off as I took in my surroundings and saw where I was sitting. The woman's eyes had a particular green color and looked friendly. I pushed myself up on my elbows, and she helped me into a sitting position.

My ears were ringing loudly, and the morning light was too bright. The beach seemed to wobble around me like a boat in a storm. I was like a shipwrecked sailor, feeling sick and disoriented. Then I saw the crowd that had gathered around me.

I felt the soft touch of a hand between my shoulder blades. The woman smiled. It was the first time I saw what she looked like. Long eyelashes adorned her green almond shaped eyes. I was mesmerized by the kind intensity in her eyes. Her face was only a few centimeters from mine. Some of her long, dark and slightly curling hair was touching my cheek. Her skin was a light tone of amber.

"Can you stand up?" she asked in perfect English.

"I guess," I answered weakly.

She reached out and helped me to my feet. Her hand felt warm and soft.

"Thank you."

"You're welcome," she said, a bright smile lighting up her face.

The people, who had been standing by, curious about what had happened to that westerner were losing interest, and soon I was alone with the woman. She stood silently next to me until we had to move away from the path of a red and blue fishing boat manhandled towards the water by a group of men.

The water was rising rapidly into the beach. As we walked, I got a full view of her, and saw that she was beautiful. Her dark hair was flowing naturally around her face. What struck me most, were her intense sparkling eyes, full of life and kindness. I felt instinctively drawn to her.

When she looked at me inquiringly, I stammered, "Thank you for your help! I'm feeling better now."

I wasn't sure, whether this was true. Searching for a way to relate to her I asked, "What are you doing here on the beach?"

A smile flickered across the woman's face.

"Enjoying the morning sun, and being at the right place at the right time."

Something about the way she had pronounced those words made me ask, "Do I know you?"

The woman looked at me in a strange way, as if she

was about to say something. But then she only asked, "What happened to you?"

I took a deep breath. "What you saw was because of a sad old story, and I fear, that I'm still caught up in it."

"If you feel like it, you can tell me the story. My name is Alma," she said.

"Mine is Luke." I awkwardly shook her hand.

I felt uncomfortable remaining on the beach, that was getting busier by the minute. As I looked around, I saw a small food stall up near the road.

Pointing towards that place I asked hesitantly, "Would you like to have breakfast with me?"

"Yes, thank you, I'd like that," she replied.

I felt relief, sitting in the little shed-like place, away from the busy beach. A woman in a cluttered corner was cooking on a stove made of clay. A friendly teenage boy took our orders of tea, tomato omelet and masala dosa, a local specialty. After drinking some bottled water, we both remained silent. I was grateful for the break, as I still felt like a shipwrecked man having just reached land.

"I'm happy to listen if you want to tell me your story," she said after a while.

I did not know what to say and took a long time to gather my thoughts. Getting lost in my memories and not knowing how to start, I uttered, "I would also like to hear about you. Where do you come from, and what are you doing here?"

"You first!" she said with conviction and an engaging smile.

"Well, I don't know. I lost my wife and kids here, more than ten years ago. Though I'm still physically alive I feel dead most of the time. Like living in a no man's land from which I find no way out. It took me all those years to manage to come back to this place. Doesn't that sound crazy?"

"No," she said, her eyes boring deeper into mine.

"My life is empty. I lost so much time, trying to find my way back. I had a life and a family before. I was sure of my world, of who I was... I lost it all..."

As she kept her unwavering gaze on me, I continued, "I had dreams, projects, goals. Now I do not even know what that means."

"What kind of dreams did you have?" she asked.

"I barely remember. Maybe dreams about traveling the world... having a summer house... spending more time with my kids...," a wave of pain poured from my guts, strangled my voice.

"I guess if I can feel pain, I'm still alive..." I croaked, wiping my wet eyes.

A young boy carrying steaming pots served our breakfast. He poured the food on big banana tree leaves which were laid down in front of us. We ate in silence, using our right hand in the Indian way.

Savoring the food as best I could, I was trying to make some sense of what was happening.

'Who was this woman who had magically appeared straight into my empty life?'

She already felt incredibly present and real. My fainting

on the beach, and the subsequent contact with her had brought me back to some 'normal' reality. The dreadful visions had ceased to plague me. I felt my inner chill soften with the warmth of the spicy meal and the woman's presence.

"Please tell me something about you," I said tentatively.

As she leaned back into her seat, I admired her graceful movements and enjoyed the soft patchouli fragrance emanating from her.

"Well, in a nutshell it's this: Ten years ago, I was working for a British help organization that was here to assist western tourists after the big tsunami hit the Indian coast. They sent me as I'm native from the region. Right now I'm here to visit my family, and like you, I felt drawn to return to this place. Lots of people have come back, in an attempt to work through their trauma and pain. I have talked to many individuals as I am a psychologist."

I instantly felt a knot in my chest, as her words threw me back to the endless therapeutic sessions I had to endure.

Sensing my mood swing, she said, "My contract ended years ago, today I'm here privately, not as a psychologist."

"I'm sorry," I said, my voice getting hoarse, "I have grown weary of psychologists and psychiatrists…, I was in a really bad shape, and they put me through an intense program, which was very challenging."

"Did it help?"

"I guess, otherwise I probably would not be here today, but still in Paris, living a secluded life."

Alma stood up. "Why don't we go for a walk? she suggested.

Then she added, "My life has changed a lot since that time, and I'm not practicing as a psychologist anymore."

As we went out of the hut the sun had risen high and the moist air was already very hot.

Seeing the woman walk with me, it struck me that she was the first person in all those years who had touched my heart beyond the walls I had built around it. Something new had found its way in, and it felt both delightful and scary.

"I enjoyed that breakfast with you," I said, looking at her shyly.

As a response, she smiled again. Her smile made her whole face shine, and it felt like a fresh shower in the rising heat.

We walked towards another part of the beach. There were mostly women and children left on the beach. They were cleaning containers and repairing nets. The typical smell of the fishery utensils floated in the light breeze coming from the sea. Most boats were already far out, on their way to the horizon line, where they would soon drop out of sight.

"Why do you feel so familiar when I'm sure I've never seen you before?" I said, more to myself than to the beautiful woman who walked at my side.

Not waiting for an answer, I continued in a low voice. "Maybe it's because I felt so lost before I met you. You are very kind to me. Being here hurts…"

"You also look familiar," she said, pausing for a moment, then continued, "but it's not from the past, maybe it's from the future?"

I felt an inner vertigo hearing her words. They rang true, and I left them hanging in my mind that had gone blank.

We continued to walk, zigzagging around people and boats, towards a calmer part of the shore. The woman's caring presence by my side was slowly filling my empty world.

We reached an area of the beach, where rocks and big boulders seemed to grow out of the sand. I remembered the place. There were kids running, shouting; some of them pulled self-made kites.

The hot, humid air was heavy, despite the proximity of the water. The coarse sand ground noisily under my feet. As I watched the kids running and playing, my wounded mind went back in time, and I saw my two little girls running just like that. A red hot searing pain pierced my chest, and it hurt like hell.

As the remaining walls around my heart crumbled, I felt the woman as she took my hand and put her arm around my shoulders. Her touch and warm presence gave the final blow to the cracking walls, releasing an unstoppable torrent of tears. She held me as the dam broke, a tsunami of grief poured out, submerging everything.

I barely remember what followed; a rickshaw ride to my hotel, worried faces. The woman supporting me, talking. The tsunami rolled away, letting me feel smaller waves, less scary ones, strangely sweet and bitter; waves of the grief, guilt for still being alive, for having been unable to save my wife Simone, and my two little girls,

Noémie and Camille. I felt their loving presence, the life we had shared.

As I opened my eyes, I saw the woman sitting next to the bed on which I was lying. Who was she? The woman smiled. I remembered her name, Alma! The colors of her sari appeared to be alive, dancing in the rays of the afternoon sun falling in through the room's small window. But what made my head spin was her delicious perfume. I felt I could get drunk on it.

"Welcome back," she said, "how are you feeling?"

She was bending over me, her long hair touching my arm. I could see all the details of her amber skin. I looked into her green eyes, and my heart exploded towards this woman I had met only a few hours ago.

"I love you, you are the most beautiful being I've ever seen." The words had come out without the usual mental censoring.

She smiled, but some seriousness entered her eyes.

"So, you are feeling better!"

I felt vulnerable, and did not know what to say.

She sat next to me on the bed. I rested my head against her, loosing myself in her fragrance and her warm presence, and I gradually slid into a deep sleep.

I woke up from the buzzing of my phone. I felt disoriented, at first not knowing where I was. I switched off the alarm and saw it was four in the morning. I remembered setting it in the plane, before arriving in Chennai.

The room was dimly lit by the golden light of a candle, but there was no trace of Alma.

'Has this all been a dream?' I wondered. But Alma's rich perfume still lingered in the room. I eagerly breathed it in, but then a sense of dread filled me at the thought, that I might never see her again.

Despite the early hour, I put on fresh clothes and went outside, hoping to see her somewhere. It was a typical Indian shopping street. Big colorful signs written in alien looking Tamil characters were advertising small shops and food places. Many of them were tiny, their narrow front side squeezed into the spaces between bigger constructions. Most of the shops had their painted blinders still down. A few street lamps, looking old and worn, diffused a dim light. I shivered and closed the jacket around my neck.

An early cycle rickshaw squeaked by in unison with the rumbling of my hungry stomach. I realized that I had not eaten anything since my breakfast with Alma the previous morning. I looked around, but could not see any food or tea vendors, nor any trace of Alma. So, I continued to walk, enjoying the fresh morning breeze.

Suddenly I heard a faraway voice calling my name, and turned to see Alma waving from down the street.

"I went out to get us some food. I'm glad I did not miss you!" she said happily as we reached each other.

I was overjoyed to see her radiant face. Part of me was surprised to see her there, in flesh and blood. She had not been a fantasy after all!

"Look what I have!" she said, waving a green cotton bag.

"Let's go and sit in that park," she said, pointing down

the street. It was a small square patch of dry lawn with a few sad looking shrubs and a couple of palm trees. We sat down on a bench behind a leafy bush. Alma unpacked the richly smelling food and we ate in silence. It was heavenly delicious and spicy.

I looked at her, grinning happily.

The first rays of the rapidly rising sun lighted Alma's face. Everything was intensely present in these early morning rays of light.

"Alma, are you real? You feel like you come from a different world."

"That's an intriguing thought, Luke, who knows, maybe you're right," she said, a mischievous look on her face."

"Why did you stay with me? I don't understand. You are an unusual Indian woman…"

"Do you always need to understand?"

"I guess not, as long as you do not vanish in a big puff of smoke."

She laughed. "I'm as real as you; what makes you think otherwise?"

"There's something unusual emanating from you, something I have never felt before. And you are very beautiful…"

"Come on…" she said, giving me a friendly punch in the ribs, "let's move a bit."

She took my hand, and led me across the street. The town had finally woken up. The street was rapidly filling with people on bikes, scooters, rickshaws, cars and all sorts of man- or animal-pulled vehicles.

A big bus came roaring and honking into the already crammed street, spreading a cloud of dark fumes and dust in its tracks. It looked like the driver had no intention of slowing down the clunky bus, expecting all other vehicles and people to magically move out of its path; which amazingly they did, some of them by the tiniest of margins.

"One has to be completely nuts to drive here," I said, looking at the noisy chaos left in the bus's trail.

"Or one has to think differently and have no fear," Alma replied, the corners of her mouth twitching slightly.

"I call that insanity," I insisted stubbornly, covering my nose against the smoke and dust.

Without a further reply Alma turned into a small sidestreet. Happy to leave the noise and dust behind, I followed her down the narrow alley. The sun was rising above the houses. We had to move out of the way of a pushcart that appeared from an alley; two men hidden behind a thick load of long fabric rolls were pushing it wherever it could pass.

"Where are we going?" I asked trying to keep level with Alma in the crowded street.

"There's an interesting place with temples near the river, not far from here. Let's go there!"

"Sounds good to me," I said, relaxing, surrendering to the present and its unfolding events.

We continued our walk through the intensifying activities of the streets. It was like a flowing dance around changing obstacles, who themselves were caught in the same process of moving around each other. Even after having been in India and other Asian countries before, I was still dazed by the sheer sensory overload.

As we left the streets behind, the land was beginning to slope towards the banks of a river. There was a herd of water buffaloes lazily moving about on the shore. They were huge animals with enormous pointy horns.

When we reached the river, I walked toward the mighty animals. I wanted to have a closer look at them.

"Be careful, they can be unpredictable towards strangers!" Alma said, pulling me away.

"Hey, I think I can take care of myself, and it's not the first time I'm in India!" I said, a little more irritably than I had intended.

She took my hand, and held it in a firm grip. "I'm sorry if I have hurt your feelings. Those buffaloes can be dangerous."

"No need to be sorry," I said, "I reacted stupidly, and I do love your care… it's just… I'm quite confused, and I don't know what's happening to me, nor what I'm going to do with my life."

Alma gently pulled me away from the grazing buffaloes, and said, "I also have had challenging times, years ago, and it led me to an entirely new world."

"What kind of world did you find?" I asked.

"A world where people are happy and wise, where everything is connected, abundant and in tune with the true nature of life."

"Wow! That sounds great, but isn't that a utopia we are very far from?"

She took both my hands, her gaze intense, as if she was sizing me up. "That world exists, and I have the feeling you are going to find it."

I was not sure what she had meant by finding that world, but her words touched my heart and left me with a new inner warmth.

We followed the river out of town for a while, passing women washing clothes on the shore. At that moment, that particular reality, a South Indian town, a woman named Alma, a river, was all I had. I was like a child again, fresh to the world. There was this intensity and immediacy of reality.

We went by several temples bordering the shore, but did not stop. We continued our walk towards an area from which swirling, dense smoke was rising. It was packed with people.

"These are the local cremation grounds," she said, holding my hand firmly, "it's the place where the bodies of people who have died are burned on wood pyres next to the water."

We passed a procession of chanting men carrying a body wrapped in a white cloth. Nearby, flames and a dark funnel of smoke were rising from a pyre. The whole area had a very particular smell of burned wood and spices mixed with musky sweet odors that were undoubtedly related to the burning of bodies. It was surreal, but to my surprise, I felt at ease, as something sacred emanated from the place.

A family was putting a corpse on a pyre that had been prepared near the water. They were around twenty men of different generations, their hair color ranging from deep shiny black to brilliant white. They opened the shroud, exposing the face of the dead. Then each man went around the body, putting ointments on it and sprinkling the face with water. I was mesmerized by the scene. Alma took my hand, and instantly I felt a flow of warm energy.

I caught sight of a man observing us from his place next to one of the pyres. He was a naked sadhu, one of those ancient holy men of India who want to transcend all attachments as well as their own physical body.

The burning of the fires was reflected in the sadhu's eyes. His matted hair came down in long unruly dreadlocks. His brown body was smeared with ashes, a reminder to what it would become. He was sitting cross-legged in a meditative posture, but all about him felt fierce and wild. Ashes were still smoldering next to him. I could distinguish the remains of a skull and a leg bone.

I was intimidated by the scene and all the more shocked as Alma pulled me along towards the sadhu. Before I realized, we were standing in front of him.

Alma folded her hands and bowed her head.

"Namaste."

He silently returned the greeting and made a gesture for us to sit in front of him.

Alma did so without hesitation, lowering herself to the dusty ground in one gracious movement. I remained standing and looked at the flowing river in front of me. I tried to take a deep breath, but the air was thick with heavy fumes and smells. Finally, I reluctantly sat down.

My unease increased as the sadhu's gaze bore right onto me. As a protection, I instinctively closed my eyes. I could still sense the sadhu's presence, but it shifted from something threatening, to a powerful inner presence I could clearly feel. I gradually relaxed, and the inner chatting and turmoil of my mind faded into silence. A wide inner space opened up, that I had never felt before. Then something else shifted in my awareness.

I felt as if I had risen from the ground, until I hovered above the sadhu. My instinct was to try and hold on to something, but my body did not move. I was seeing the sadhu very distinctly, several meters beneath. In front of him, Alma was sitting crosslegged. Then I saw the man next to Alma. His eyes were closed. It was me. But I, the observer, was so much more, in that vast, vibrant dimension I had just entered.

My view expanded an I realized, that I was leaving the Earth. I had an inner knowing that I was following the light back to its origin in the Sun. As I approached the gigantic solar body I could sense its enormous energy, not as heat, but as something burning in my own heart and radiating outwards. I could call it love, but it felt much bigger than that word. Finally, the radiating energy that had expanded from my heart reunited with its source as I dove into the Sun. Her fiery body absorbed my tiny speckle and I became pure radiant light energy.

The duration of that inner journey could have been seconds or as much as years. I had been in a realm where there is no time. But then, as suddenly as the vision had started, I was back on the noisy river shore, sitting next to Alma, facing the old sadhu.

I was disoriented and dazed by the sounds that felt very loud. As I looked around, I had a sense of recognition. It was like coming back from a long journey. As my rational mind kicked in again my first thought was that I must have breathed in toxic fumes that were surely floating around the place. Somebody had burned some powerful stuff that had caused these hallucinations.

Alma and the sadhu had not changed their positions. She had her eyes closed. The fire next to us had stopped smoldering. The sadhu's gaze was still resting on me. I looked straight at him, but his eyes were like flames burning my mind. I quickly averted my eyes.

Lost in an inner vertigo, I had not noticed that Alma was looking at me. I started to open my mouth to say something, but she put a finger on my lips, motioning me to get up. After bowing again to the sadhu, we left.

Chapter Two

I was glad to walk away from the cremation fires and its steady stream of ernest looking people doing their business.

The thrifty and lively Indian street life rapidly surrounded us again. Alma bought two bottles of mineral water from a stall. "Drink!" she said, handing me the water which I eagerly drank.

We continued to walk towards the town center until we reached the temples. Alma broke the silence.

"Do you want to sit somewhere?"

"Yes, I would not mind getting a break, how about that temple over there?" I asked pointing to a Hanuman temple we had just passed.

We entered the first yard of the temple and sat down on a stone bench which was carved into its inner wall. Next to it were colorful statues and paintings of the Hindu monkey-god.

I welcomed the quiet space with an inward shudder, realizing how intense the whole morning had been. The incredible out-of-body experience, and the inner journey I had made at the cremation place, were still burning brightly in my mind. I closed my eyes, savoring the moment of peace. I was finding comfort in the warm presence of Alma next to me. After a while I opened my eyes.

"I had a fantastic vision."

"Tell me."

Her warm eyes were all the encouragement I needed.

"I'm not sure if it was the sadhu's presence or some psychedelic smoke I inhaled, but it felt like I had left my body, and seen us sitting there…" I trailed off my mind going back to the experience. Alma waited silently.

"It all came with an inner knowing that I was much more than that body sitting there. Then, whatever I had become, left the Earth and traveled to the Sun, like following its light rays. I literally dove into it, becoming one with it, everything was alive!"

Our eyes connected for a long moment, then Alma's soft voice broke the silence.

"That's a mighty vision you had, Luke," she said, then added after a moment, "I feel it is a sign that a new world is opening up for you."

"Alma, you mention that new world again. What do you mean by it? If there's something else out there that I was unaware of until now, I want to know!"

She took and held my hands.

"I know a world where who you really are, is part of

your life. But it will be your journey to it, and it seems you are already on your way." Her warm smile went straight to my heart.

I had no idea what she was talking about, but I felt something powerful behind her cryptic words. Resuming my old life was not an option, as that life had already died.

As I looked at her, sitting next to me, I was in awe about what my eyes were seeing. Even in the shadows of the yard, the bright Indian sun intensified all of Alma's colors. The background was this beautiful Hanuman temple, adorned with sculptures and paintings. The whole scene had a paradoxical intensity in being both dreamlike as well as intensely real. It is one of the extraordinary moments of my life.

The magic bubble was shattered by the ring tone of a phone. Alma swiftly opened a little pocket concealed inside her dress and took out a small mobile.

"Sorry, one moment," she said, looking at me apologetically, and went swiftly towards the exit of the temple, leaving me alone.

It felt a sudden chill without her warm presence. I could hear chants coming from the inside of the temple. Sweet smells of incense floated from the main entrance.

When Alma came back, I could sense a tension in her body language. Her face did not show any emotion but had lost its shine.

"Some bad news? "

"Is it that obvious?" she said, "it was a friend who is in trouble and needs my help."

"What kind of trouble? "

"I cannot tell you right now, as it is very much connected to a reality of which you are not aware. I hope I'll be able to tell you about it soon. For now, I have to leave and see some people here in India before returning to Europe as soon as possible."

I must have looked alarmed, as her expression relaxed and she took my hands. "Don't worry! We'll meet again soon. Give me your phone number and email. I'll get in touch with you as soon as I can."

I did not try to hold her back as I sensed the urgency in her voice. We exchanged our contact info. It was time to say goodbye.

As Alma stood hesitantly in front of me, I opened my arms and hugged her. I was not ready to let her go, felt scared and vulnerable at the prospect of remaining alone. Part of me wanted to hold on to her, prevent her from leaving. As my embrace became tighter than I had intended, something amazing happened.

A sudden high voltage bolt emanating from her struck where our bodies touched. The intense flash of high hot current was dazzling and painful. It left me bent over, sweating and utterly shocked.

Alma put her arm over my back.

"No! Don't touch me!" I shouted. People entering the temple looked at us in alarm.

"I'm sorry!" Alma said, taking a step back.

"What did you do?"

"I don't know," she replied, "this has never happened

to me before. My guess is that you have felt the energy of the other world," she said, trying again to touch me, this time only putting her hand on my shoulder.

"Alma, this is nuts, what are you talking about? That was the freakiest thing that has ever happened to me! Have I gone mad? Who are you? Are you some alien from another planet?"

"No Luke, I'm from planet Earth. Just like you."

"This is crazy!"

The anger I felt was getting some of the heat out of my body. It felt like the hot current had given me strength. My system had gone into overdrive.

Alma looked worried, "Come with me, let's stay together a little longer, but we need to go," she said.

She took my hand and led me down the stairs into the crowded street. She was tense. I saw her glancing around as if she was looking for something.

"What's going on?" I asked, "if you worry about me, there's no need. I'm fine now. My world is completely unhinged, but I'm starting to enjoy the ride."

"Good, but right now I'm more concerned about dragging you into problems of a nature you are unaware of, and I know that it's not the time to tell you anything about it."

"Is it connected to that other world?"

" Yes."

"Is there anything more you can tell me about it?"

"No, not yet."

"Why?"

"Because there are things that are hard to understand if not directly experienced and seen with your own eyes. But please," Alma urged, "we have no time for this now!"

"Why are you looking around?"

"I want to protect you. Staying with me puts you in danger, as there are people looking for me. Please accept for now that there will be a time when you'll get all your questions answered."

We walked for a while along the crowded street. Suddenly she grabbed my arm and swiftly pulled me into a narrow alleyway, away from the busy street. I glanced back, curious as to what had elicited her action. I could only see the crowd and small vehicles. But just as I was looking away, I saw a big white SUV, parked on the other side of the main road, behind a phone pole from which hundreds of cables randomly hung in a big spider-like cluster. Two men, tall and broad-shouldered had stepped out of the car and were heading in our direction. They both were wearing a kind of electronically enhanced glasses, connected by wires coming out of their suits.

I felt an instant knot in my gut and hastened my steps. "If what you were worried about was a big white car, there are two men from it heading our way!"

"I know." she said, pulling me along with increased speed.

The alley was narrow and had only a few tiny shops. But it was broad enough to give access to the small and very mobile auto-rickshaws. We were lucky that one of these vehicles had just delivered a passenger and was heading in the right direction honking its way through the human traffic. We ran and caught it before it could gather speed. Alma waved a five-hundred-rupee bill and shouted something in the local language. I barely got in as the small engine gave a high whine and the rickshaw speeded away.

As I looked through the tiny rear window of the vehicle, I saw the two men sprinting down the street, trying hard to catch us before we would leave the narrow lane for the larger road fifty meters ahead of us.

Never in my life had potentially hostile people chased me. This was a huge shock, and I went into full panic. My pulse was thundering in my ears and I could barely breathe. Who were these men? Why were they trying to get us? Were they criminals, police, or some government agents?

My mind was racing. I realized I knew nothing about the woman who kept shouting at the driver. Into what madness was I getting myself?

Only a dozen meters from the junction to a bigger street, the auto-rickshaw had stopped. A group of people who were just leaving a house were blocking the way. Alma urged the driver onward who had started to madly honk at the group. Honking is so much part of the Indian auditory landscape that, not seeing an immediate danger the people were not impressed and did not move faster. Several children were running around, which made things even worse.

Our pursuers were now running at top speed towards us, trying to seize their chance. One of them had stumbled over an obstacle and barely regained his balance. The other man was shoving away anything hindering his progress. He was on a direct course to reach to us in a few moments.

I had no idea what these men wanted to do to us, but panic flooded my body with adrenaline, tightening a suffocating grip around my heart.

"This is crazy! Who are these men?! What do they want?" I shouted over the vehicle's noise.

Alma was busy giving instructions to our driver and did not respond to my screams.

Like in a nerve-wracking thriller, our vehicle had started to move just in the nick of time. The people in front of us finally realizing that something out of the ordinary was happening. They had moved aside and were watching the unfolding scene.

It had been very close. The two men reached the crowd, just as our rickshaw accelerated away. They got stuck in the same group that had reformed behind us. I managed to draw a cramped breath as we reached the junction and the driver swiftly honked his way deeper into the dense traffic of the bigger street, out of sight of our pursuers.

I had collapsed into the back-seat, breathless, my heart in my throat. I felt an intense physical relief and exhilaration at our escape. I closed my eyes, grasping the door frame of the rickshaw. The drive was erratic and very bumpy. The polluted street air was rushing through the open vehicle as the little engine screamed its way into a dense background noise of motors and honks.

As I opened my eyes, I looked at Alma who sat on the

opposite seat, her hair swirling in the wind. Her eyes were resting on me, and she looked calm as if nothing out of the ordinary had happened.

We were heading out of town, putting as much distance as possible between us and our pursuers. They had probably returned to their car.

The small vehicle was having trouble with the bigger potholes in the road, but Alma kept urging the driver onwards.

We passed villages with earth huts and straw roofs, surrounded by rice fields where I could see many people working. As the road led upwards over a hill, a bigger view emerged behind us, and I was glad not to see any white SUV heading our way. There were only trucks, buses and heavily laden agricultural vehicles on the road behind us.

"What now?" I shouted through the whine of the small engine, which had become almost bearable.

"I have to meet someone near the seashore." Alma replied, "that's where we're heading now. I'm sorry we cannot spend more time together, but I have a feeling that we will meet again soon."

Despite her reassuring words I felt my stomach tighten. "You cannot leave me after what just happened! What if these men find me? What was this all about? Were they criminals or government agents? What have you done to be pursued like that?" My mind was racing and fear had gripped me again.

Alma managed to put her hand on my shoulder. "I understand that this is very upsetting, but please trust me.

I'm not one of the bad guys, nor are they, and I think it's better for you not to know right now. These men were only after me. I don't think they had any chance of identifying you."

"You don't think, but what if they have?"

"If you must know, they had a particular way to target me that only works on me. It's unlikely they are even interested in you. I know it's difficult not to understand, but, again, I ask you to trust me."

"I guess I have no other choice."

"I'm sorry that you got into this, but it's an unforeseen emergency, and it's the best I can do. I have to leave very soon."

We passed through an area of slums, a patchwork of hundreds of basic shelters, and continued to drive south until we reached the seashore. This was the area of 'my beach', where I had first met Alma. I felt my throat tighten, the pain and emotions which had overwhelmed me that day were still present. I suppressed memories of my children and my wife happily driving towards the beach on that very road.

"I cannot bear going back to this beach," I said through clenched teeth.

Alma told the driver to stop. She sat next to me on the rear bench.

"The moment has come to say goodbye," she said, taking my hand.

At that moment I felt no more resistance. I wanted to get away from the dreaded place. I felt a bone-deep tiredness and longed to have a break from all that insanity. I also had an inner sense that I would meet Alma again.

"It's ok, I guess I'll be fine."

She beamed her beautiful smile I had already begun to miss.

"If you have any problem, call a man named Sundar. He's a friend, and he'll be able to help you if you need anything." She gave me a phone number scribbled on a piece of paper.

"Even if I get in trouble with our 'men in black'?"

"Yes, even then, but I'm sure they'll leave you alone. I don't think they have enough information to identify you. But as a simple precaution, take another rickshaw to your hotel, making sure this one is out of sight. They probably have taken its number and will interrogate the driver."

I looked at her beautiful face that had turned earnest. "Sure, good idea, but you sound like the secret agents in the movies. Who are you Alma?"

She did not answer, instead asked, "When had you planned to return?"

"In a week, but I guess I can change the ticket and return with an earlier flight."

"Good, do that!" Alma's face showed relief.

After a short hug, a few more words of goodbye, she stepped out of the rickshaw and left. She swiftly walked into a small alley and was gone from sight. I was alone.

Back at the hotel, after a quick room service meal, I felt exhausted, even depressed. Life had lost all zest since Alma's departure. Even the colors looked dull. Since it was still afternoon, I decided to take a nap.

I forgot to set an alarm, and instead of the intended short siesta, I fell into a deep sleep from which I awoke with a start, confused. As I looked at my mobile, I saw it was nearly half past three, already early morning. I had slept almost ten hours.

I decided to use the early start and leave as soon as possible for Chennai, where I hoped to change my return flight. But I still had time for a walk.

I was puzzled and confused about everything that had happened in such a short time. But less about the crazy experiences and events than about my feelings for Alma. Her absence was painful; the world felt cold and hollow without her. My longing for her made me walk the same way we had gone together the day before when we went to the cremation place. This time it was even earlier, and the streets were mostly empty. Cycle rickshaws were parked at the side of the road, their drivers sleeping on the rear bench, covered by a thin blanket.

I continued to walk until I reached the place near the river, where the buffalos had been. A couple of isolated lights dimly illuminated the scene. I sat down near the water, which had become more turbulent, like my feelings, as I recalled the amazing time I had had with Alma.

I was alone, a rare thing in India. It was so quiet that I could hear the gurgling of the water. I saw a few stray dogs that were sleeping on piles of dirt and rubble gathered at the water's edge. Two animals woke up by my presence. They looked very thin and dirty. Unfortunately, I did not pay more attention to them as they appeared to be harmless. I was watching the river flow. The water was as dark as the black night sky. It was flowing heavily towards the cremation area.

A noise brought my attention back to the dogs. Meanwhile, they had gathered into a small pack of half a dozen and had moved uncomfortably close to where I was sitting. Some were growling towards me. All of a sudden, they looked much more menacing. The individual, harmless looking dogs, had become a threatening pack of wild animals. I stood up, finally realizing the danger. My sudden motion and the fact that I had risen made them move away, but their growls intensified.

This triggered an old childhood memory of having been severely bitten by a dog and it was not making things easier. Two more dogs had joined the initial group, and they were now an impressive heterogeneous pack; some dogs had visible skin problems, hairless patches showing bright on their darker fur. Others had torn ears and wounds. They barked and howled menacingly. I looked around, but could not see anybody, not even a stone or a stick I could have used as a weapon.

One of the dogs approached with upturned lips and menacing teeth. I froze, unable to move. My eyes were desperately looking around for help. The dogs were closing in on me. This was a nightmare! I was unable to move as the deadly danger steadily approached with blazing yellow eyes.

Out of nowhere, a big, tall Indian man erupted, screaming at the dogs, while waving a stick in front of him. The dogs scattered, their pack energy instantly dissolved by the new threat. The man chased them for a short distance and walked back to me, still holding the small stick that did not look very menacing.

"These poor bastards were as scared as you were," the man said, dropping the stick and folding his hands. "Namaste."

"Namaste, Sir, thank you! You saved my life!"

"I'm not sure your life was in real danger, but they could have wounded you badly."

"Well, I for sure feared for my life. I don't want to know what could have happened. I'm glad you came to my rescue!"

The man looked at me intensely, and I had an odd feeling about him.

Suddenly he smiled and stretched out his hand. "I'm also glad to have met you; my name is Sundar."

"My name is Luke, but wait a minute, are you…" I stared at him, speechless.

"Yes, Mister Luke, I am a friend of Alma's."

The man was very tall, and carried his black curly hair pulled back in a ponytail. His intense eyes were illuminating the dark complexion of his face.

"What were you doing here? Did you follow me?"

"No Mister Luke, Alma had asked me to keep an eye on you until you safely depart. I received a warning that you left the hotel in the middle of the night. That's why I was able to be here in time when you needed help."

"So, you were my guardian angel," I said, very grateful for whatever had brought him to my rescue.

"Yes, a guardian, that's what I am." he said with a broad smile and a glimmer of unspoken things in his eyes.

"I guess I should be going back to the hotel and call a taxi."

"I can take care of that, Mister Luke," Sundar said firmly, "I'll call a friend who will drive you to the airport where he has good connections. He will help you with the changing of your ticket."

I started to protest, but he explained, "It's India, things tend to be more complicated, but good connections can go a long way."

I surrendered, feeling at ease with the warm energy of the man that reminded me of Alma's. I checked out of the Hotel with a very sleepy clerk, while Sundar made his call.

As we waited outside, I asked, "Alma mentioned another world. Are you also part of that other world?"

Sundar's eyes lit up even more. "Did she? She must trust you very much! I can only tell you so much of the truth: yes, I am, and yes, I hope you'll find your way to it. I hope we'll meet there in the future."

With these final words, he bowed and shook my hand, leaving me waiting for my ride.

Chapter Three

Sundar's friend had been a great help at the airport. The next flight was already fully booked, but with the appropriate connections, I got a free upgrade to business class that still had an empty seat. The luxury and space on the upper deck of the already aging Air France 747 aircraft was perfect to relax and reflect on the recent events that had begun to change my life.

At some point during the flight, I woke up and opened my eyes to endless mountains, illuminated by the silver light of a nearly full moon. The screen monitoring the flight told me that we were above Iran. As I looked through the porthole, the cloudless moonlit night sky looked mysteriously alien. The endless arid and partially snow-covered mountains looked like the rough skin of a gigantic prehistoric animal. The endless shapes unfolding under the plane were in constant flux. From that height, illuminated by the moonlight, the Earth looked alive.

The plane broke through the polluted Parisian haze in

the early morning and landed at Charles de Gaulle. The sun had not yet sent her first dawning beams to the city that contained my home where nobody awaited me.

As I was standing in the 'non-EU' queue at the passport check, under the watchful eyes of customs officers, I felt a growing anxiety which rapidly became a panic that I barely managed to control. The long queue in front of me was moving at a snail's pace. The officers took forever scrutinizing the passports, matching them with the persons in front of them. What unsettled me most was the fact that they systematically scanned the passport data into their system. The whole setting was under the watchful eyes of grim looking soldiers carrying machine guns. They were positioned on each side of the exit doorways.

My mind raced back to the men who had chased Alma. Had they been from the police or some secret service? What if in the meantime they had managed to identify me? Perhaps they flagged me as a dangerous criminal or terrorist? As the queue in front of me grew smaller, my fertile mind was weaving bigger and more terrifying scenarios of what would soon happen.

When I finally stood in front of the customs officer in his booth, my hand that handed him my Canadian passport was damp and shaky. The man barely looked up, took my passport and slid it into the scanner. I held my breath; it seemed to take much longer than for the people who had passed before me. At last, he looked straight into my eyes, and without a word handed back my passport. I moved on, my lungs pumping oxygen into a stressed organism. *'I'm completely nuts, totally paranoid,'* I told myself and hurried out, looking straight past the soldiers.

As I went through the arrivals gate, for an instant, I traveled back in time. I saw my family stand there, my girls, four and seven, all smile and curly hair. They were waving, my wife barely managed to hold them back. They stormed towards me as soon as the last barrier had opened. I kneeled and they jumped on me. We hugged and kissed. My arms and hands remembered holding them, how they had been teeming with joy and life.

The pain struck hard, and I was glad to feel it, as, for a moment it took away the horrible distance of my heart. I took a deep breath and walked towards the taxi terminal.

When the taxi dropped me off in front of my apartment, rue Monge, in the fifth arrondissement, I had regained some precarious balance. I was going back to a home that had become an empty shell. This moment was one of the hardest of my journey. But then I did not know that it would soon get much worse.

The elevator took me up to the fifth floor where I owned a comfortable duplex apartment. My stomach was a knotted up in apprehension. When the key turned in the lock, I asked myself, '*Is this still my home?*'.

The response to that question was lurking behind the thick door, which was only snapped close, not fully locked, several turns, as I always did. When it opened, I nearly slammed it shut again, not believing what I saw. Behind the door was a war zone. Upturned, broken furniture, pictures ripped from the walls and their canvases. Everything lay smashed on the floor. The fabric of the sofa and chairs had been ripped off and was hanging in tangles from a maze of broken wood pieces.

The sight of destruction hit me like a punch in the

solar plexus. I gripped the door frame, as the ground started to shake under my feet. It was as if I had to absorb the kinetic force of the violence which had caused all the destruction. My first impulse was to defend, to push back, to destroy the attacker. But all had already been done, and the cowardly attacker had fled, unchallenged. The only thing I could do was to scream my despair.

I could not believe what I saw; nearly everything had systematically been ripped apart, destroyed. I walked around, my face wet with tears. Eventually, I called the police.

They were supportive, and did not ask too many questions. They seemed to care for how I was doing and what kind of support I needed. I did not have any family or relatives in Paris. My father is Canadian, and my mother is French, at that time they already lived on the west coast in Vancouver.

As a child, I had frequently spent my holidays in Paris, where my grandmother lived. I also studied in Paris and met my wife at the Sorbonne University.

I have lived most of my adult life in Paris, which means that I knew many people. I also had some close relationships, including people from my wife's family who lived in France. But since her death, I had avoided them all, as much as I could, and they had gradually given up on me.

I told the police that I would contact a friend to evade their psychological counseling. I had decided to go to a nearby hotel for the night and rest. I felt exhausted by the jet lag and the shock of all the destruction.

It was weird to take a hotel room so near to where I had lived, but I had not much energy to ponder on it. After a long shower, I collapsed into the bed, where I remained unmoving for a very long time.

I woke up feeling refreshed and rested. But my stomach contracted as my first waking thoughts brought back the incredible wreckage of my apartment.

The police had told me to contact them as soon as possible, but I felt I needed more time to regain my balance. Had the destruction anything to do with what had happened in India? I could not help thinking of the men who had chased Alma. These thoughts brought back the vivid memories of the hours spent with her.

Where was she right now? I missed her; she had been the only person who had touched my heart since a very long time. On impulse, I took out the phone number she had given to me at the temple and dialed it on my mobile. The phone kept ringing for a long time. Just before I was going to give up, a mailbox message started, with her voice asking to leave a message. I got goosebumps as I heard her warm voice on the recorded message.

In my loneliness, talking to her via voicemail felt like a close substitute for the real connection I craved. With a voice that betrayed my emotions, I told the recorder what had happened and what my current situation was. I ended the message with the wish to hear from her.

I left the hotel and strolled down towards rue Mouffetard, a street market area. I love that street, its liveliness, the odors floating in the air, the food vendors shouting the merits of their goods to the passing crowd.

This place always managed to lift my spirits, and that

day was no exception. For a while, I forgot my ruined apartment and the upcoming police investigation. I was just present to the life pulsating all around me.

'When will Alma call me back?' I wondered. *'What is she doing? What kind of situation is she in at the moment? And what did all her allusions to this mysterious other world mean? Did that world really exist?'*

There had been something consistently authentic in everything she had shared. I continued to feel the instinctive trust I had felt for her in India.

Barely audible in the surrounding noise, my mobile rang. Afraid I would miss the call, I fumbled hastily in my pocket and picked it up in time. Convinced that it was Alma calling back, I was disappointed to hear a male voice instead, asking if I was Luke.

"Yes, of course, that's me," I said with some frustration. I was wondering who knew my private number and my first name.

"I'm a friend of Alma's." the man said, immediately getting my full attention. It was not that long ago that another man had said the same words.

"Unfortunately she is busy right now and asked me to give you any possible assistance."

"Thank you," I said, not knowing what to say. The situation was unexpected.

"My name is Michael, by the way. I live here in Paris." After a short pause, the man continued, "I suggest we meet somewhere soon, and see what we can do."

The man's voice was deep and melodious, maybe a middle-aged man I guessed. His British English had a subtle hint of a Scottish accent.

"Yes, that would be great." I said, gratefully taking up his offer, then added, "I have to go to the police commissariat, before anything else. As soon as I'm done with that, I'll get back to you."

I called the police inspector I had been given as a contact and he told me to meet him at once at the apartment.

The police had investigated the whole morning. It seemed that the intention of the perpetrators had been to destroy as much as possible. The inspector asked me to check for missing objects and valuables. That was very difficult and painful, considering how much was scattered and smashed to pieces. But part of me did not care any longer about those things. It felt as if the place had died and would soon be gone forever. The furniture, objects and personal items were from a past life which had left me.

I gathered some pictures and a few personal items that found me, more than I found them.

The inspector reported, that nobody in the neighborhood had heard anything. The flat beneath was empty; it had been for sale for a while. He also told me that there were gangs of frustrated young people from the suburbs, who would occasionally break into houses and perform that kind of destruction. He considered this the most likely explanation, as theft had evidently not been the prime motivation. He took my fingerprints to match them against the few they had found.

The inspector asked me some questions about my life and whether I was aware of having enemies. I had to take a deep breath before responding, my mind racing back to

India, making all sorts of connections to the mysterious people Alma had been worried about.

I must have been unresponsive for more than a few moments. When I came back to reality, the inspector was silently staring at me.

"Are you sure, you have no enemies who would do this to you?" he asked with an edge of sharpness in his voice.

"I'm sorry, I drifted off, I'm exhausted." I said, "Of course I have no enemies of that sort, I'm just a mere citizen with a rather conventional life."

I knew when I spoke these words, that this was the description of my past self. But the new self had yet to be revealed. Another big part of my former life had disappeared with the destruction of my apartment.

The inspector knew that I had lost my family. He urged me to get help, talk to somebody. He said he would communicate a report to my insurance company and ask them to get in touch with me. Finally, he promised to keep me informed about anything connected to my case.

I put the pictures, a few personal items and some clothes I had gathered, into an old leather bag and left at the same time as the police. I was unable to remain there alone. I probably would never come back to the place, I thought. I did not look back as I walked towards the hotel, feeling disoriented and lonely.

As I watched people passing by on the sidewalk, I reflected that most of them seemed to have a purpose. They were on their way to places, doing errands, meeting somebody, going home. I realized, I was trying to list all those possibilities that were no longer applicable to me.

Then I remembered the man who had called. I still had something on my agenda, I thought, finding comfort in it. I took out my phone and dialed his number. This time there was no more excitement, I felt detached. I was a mere observer of the unfolding of my personal story.

The deep voice answered. "Yes, Michael here."

"I'm done with the police. If it suits you, we can meet anytime."

"Good, tell me where you are, I can come right now." he said, as if it had been the only thing he had been waiting for.

I told him where I was and asked how long it would take. "About ten to fifteen minutes," he said.

"Ok, I'm in front of a brasserie, I'll sit here at the terrace."

The outdoor tables were bathed in the early spring sunshine. The air was still fresh but already carried a promise of warmer times. I enjoyed sitting in the cane chair, slowly sipping the strong black coffee I had ordered.

'Life is good, despite all the other stuff,' I thought, feeling grateful. At that moment, I remembered a famous Zen story about a man being chased by a tiger. To avoid being eaten alive, the man leaped off a cliff and grabbed a vine where he hung precariously. As the tiger tried to catch him from above, he looked down and saw another tiger far below waiting for him to fall. To make matters worse, a mouse began chewing on the vine. At that very moment, the man spotted a luscious wild strawberry growing

out of the cliff side. He then held the vine with one hand, picked the fruit and ate it. '*Delicious*,' he thought.

I considered the story was somehow relevant to my current situation. I also felt a bit like hanging on a vine, only that in my case, no real tiger threatened to devour me. Or were Alma and her people predators ready to swallow me into their mysterious world?

Chapter Four

I was enjoying my "wild strawberry" when I heard a discrete honk on the street in front of me.

It came from a fancy, dark red Peugeot, whose elegant surfaces reflected the sunshine.

The driver's window slid down, and Michael's voice received a face. My fantasies about how people look from hearing their voices rarely match reality, but here I thought it was fitting. It was a positive first impression. He was smiling, and his eyes were friendly.

"Jump in!" he said.

I climbed into the car, that welcomed me with a warm smell of fine leather.

"Hi, Michael, great to meet you," I said, stretching out my hand.

He looked younger than the middle-aged man I had expected, but was probably older than he looked. His lively blue eyes were surrounded by fine laughing lines.

His curly, mostly dark blond hair still retained the shine of youth. The grip of his hand was strong and energetic. I immediately liked him and relaxed into the comfortable passenger seat.

"How has it been going with your apartment and the police? You brought some things?" he asked, pointing at the bag on my lap.

"Yes, this is all I'll keep from it," I replied with a firmness in my voice which surprised me. "My old life has left me. Apart from my memories I retain very little from it."

"I'm sorry to hear that." Michael said, "but, with the risk of sounding corny, I would say that this is a great opportunity for a new beginning."

"I have only known Alma for two days, but I'm sure that she would have said the same." We both laughed, and I felt my spirits rise.

"Where are we going? What can you do for me?"

"I think you need a new place stay, as you can't be forever at a hotel. I suggest you check out and get your things. I have a lovely apartment I can let you borrow for a while. There you will be more at ease."

"Ok, thank you!" I said, readily accepting his generous offer, while admiring the car's wooden dashboard.

We drove back to my hotel, and I rapidly checked out. Soon we were on our way to what started to feel like new adventures.

Curiosity and excitement had replaced my loneliness. I felt stronger, ready for whatever would come next. There was nothing left to lose. The cup was empty. It could only be filled.

We drove silently for a while and were leaving the 'quartier latin', heading towards the Seine river, and shortly after, we reached its busy sunlit banks.

As the car glided effortlessly through the familiar scenery bathed in the bright sunlight, I enjoyed seeing the spectacular historical background of Paris. It was like seeing it all again for the first time.

Finally, we crossed the Seine and passed the Paris City Hall. We were heading towards the Bastille area where once had stood the infamous prison that was stormed in the very beginnings of the French revolution. But before we got there Michael took a left turn, into the "Marais" one of the oldest and most picturesque areas of Paris.

"Here we are!" Michael said, when we finally turned into a rounded portal. A heavy gate swung open into the paved courtyard, revealing one of the old so-called private hotels from the 17th century.

The massive door of the mansion opened, and a smartly dressed man came out, and walked towards the car. His steps were oddly stiff and regular, and he kept his body straighter than was natural. As he opened the car doors, making a nearly imperceptible bow with the head, I realized that he must be a butler. He looked Japanese or Korean, I was not sure, but he was surprisingly tall, nearly as tall as I. His black hair was cut short. His round face looked as if barely succeeding at looking serious.

"Bienvenue Monsieur" he said, taking my luggage in a swift gesture which left me no choice.

"May I introduce you to Chul, he is the guardian angel of this place."

I was impressed by the sight of the old building and a genuine butler, the first I have ever met in person.

"You are living here?" I asked, letting my voice betray how impressed I was.

Michael made a sweeping gesture over the property. "Yes, this is where I live and work. The house has been in my family for six generations. I consider myself the temporary custodian rather than the owner of this house. But please come in, you must be tired, we'll have plenty of time to chat later."

He took my arm in an unusually friendly gesture, and we went the few steps up into the house. After walking through an artfully decorated lobby, we came to a short hallway lined with mirrors, leading to an elevator.

"Chul will take you to your accommodation on the second floor," Michael said, opening an old style sliding grid, "we can meet later, whenever you are ready."

I thanked my generous landlord, and the butler took me to what looked like a huge, luxurious suite, comprising lobby, bedroom, office, tv room, spacious bathroom, kitchen and dining room.

Though I appreciated the beauty of the place, I was starting to be a bit overwhelmed by it's display of wealth. I was feeling apprehensive and suspicious, but realized the paradox that these people were actually helping me. I had an overwhelming sense of untold things I did not know.

I took a shower and lay down on a bed where a full extended Indian family could have comfortably rested. I closed my eyes, and let my many thoughts roam freely inside my mind.

What was I doing in that place? I had been rather detached and relaxed about my fate in the last hour. This unusual place had managed to shake the precarious balance I had barely had time to enjoy.

After a while, I felt calmer. When somebody knocked on the door I reluctantly got up. It was the butler.

"Is everything to your liking, Monsieur?"

"Yes, thank you." I replied, but then, as the man looked so friendly, I admitted, "I have not managed to relax."

His response was unexpected, "I believe, Monsieur, that a good massage will help relieve the tensions in your body," he said, a huge smile spreading all over his Asian face. He had a calm and soothing presence inviting trust.

"Well, yes, I would certainly love a massage, after all these crazy days. Do you have someone doing house visits?"

"No need, everybody and everything is already here, you can have a massage right away." he said as he opened a narrow wall cupboard which revealed a folded massage table and all the required accessories, which he swiftly set up in the bedroom.

"Please get ready and lay down."

"You really are an extraordinary butler!"

"Who told you I'm a butler?" he chuckled.

As Chul massaged my back, I felt a wild mixture of pain and pleasure. It was as if he were touching several layers of my body that was dissolving under his hands.

After a while I felt like a floating body-less entity, barely feeling Chul making tiny movements along my spine. Suddenly a flash of potent electric current jolted through my body. It nearly made me fall off the massage table. I screamed in pain as if I was on fire.

I started to cough, feeling angry and frightened. "What did you do?" I screamed, starting to cough.

"I'm sorry, Monsieur. What happened?" Chul said, bringing me a glass of water.

"You electrocuted me, just like Alma did! Who are you guys?" I was still screaming.

"I'm sorry, Monsieur, this has never happened to me before."

"That's exactly what Alma said when it happened!"

"Monsieur Luke, believe me, everything is OK. Take a rest. Whenever you want you can come down to the lobby where Mister Michael will meet you."

I could not relax anymore. My heart was pounding, and I felt upset and worried. Who were these people who produced this incredible energy I had felt? I realized that after having been so much immersed in the pain of my past, I had eagerly welcomed the diversion created by Alma and her friends.

With a new resolve, I dressed and went down the stairways towards the lobby. The big mansion was silent. I seemed to be the only person in the huge building.

I saw Michael reflected in one of the golden mirrors of the lobby. He was sitting with a tablet in a corner behind a big marble column. I hesitated for a few moments, observing him, but he caught my eyes in the mirror and laughed.

"Hello Luke, I had a feeling you would come. Please take a seat!" He took my hand and guided me to a Louis XIV chair with complicated rounded legs and armrests.

We looked at each other silently for a few long seconds.

"I guess you have some questions," he said, as if he had just read my mind. Without waiting for an answer, he continued, "If it's ok with you, I'd like to take you on a ride!"

He stood up, barely giving me time to feel how uncomfortable the old chair had been.

I saw in his eyes that he was evaluating me. It felt quite uncomfortable, as he had an intense unapologetic presence.

"Where would you like to take me?" I asked, my voice giving away the excitement and anxiety I was feeling.

"I'd like to surprise you with an interesting place, as an appetizer before we have lunch." The warm smile which came back to his face took away any doubts that were still lingering in the back of my mind.

"That sounds good to me," I said, following him out of the house to his car.

After a long drive through dense Parisian traffic, Michael parked the car in a street adjacent to the boulevard Montmartre.

"Where are we going?" I asked, as I unlocked my seatbelt.

"We are going to the Musée Grévin; have you been

there before?"

"No, it's the famous wax museum, I've never been there…" I trailed off, as I nearly mentioned that my kids had been too young for that kind of place.

We walked down the noisy boulevard, and arrived at the rather small entrance of the museum. The mirrored walls of the hall were lined with life size pictures of famous people. It looked more like the entrance of a music hall than a museum.

"Why are we here?"

"Good question! Of all the places, why on Earth would I bring you here?" Michael replied, looking amused.

I felt Michael's gaze, as I was pondering his question.

"This place is about famous people, what they look like. So maybe you want to tell me that you are different, and tell me why I got electric shocks from Alma and Chul?"

I saw a flicker of reaction in his eyes.

"Yes, it's about all these things!" he said, holding my gaze, then he looked around as if trying to figure out what to do next.

"I want to know what this is all about!" I exclaimed, as I was exasperated with all these mysteries.

"Are you sure? Knowing certain things will change you and your life forever. Once you know them, there will be no un-knowing, no turning back," his eyes had narrowed, lines appearing on his forehead.

"Yes," I replied, "life has cleaned my slate, brought me

back to zero. I have nothing left to lose."

Michael nodded, and continued, "There is a reality only a small number of people on Earth are aware of. Are you interested?"

"Yes! Right now I'm drawn to it like a moth to the flame!"

"Nice analogy, but I'll make sure not all of you gets burned away," he said with a smile and started to walk around.

"As you said, our little tour here is about us humans. What do you think makes us who we are?"

"Our outer appearance, our inner sense of self, our memories," I ventured, then added, "some people would say our souls."

"Why does a person look like she does?" Michael asked, pointing at a famous French actress immortalized in wax.

"I guess it's about genes and what the person has experienced and done in life," I replied, not sure where the conversation was going.

"Yes, this seems a reasonable explanation, and it's also what your science tells you."

"Why do you say 'your science,'" I looked at him suspiciously, "do you have another science?"

Michael had a mischievous smile. "Possibly, but that's not the point right now. Let's continue with our subject."

He made a sweeping gesture. "All these figures are made from the same material. Their outer skin is of different kinds of wax. If we melted them, they would become some undefined sticky liquid. But right now, these forms are recognizable, mainly because we know the people they represent, we have their pattern stored in our minds."

"Yes, that's quite obvious." I snapped, getting impatient.

"Let's go to the workshop where they produce these guys!"

Michael led me away from the main exhibition into a narrow and dark hallway that led to a closed door.

"You seem to know your way," I said, "have you come with people like me before?"

"Yes, a few times." he said, not volunteering more details.

A big "Keep Out" sign in French did not stop Michael from opening the door. I followed him hesitantly into a big, messy looking room.

All around there were work tables littered with an impressive number of tools. I distinguished electric metal cutters, manual drills, paint brushes, pots of glue and paint. In the middle of the room, several humanoid figures were strapped on vertical holders. They were at different stages of development. The scene was unsettling to somebody unprepared, as unlike stone sculptures, they had the color of human skin.

Michael went to a life-size body at the center of the room.

"What impression do you get from this?" he asked, pointing at the figure which only had the general shape of a human being.

It was a rough sculpture just beginning to express the details of a human body. In some parts of the torso and the legs, one could see a metallic structure not yet covered by the pinkish wax. The head was already well formed, and the face was merely outlining what would become a nose, a mouth, and eyes.

"It's just a human shape without any precise details," I said, feeling like an intruder.

"Yes, it's like an early stage of a fetus, where you begin to see that it's human. What do you feel when you look at this body?" Michael asked, touching the figure at the back of its head.

"Nothing much. It's lifeless. I only feel some curiosity about what it's becoming."

Michael then turned and went to another figure which was hidden in a corner near the door. It was covered by black fabric.

"This one is a special prototype."

He waited a few seconds, creating a dramatic anticipation. Then he slowly pulled at a corner of the velvety fabric.

"This is incredible!" I whispered on a long withheld out-breath.

Most of the wax people I had seen so far in the museum were well made, but they had the distinct sense of being wax figures. Many details felt slightly off, and their body language did not appear natural. But looking at the figure of Cate Blanchett in front of me, I almost expected her to continue her arm movement in support of something she was about to tell me.

My heart tightened, as it took me instantly to a scene in "The Lord of the Rings," the last movie I had seen with my wife.

"I have never seen anything like this," I said, unable to take my eyes away from the actress.

Michael nodded, "The artist is a special friend of mine. He wants to express the essence of a person," he paused, then added, "it's part of a project to stimulate a new awareness."

"What makes that amazing difference?" I asked in a low voice.

"He taps into and connects with what you call the soul, the spirit part of the person."

The unease and the anger I had felt in the morning were coming back.

"Why did you take me here? I've had enough of going around in circles, and not knowing anything about what is really going on! What is the point of all this?" I stopped, out of breath, my face flushed.

Michael looked at me, his clear eyes wide. "This is exactly my point, and why I'm taking it slowly. I'm preparing you for a big transition."

"Are we talking here about alien invaders and instantaneous travel through the galaxy?" I replied, not able to keep the sarcasm out of my voice.

As he laughed in a very disarming way, I could not help but smile. He was driving me crazy, but I had decided to trust the man. "Why don't you just tell me? I have nothing to lose!"

"You are not yet ready, and it's lunchtime. Let's go and have lunch. Then we'll talk, and do some experiments."

I did not ask what he meant by 'some experiments', as I was glad to leave the creepy workshop.

Back in the car I closed my eyes and tried to relax. We had not spoken since leaving the workshop. I still instinctively trusted Michael, and I could not find anything I disliked about the man. The personal vitality he radiated reminded me of Alma. I was both apprehensive and excited at the prospect of discovering something new.

We drove for a while and finally stopped at the quai de la Tournelle, next to the Seine river. A big door immediately opened in the elegant building in front of which we had parked. A uniformed porter came out to meet us and waited beside the car.

"We can't be going to the "Tour d'Argent", I cried in alarm, when I saw the restaurant's name, "that's a posh, overpriced VIP restaurant for rich Americans tourists!"

My voice betrayed fear as if it was a genuinely dangerous place.

"What's wrong with overpriced restaurants? Value is just a mind game," he replied, his tone nearly solemn.

"But that will cost a fortune, just for a simple meal!"

"That meal will not be simple, and anyway I'm going to pay the bill, relax!"

Far from relaxing, I became acutely aware of my clothes, and my slightly unshaved chin.

"But I need to change before I can go to that kind of place! They will want me to wear a tie!" I squeaked.

"Real VIPs don't change, they don't care about these details," Michael replied matter-of-factly.

"Easy for you to say, dressed as you are in a very 'casual' Armani suit!"

"It's not an Armani suit," he said with an amused grin, "it's from Christian Dior, custom made."

I looked at him incredulously, and the tension evaporated, as we broke into a hearty laugh. I surrendered to the disarming charm of the man and his singular perspective on reality. It was consistent with the kind of place he called home.

As we entered the restaurant on the upper floor, the chief waiter greeted Michael by name, and without even a glance at me, showed us to a table right in front of a huge window that had a gorgeous outlook on Notre Dame cathedral.

We settled down comfortably, enjoying the view. I took a miniature baguette from a small basket, a waiter had just put on our table. I slowly broke the brown crust, revealing the white bread inside.

Michael handed me the butter and said, "This is a good time to connect and get to know each other. I'm very happy to hear from your recent experiences."

The setting was gorgeous, and what I felt from Michael was only warmth and friendship. I took a deep breath and started to speak.

"Since I met Alma in India, crazy things keep happening. Things like an out-of-body experience, running from men looking like secret service. There also was a hug with Alma and a massage from Chul, both giving me an incredible electric shock. And, last but not least, the destruction of my apartment…" I paused, and looked into Michael's blue eyes which were unblinking.

"All this tells me that you're no ordinary people and that some other folks are trying to catch you. Something is different with you guys, and I have no clue what it is. Alma also spoke of another world. All this is very mysterious."

Michael looked squarely into my eyes with a gaze from which I could not move away, and said, "These are indeed quite crazy things. From my perspective, they are uniquely linked to your person, and how your life is unfolding. Being highly unusual, I can nevertheless confirm that the electrical shocks you received are directly connected to what you call the other world."

I interrupted Michael, shivers running down my spine, "And what about the wrecking of my apartment? Is that also related to that world?"

Michael put his hand on my arm, in what felt like a very friendly gesture. "It was a bad and strange thing that happened, but I am nearly sure, that it's one of those synchronistic events that happen as an expression of life's own intelligence."

"What do you mean by that?"

"I mean that your life has started to move into a totally new direction, and that the destruction of your old home is a clear sign that there's no going back."

"So what you say is that it's not related to the guys pursuing Alma, and that it happened by pure coincidence?"

"Luke, I can only say, from my own life experience, that life is much too big, to allow for something like pure random chance."

I looked at Michael, sitting opposite to me, an amazing view of Notre Dame cathedral as a background, and I felt, that my life had indeed taken a very different path. My rational mind could not agree, but my heart felt that what he just said was true.

Our conversation was interrupted by an invasion of waiters who carried cloche covered plates, which they theatrically unveiled.

Michael made a sweeping gesture towards the refined starters in front of us.

"Let's continue our conversation later! Now's the time to enjoy the lovely meal they prepared for us."

Chapter Five

I savored the delicious four-course meal in such an upscale place. I particularly enjoyed their famous duck dish. The easy and joyous conversation we had during the meal strengthened my growing friendship and trust I felt for Michael. I had stopped worrying about high voltage hugs and secret services.

Michael did not ask for the bill, nor pay, which struck me as odd, but I was beyond remarking on it. We got up, and he led me to an elevator. As we arrived at the second underground floor, the door opened straight into a swimming pool and sauna area. Light beams behind big tropical leafy plants created an intricate pattern that bounced all over the place. The air was moist and carried a pleasant fragrance.

Michael guided me to a rounded room, adjacent to the pool area. It was decorated with ornate roman style couches and colorful tropical flowers.

"Are you still sure you want to jump off the cliff of

the known world?" he asked.

I tried to ease my tension with a joke, "And find out that the world is carried on the back of a giant cosmic tortoise?"

Michael laughed, "Yes, something of that amplitude!" he said.

I sat down on a couch and looked at the dimly lit, unusual room. *'I have already left my known world.'* I thought, then exhaled the air that I had blocked in my lungs.

"What are you talking about? You sound as if I'm from the Middle Ages and you're about to tell me that the Earth is round and travels around the Sun."

"Yes, absolutely!" replied Michael, while sitting on the couch opposite to me. "But, with a difference: this first leap is going to be bigger, and there will be more following, one greater than the other."

I was stunned, as I realized what he was saying, and that he meant it. The bees of fear and excitement were again twirling inside my entrails. Did I want to change my perspective of the world that much?

In a vain attempt to bargain with Michael, I said, "I'm not aware of science being anywhere near that kind of breakthrough discovery!"

"That's because there is still a separation between the physical sciences and what I would call the mind and spirit dimension."

I stood up as if I was going to leave, but remained there, standing. "What are you going to do now?"

"Nothing, if that's what you want." He seemed more

detached, his focus going inwards.

"I have not come this far, to get no answers!" I exclaimed.

"What kind of answer do you want? Do you want food for your mind, or do you want me to blow your mind away?"

"From where I am right now, I'd say blow whatever's left of of it!" I said, sitting down.

Michael stood up, and without a word began to undress. He did it so naturally, so matter-of-factly, that I felt no big surprise or discomfort. One by one his elegant clothes landed on the couch. He even took off a ring he was wearing. Finally, Michael stood in front of me, as naked as on the day he was born. His body looked well exercised and lightly tanned. He closed his eyes.

For a long minute nothing happened. I waited, gripping the ornate arm rest, taking deep gulps of moist air.

'What is he doing?'

Faintly at first, but increasing rapidly, I felt the room becoming electric, as if the air had charged with energy. The sensation reminded me of what I had felt during the hug with Alma and the massage with Chul. But nothing happened for another long minute. I was starting to feel the electricity on my skin.

All of a sudden it happened. With a rush of air Michael disappeared. His absence only lasted a very brief instant, then with a another ripple of air, another body materialized. A smaller body, with darker skin. Female, with long black hair, slightly curling. I could not believe my eyes. It was Alma!

She was standing in front of me, her eyes closed, immobile, naked. Time was standing still.

As she opened her eyes, I lost my inner balance, nearly falling off the couch. She moved her arms and took a step forward in my direction.

My heart was pounding wildly. I tried to shake off my vertigo and held on to the headboard of the couch.

Alma looked straight at me and smiled. My ears were ringing loudly, and my mind had gone blank. I was just staring at her.

She stretched her arm and her hand touched my shoulder. I heard her speak, but her words did not make sense. It was just noise, in what felt like a big empty space. Then her hands were shaking me. I heard a familiar word. "Luke! Luke!"

Then, in one flash of awakening, it all came back, Michael, the restaurant, the basement, his body disappearing, replaced by… Alma's! Alma, who was now standing in front of me, shaking me.

"Alma! What are you doing here? Where's Michael?"

Alma's response threw me right back into the land of no-mind.

"I am Michael!"

My eyes looked at Alma, pleading. I had lost my sanity.

She seemed to read my mind. "No, Luke, you're not crazy. Your mind just needs to catch up with what you saw."

She stood in front of me, waiting patiently.

I could only stare at her, as my inner vertigo slowly receded. Finally, I managed to pronounce something coherent.

"Are you saying that you switched your body with Alma's like they do in sci-fi movies? Does it mean that Alma got your body?"

"No, Alma is unaware of all this. This is no sci-fi, but a way into my reality that I am opening up for you! "

Michael/Alma was standing very close to me, naked. I was starting to feel the awkwardness of the situation.

"Ok, so how do I relate to you? Are you going to put on Michael's clothes?" I pointed at the pile lying on the couch.

"No, Luke, I'm going to put on the clothes which have been prepared for me in the dressing room. I could change back into my own body, but I think it's more useful for us if I remain as Alma for a while longer. How are you doing, Luke?"

"I don't know, I'm feeling agitated, upset, in the truest sense of the word! I feel like screaming, howling, like smashing things, that's how I'm doing!"

"I warned you!"

"But I did not expect it to be something like that!"

"You expected some magical trick, but this is very real. It's at the core of life, organic, essential, connected to the very fabric of this universe!"

"Yes, it feels indeed like the fabric of my being has been ripped open. Nothing makes sense anymore."

Alma put both her hands back on my shoulders, and I

felt them strong and warm. Despite the bizarre situation, I felt comforted by the touch.

"I understand how you feel, Luke. Trust me, it's going to make sense again, when you have shifted your perspective."

She went to the changing room and soon came back, elegantly clad in a sky-blue silk dress. She looked like the Alma I had known a couple of days ago, beautiful, for me at that moment disturbingly feminine.

"How can you be Michael in Alma's body?" I asked, still not able to wrap my mind around it.

"Let's get out of here, and go for a walk. This will create a more suitable space for such a conversation."

She took my hand and lead me towards the elevator, not giving a glance to Michael's clothes she was leaving behind.

We exited on the ground floor and went straight to the main door. Seeing us coming, the porter hurriedly opened the door for us.

We crossed the street, and went down a flight of stairs leading to the Seine river banks.

"Let's walk towards Notre Dame!" Alma/Michael pointed straight ahead where the towers of the Paris cathedral were already visible.

She walked swiftly, a happy spring in her steps, exactly as I remembered Alma walk, not as I saw Michael only minutes ago. I still could not believe what I was seeing.

'When am I going to wake up from this crazy dream?' I thought.

I hurried my pace to keep level with her. "What should I call you? Alma, Michael, or would Michelle be more fitting?"

She stopped and turned to the flowing river where one of these long tourist's boats was passing. I could hear a voice commenting in English over loudspeakers.

She finished her half circle toward me.

"This is all easier than it seems and more complicated than you would ever expect. Complicated in terms of involving things you have not any concept of, making it rather challenging to explain."

"Maybe you start with the 'easier than it seems' part of it." I ventured, trying to sound cheerful.

She threw her arms up, her eyes wide. She whirled around herself, and shouted. "Life's so good, you have no idea! It's very energizing to do this little exercise! Hey, Luke, relax, enjoy the ride, let's seize the day!"

I looked at her, a bit nonplussed. "Little exercise… I'm not sure I can follow. What's happening to you?"

"Come, shut up and let's walk, I'm not ready to talk."

This was as much out of character for Michael, for the little I knew him, but part of me was going along with that new energy. Again, I tried to match Alma's swift pace.

As the towers of Notre Dame grew bigger on our right, Alma slowed her pace and went to a bench that faced the cathedral on the other side of the river.

"I love this place!" she said, sitting down.

As I sat next to her, I felt relief after the brisk walk.

The air smelled of the dirty water, and of the plant life living on the banks. The noise of the city was subdued because of the lower position of the river

I closed my eyes, and enjoyed the sun rays glowing red through my eyelids. I could feel an unusually high energy emanating from Alma/Michael next to me. It was a physical sensation, like feeling warm next to a heat source.

'That energy connects all my crazy experiences to Alma's other world.' I thought.

We sat quietly for a long time before I heard Alma's voice.

"How are you doing, my friend?"

"I'm good."

"How are your questions doing?"

"They're gone, seems they took a vacation since your little demonstration."

"Would you like to discover more?"

"You keep asking the same question. Have I not been clear enough before? I can see that you have been evaluating me. Have I not passed your tests?"

"Yes, you're right, I have been evaluating you. You are facing a big change of paradigm, a polar shift in most of your basic assumptions concerning your life and your world."

"Do you want to train me into becoming somebody like you, who can change his body?"

She laughed in Alma's light and charming way, and I had to shake off my inner confusion to hear her response.

"Far from that! The faculty of changing into another body is only a side effect of the energy of my world. I am using it to train your mind to accept that physical matter is not what it appears to be."

"You succeeded in that, but what now?" I said, somewhat irritated, "how long can you maintain Alma's appearance?"

"As long as I want to, I am connected to the essence, the spirit of my friend Alma and I am expressing her physical appearance using the true nature of the power that creates everything in this universe."

She stood up and walked towards stairs leading to the upper walkway. I followed my incredible companion. We crossed the bridge and walked to the big plaza in front of the cathedral.

"Are you taking me to Notre Dame?" I asked.

"I'm only guiding you towards the cathedral, Luke, you are free to go wherever you like!" She said with a mischievous smile. I did not respond, just continued walking.

I must note here, that I have mostly been referring to my companion in the feminine form, as Alma. My awareness of her/him having been the man called Michael, less than an hour ago had started to conveniently fade into my immediate perception of how things appeared.

We passed in front of the outer gates of the immense cathedral, where beggars were pursuing their trade. We went straight around the left edge of the ancient building, towards the entrance to the cathedral towers. A sign warned the visitors that there are 387 steps to the top.

"So now, you want to test my fitness," I joked, "is that part of your standard curriculum?"

She just laughed, and I followed her inside the old building to a narrow wooden staircase that was winding upwards. I followed her silently, mesmerized by the slow rhythm of turning along the spiraling staircase.

As we arrived on the highest landing, bright daylight flooded the dimly lit staircase.

I was dizzy from the long climb. Blinded by the light, I had to grab the railing on the narrow walkway to steady myself. Everything was blurry as I stepped outside. As I turned, looking for Alma, and my heart nearly skipped a beat, as a monstrously horned creature had appeared in front of me.

Alma who had advanced along the platform was laughing, and I knew she had seen my reaction.

"Did you seriously think I had changed into a gargoyle?"

"Who am I to know? Maybe you brought me here, just for that purpose?" I said, my face flushing.

Without answering she continued to walk along the narrow walkway. I followed her silently, lost in an endless loop of vague impressions and confused feelings.

I had thought I had the main keys to the knowledge about the nature of the Universe. Now it seemed that I needed to start all over again, right from the beginning. The scientist in me was excited about the prospect of making new discoveries, but my ego had a hard time letting go of all the foundations I had taken so much time and work to construct.

I felt vulnerable. As I was searching for something familiar in my mind, the memories of my wife and children came flooding back. I felt an overwhelming longing for my old happy life to be restored. But even the last remnants of it were gone.

She sensed my mental turmoil and said very softly: "I know, Luke, it's not easy to let go of the old sure knowing, things you have never doubted. It shakes your identity, the sense of who you are as a person."

She stopped walking. The wind was blowing hair into her face.

"Nothing is really as it seems, and everything is much more than it appears," she said as if talking to herself.

"Having spent the last hours with you, I tend to agree." I said, with a thin smile, glad to feel some humor.

On an impulse, I grabbed both her arms and held her in a firm grip. "Just tell me who you are! Are you from that other world?"

Her arms felt warm and firm in my hands.

"I am a human being, just like you!"

"Who are you?" I repeated, "are you Michael, or are you Alma, just tell me the truth. You drive me crazy!"

A group of German tourists was trying to squeeze around us, as we were taking up much space on the narrow balcony.

She also took my arms in her hands, locking us in a double grip.

"We humans are so much more than we commonly think we are. We are an outer being of flesh, and we are a vast inner being who in reality lives in the Spirit World. We are fields of energy and streams of being and consciousness, manifesting through the very fabric of the universe that we co-create, that's in short who you and I, and all human beings are."

"But how could you become Alma, so amazingly, so incredibly... " I trailed off, not finding words which could express the turmoil of emotions I was feeling.

She tightened her grip on my arms, and feeling the warmth of her hands, added to my confusion.

"This has to do with the stream of consciousness located in the spirit dimension. I can only do this in a very limited way, and only with people I have a special connection to, like I have with Alma. I have done that to create an opening in your mind and so prepare you for more things to come that are beyond your world."

"Why did you pick me? What are your intentions?"

"Nobody picked you; it was Alma who saw you on the beach in India. Her only intension at first, was to help a man who was obviously distressed."

"But how different are you from ordinary humans?"

"We are genetically and physically absolutely identical with all people on this planet, the only difference being that our bodies have a higher dimensional essence. We are in many ways the future of humanity."

"How many humans are there like you?"

"This is a question that right now I cannot truthfully answer, as there is a major fact concerning us, of which you are not yet aware."

"But how do you explain that up to now, no significant information about your kind of people has spread all over the internet and other medias?"

"There have been very rare occurrences in the past where this nearly happened, but each time they have been contained by the likes of Alma and me."

"Why are you keeping it secret?"

"Simply to protect ourselves, as these two worlds, are too much apart in how they view life, their connection to the planet and the inner dimensions of spirit. We hope there will be a future where secrecy is no more necessary. I hope I'll be able to show you that other world very soon, then things will become much clearer for you."

My emotions were welling up again "Soon, soon, always later! What am I to you? A guinea pig that you string along, doing your tests at your leisure? What is this world you are talking about? Is it real, or is it merely a metaphor?"

She let go of my arms, and looked at me, with an intense and worried expression.

"I keep telling you, Luke, that you are a free person, with a reasonable amount of free will. You can leave this whole adventure now, or at any point in the future. But if you decide to continue this journey, the truth is, that I am testing you. I am getting to know you, and see if you can deal with the reality of that other world, and whether I can trust you with that secret."

"You sound like you are from the Martian secret services, planning to take over our world!"

I nearly shouted, I was getting upset again. What on

Earth was I doing with that creature, on Notre Dame's tower? I was getting scared, losing my ground again.

"Luke!" she shook me lightly, "I understand that you are upset, but we need to be in a different space to bring clarity instead of more confusion! Come, let's go! And remember, it's your choice!" She just turned and left.

I froze, overcome by panic. At that moment, it did not feel like I had any choice. What choice was there to be left hanging with the biggest mystery and revelations only to be hinted at and not resolved. How could I live with that? I was scared and upset, but it became clear to me at that very moment that I had never desired anything more than continuing on that path. There was no more turning back. I straightened myself and hurried towards the stairs.

Chapter Six

Rushing down the stairs I bumped into several people who were on their way up. I was straining to catch sight of Alma, who had left me just a minute ago.

"What if she disappears, just vanishes without creating another body?" My heart was thumping hard.

I nearly missed a step, when I passed one of the windowed alcoves. Grabbing the railing I stopped my downward flight in an awkward freeze. Here I was, my legs and arms were thrown into an unlikely and comical posture staring at an Indian woman who was just closing a small foldable phone.

"So, you decided to continue your journey with me!" she said, smiling down at me from her position on the landing between floors.

A security guard who had just come up the stairs stopped for a second and looked at me suspiciously, but then decided to move on. I was breathing hard and adjusted my balance from my uncomfortable position.

As I regained my balance I looked at the old, eroded wooden stairs. The rugged iron railing felt cold in my hand. Time stood still for a rare instant of intense presence. All the history and complexities of my life contained in a heartbeat's moment.

Then I laughed and felt a lump of tension dissolve.

"Yes, you're stuck with me!" I said.

"Great!" she said, smiling. "Let's go and have a coffee!"

I was glad to leave the narrow old tower. We walked towards the rear of Notre Dame, and continued on the street bordering the river.

We sat on the terrace of a café that was on the sunny side of the street. The fresh air was competing with the heat of the sunny sky.

She asked abruptly "So, what would you like to do now?"

I looked at her, magnificent in her sky-blue silk dress. She had crossed her legs and angled her head backwards, to catch the sun rays on her closed eyes. It was crazy to feel what I was feeling for that woman while twisting my mind around the fact that the person in front of me was in reality Michael. I even thought I was getting a hint of that patchouli scent Alma had worn in India, but I knew it was just my imagination.

Then with an effort, I turned my attention back to her question.

"Continue to explore and discover this glorious other world of yours?" I ventured, aware I was being sarcastic.

"When you say it like that it sounds rather boring!" She had a mischievous glimmer in her eyes. "You know what? The best way to explore any world is to see it with your own eyes."

"Are you going to take me there?" I said, gulping.

"Yes, probably!" she said and stood up. "Just throw a few coins on the table and come with me!"

She was already on her way. I hurriedly paid for the coffee and ran towards her walking shape bathed in midday sun rays. She was walking towards the next street junction.

"Where are we going?" I shouted, catching my breath.

"To the butterfly island, where it all began!" Her eyes were beaming, her whole bodily appearance was sparkling with energy.

"What island?"

"You will see! I have called Chul, and he's taking us there right away."

We walked towards the other side of the river island on which Notre Dame was built and arrived at the "quai aux fleurs", which is lined by a permanent flower market. Alma did not stop and swiftly walked towards a bridge linking both islands in the oldest heart of the city.

At the corner of the bridge, I saw Michael's dark red Peugeot parked halfway on the sidewalk. The driver's door opened, revealing Chul, dressed in a blue, uniform-like suit. With a broad smile he opened the back door, where I dropped into the comfortable seats, grunting with relief. Chul did not seem to be surprised by Michael's changed appearance.

I closed my eyes, and felt the powerful car move us on the old Parisian pavement. I barely heard the characteristic rumbling noise. I felt the inner distance from the world that had been mine.

After a while I opened the corner of my right eye and saw Alma, or should I say "Malma", looking at the road ahead. She sensed my glance and turned. Her eyes were still blazing with energy.

"I'm happy you decided to come on this journey, and I'm glad to take you." she said.

"I'm no less confused!" I exclaimed, "I don't even know where we're going. I must be nuts to trust you like that, but that's all I got!"

"Trust is essential on both sides, without it, this particular journey is impossible!"

"Where are we going?"

"Right now, we are heading to Le Bourget airport where our journey continues to another part of this planet"

"Why are you doing this with me? Why take all that trouble? Don't you have more important things to do?"

"No! Right now, this is what I'm doing, and I'll dedicate all my time and attention to it until it's done."

"But what is so important about it? I'm a rather average, unimportant individual!"

"Luke, the great thing about you is that you have shown inner strength, the capacity and willingness to be open-minded, and to see things differently. Because of that, I trust you, and I know that you are capable of doing the journey."

Traffic grew dense as we neared the airport. After passing big warehouses and parking facilities, we arrived at a small inconspicuous looking gate.

Chul flashed a badge at a security agent, and the gate went up with a high pitched metallic sound, piercing the car's sound insulation.

"Butterfly island sounds like the Caribbean," I said, as the car drove past airplane hangars of various sizes.

"You'll see!" she said, smiling, "Why don't you enjoy not knowing for a while longer. Sometimes it's a good state of mind to be in."

I was reluctantly getting used to my companion's sibylline ways. My state of mind was becoming less rebellious, the more I accepted, that I had become a student again, and that Alma/Michael was teaching me something.

After a short drive Chul parked the car in front of one of the bigger hangars. The sudden cooler and kerosene smelling air tore me out of my reverie, as Alma opened her door. The massive sliding gates of the hangar were closed, but bright light was emanating from a small entrance on the side of the building.

I saw Alma walking straight towards the door and disappear through the luminous frame. As I turned to our driver, I saw that he also had left the car without me noticing. For a moment I resisted leaving the safe comfort of the vehicle. I realized that I was probably going to leave the country, to a destination my incredible companion had decided to take me.

Finally I got out of the car and walked to the door, where I stopped right within the frame. The sight of the brightly lit, golden, gleaming big private jet took my breath away.

Alma was standing next to the lowered stairs of the plane. She was speaking to Chul and another person in a pilot uniform. As I approached I saw that she was a tall woman. Her braided hair was held in the back by a rainbow-colored clip, contrasting with the formality of her uniform.

"Meet Anne-Marie, our co-pilot." Alma said then looked at me with a particular intensity, as she added, "get yourself comfortable in the front part of the plane, I'll be with you shortly!"

I wondered what she was up to, but had to turn to the woman next to me.

"Hi, nice to meet you!" I said, shaking her hand. She had a pleasant, joyous face, impression reinforced by her prominent cheekbones. Her skin was a light tone of brown.

"This is an amazing aircraft!" I said, looking at her expectantly.

"Yes," she confirmed enthusiastically, "it's a top of the line Gulfstream jet. It can fly at nearly the speed of sound to any destination almost half across the globe without refueling... but please come in and see for yourself!" she said enthusiastically, with a pronounced French accent, and pointed me up the stairs.

As I stepped into the body of the aircraft, my steps froze again, and my language capacity was instantly reduced to one word, "Wow!" which I kept repeating until the co-pilot gently nudged me forward.

I blushed and apologized, feeling a bit like the country mouse discovering the town.

"It's quite a sight when you come in!" she laughed.

I could see the area Alma had asked me to go to. It was furnished with big individual seats, draped in white leather. In front of the seats, attached to the walls were shiny tables made of precious wood. It all made a shocking impression of wealth.

I took my seat and closed my eyes. I felt tired and needed some quiet space and forget all that was around. The subtle smell of leather was the only reminder of where I was. My thoughts drifted away, and I fell asleep.

I heard a voice calling my name. The voice was familiar, but I could not put a name to it. I reluctantly opened my eyes, and saw the person sitting in front of me. I was instantly fully awake, as my mind caught up: It was Michael! The last time I had seen him, he was naked, and had disappeared in front of my eyes.

I felt dizzy with the thought that the person in front of me was the same I had been with the whole day. Only his appearance had changed twice. Now he was back in his original body.

"You always have been Michael, even when you looked like Alma!" I exclaimed as if I was only now catching up with that truth.

"Yes, put in the simplest terms, that's true," he paused, giving me time to gather my wits, then continued with his deep masculine voice, "but, as I told you before, I also have been connected to the spirit and energy which is the essence of Alma. That is why it was such a disconcerting experience for you. Your mind could intellectually understand that I was Michael, but you could also feel Alma's energy."

I looked out of one of the big windows, as the plane had started to move.

"We are taxiing to the runway," Michael said, as he fastened his seatbelt.

I did likewise, and closed my eyes again, reluctant to engage in more discussions with him. My mind was screaming "Give me a break!"

Keeping my eyes closed during takeoff, I drifted back into sleep while we rose to cruise altitude.

I woke up as my head jolted sideways. I was immediately wide awake and felt the plane rocking from side to side. Michael was still sitting in front of me, holding a tablet.

"We are flying through heavy turbulence," he said calmly.

The plane, in unison with my stomach seemed to be moving in all directions at once. I was starting to feel sick.

"This is more like we hit a storm," I said, grabbing the armrests, "I just hope your pilot knows what he's doing!"

Michael laughed, "Maybe next time you can join Chul in the cockpit. That's the best place during turbulences."

"I think I'll skip that!" I said, straightening my posture. I looked out of the window and saw that the sky was divided between an area nearly free of clouds, with visibility going down to sea level, and another area ahead of us that looked dark and dense with a scary looking cloud formation shaped like an anvil. I felt the plane change course, slowly turning to the right.

"I think our pilot has just decided to fly around the storm," Michael said, "come, let's have a look!"

He unfastened his seatbelt and went straight to the cockpit. I hesitated, as the plane was still shaking massively, but then, curiosity got the better of me, I stood up and entered the pilot's lair.

The space was small, filled with displays and controls. Both pilots were looking straight ahead. In front of them were four big screens. The ones directly in front of each pilot were showing what looked like a live map with weather radar information, which I recognized, as I worked in the field of climate research.

Michael and I were standing in a tiny space just beyond the door. Chul turned around and freed one ear from his headset.

"There's a pretty nasty storm ahead of us, as you can feel. It's not too spread out yet, so we are going to fly around. It'll cost us half an hour flight time. I just got the course change approval."

"No problem, Chul! We are in no hurry. I was showing Luke around."

Anne-Marie, the co-pilot turned around and flashed us a smile. "You can see, Luke, we are in very good hands," she said.

"I was never really worried." I lied, happy to walk back

towards my seat where I hurriedly fastened the seatbelt.

The new flight route gave us calmer skies. We spent the last hours relaxing and of course, having an excellent meal, professionally served by Chul the most versatile person I have ever met.

All traces of the storm had disappeared. There was an unhindered visibility down to sea level.

"During this season, thunderstorms and cyclones show us the power and aliveness of the planet," Michael said.

The plane had started its slow descent towards our destination, which, I realized, was still unknown to me. Looking out of the window, I still saw only water, stretching endlessly.

"If you want to see where we'll soon be landing, before knowing the name, just go to the cockpit, and ask Chul to show you the butterfly," Michael suggested, pointing at the horizon.

"Another one of your tricks!" I said, matching Michael's smile, "how fitting to have a butterfly! Is it going to metamorphose into a spaceship and fly us to another planet?"

Michael burst out laughing: "Wow! What an imagination you have! You should write novels!"

"Maybe that's exactly what I'll be doing if one day I live to tell what happened to me these days. But who would believe that this was no fiction?"

As I entered the cockpit, the co-pilot took off her headphones. "Ah! My replacement has arrived!"

"Another new experience for the day," I said, getting excited.

I climbed into the vacated seat and strapped in. Anne-Marie helped me with the headset, and before long I was comfortable, sitting in front of the huge navigation panels.

"You have come for the butterfly?" Chul's voice was crystal clear in my headphones.

"Yes! I'm bracing myself for one of your magic tricks!"

"No magic trick here, just technology! We would need to be at more than double our maximum altitude, something like ninety-five thousand feet, for you to see the live image, but I can show you a satellite view of our position on your monitor."

The panel in front of me switched to an image showing the local area as seen from a considerable height. There, in the middle of the screen, lay a big island. It was clearly shaped like a green-brown butterfly, with its right wing slightly higher than the left.

"Wow!"

"Now look out of the window! In front of us is the middle part where the wings join, that's where we're going to land."

I stretched my neck to see above the panels. Ahead of us, a land mass was approaching. Having seen the satellite picture, I could figure the big central bay, from which the huge wings were spreading.

Instantly I knew that this was Guadeloupe, a Caribbean island that is part of overseas France and that we would soon land at Pointe-à-Pitre airport. A wave of excitement washed over me. I was eager for the next ride with Michael on the wings of that huge butterfly.

Chapter Seven

The co-pilot's seat is definitely the best place on a plane! The approach to the airport and the landing had me nearly stand upright in my seat. I wanted to see it all. Chul had demonstratively raised his hands from the controls and let the high-tech plane do it all by itself.

Minutes later we were taxiing to a hangar, which looked like the one in Paris. The air was warm, and a light tropical rain enhanced the subtle exotic fragrances I could smell above the airport stink. A big white car was waiting. We left the co-pilot with the plane, and Chul switched roles again taking the driver seat, and we were promptly on our way. I noticed that we did not pass any passport controls, nor did we do any paperwork. We were still on French territory, and Michael's obvious VIP status surely had its advantages.

The car was a large Renault Espace, fitted in the back like a limousine with two rows of seats facing each other. Michael opened a fridge placed in a panel between the seats, and filled two glasses with an orange beverage and ice.

"Here, have a local drink, to celebrate our arrival in Guadeloupe! They make it from local fruits and Rum!"

We left the airport area and drove a long time on busy urban roads and motorways before finally leaving the city behind. Our itinerary led through villages where the local Caribbean culture became more visible. Men and some women in colorful clothes were hanging out in small groups around shops and cafés. We were approaching the coastal area, driving north from Pointe-a-Pitre, on the left wing of the butterfly.

The road was winding down from a higher plateau, green and rich in tropical vegetation, towards the sea that I could see glimmering ahead of us. Michael had chosen to open the windows instead of using air conditioning. The warm moist air was richly perfumed by the surrounding vegetation.

As the road started to follow the shore, the air became fresher and dryer. There were small beaches separated by rocky areas and patches of palm trees growing right next to the high tide water line.

It looked wild and rugged, barely touched by human activity. The road stopped abruptly and finished in an empty rocky patch big enough for several cars to park. There were no visible constructions around.

Michael stepped out, and I swiftly followed, happy to stretch my legs after what had felt like a long drive. In front of us was the half circle of a pristine Caribbean bay with its palm trees, white sand, and turquoise water.

"Let's have a dip!" he called out to me.

He stripped while running over the hot sand. The waves were high, the tide climbing. I had the odd feeling of time slowing down. I witnessed his actions as he ran, took off his clothes, dove headfirst. I froze as he disappeared into the foaming waves. I used to love the sea…

I sat in the hot sand, breathing hard. Part of me longed for the fresh water, while another was about to run for his life. Out of the corner of my eye, I saw Michael jumping waves. As if in a dream, I slowly took off my clothes, and walked to the water's edge. The waves were licking at my ankles. I took a step into the water and sat down. My body shuddered at the contact. Michael was rolling out of an enormous wave and splashed water towards me. Overcoming the heaviness that I was feeling, I sprayed some water in his direction, but it felt like lead.

Michael gave me a friendly tap on the shoulder, his eyes filled with compassion.

"It's ok, Luke, take it slowly," he said. Then he walked out of the water.

Chul was sitting on the beach, like the vigilant guardian he was.

For a while, I sat silently, with the power of the waves touching my legs. Slowly I stretched out on the wet sand, my body finally relaxing.

When I got up, I saw Michael and Chul, sitting nearby. They both were smiling, and I saw friendship and empathy in their eyes.

I turned back to the sea that was on fire with bright glittering sun rays. I closed my eyes and relished in the warmth and the intense light, colored red by my eyelids.

When I reopened my eyes, I saw an indigenous looking man standing next to my two companions. They were looking in my direction. The man was unusually tall for a native. Age showed with his long curly white hair cascading freely over his shoulders. His eyes were bright power spots in his darker face. He wore a long red tee-shirt which were the only visible clothes.

Time stopped for a moment when our eyes met. Then I continued to walk towards the group.

'That's probably the man we came all the way to see,' I thought., feeling excited and curious as I approached. The man had not moved, he kept looking straight at me, making me feel uncomfortable.

Fortunately, Michael stepped in, "This is Cledor, venerable guardian of this place."

As the man did not stretch out his hand towards me, I just made a little bow with my head.

"Glad to meet you Mr. Cledor, my name is Luke."

His voice was deep and melodious when he spoke.

"Yes, Luke, welcome. I was expecting you, come, let's go to my house!"

At that moment Michael turned to Chul.

"It's time for you to go back and fly the Gulfstream home!"

I could not help asking, "Do you mean to fly the plane back to Paris? Are we going to stay here?" Instantly I felt a rush of anxiety, not understanding what was going on.

"Don't worry Luke, from now on we won't need the plane any longer, there are much better and faster transportation means than planes!" Michael said with a mischievous smile.

"I don't understand."

"You will soon enough!"

Without waiting, he he took a small backpack and started to follow the black man who was already on his way.

I turned to Chul who was watching; his face displaying amused calmness. I realized there was no use asking explanations from him.

"Goodbye Chul! Are we going to meet again?"

"Yes, I'm sure! Please take this backpack. I took the liberty to fill it with some essentials for you. Bon voyage Mister Luke!" he turned and walked towards the car.

I quickly dressed, took the backpack, and jogged to catch up with the two men who were walking towards a hill overlooking the beach from the upper end of the bay. It was broad with a round top, like the head of a huge giant whose body might still be buried underneath. It was covered by trees, but at what would be the very center of the giant's cranium I could see a small patch of orange-red color contrasting with the lush green of the jungle covering the hill. It was too far to see any details, but I was sure I was seeing the roof of Cledor's house.

'A nice climb!' I thought.

As I had expected, we left the beach and went up a narrow path spiraling up the hill. We moved in semi-darkness, everything was green, even the light. The dense jungle on both sides gave me the impression of walking through a tunnel. The moist air was smelling of earth and rotting leaves. High in the trees, tropical birds were having loud discussions.

It was like wandering into a different world. We were walking in silence, one behind the other, following the spiraling path. Again I had the feeling that I was leaving my familiar world behind. After a long walk, we reached the top of the hill.

At the outer edge of a small clearing stood a house. It was a broad, one storied traditional Creole house with a covered porch. The door and all the windows were open. As I entered the big square room I was struck by a painting on a wall. It showed a huge sun in intense tones of yellow and orange, with rays like spirals radiating outwards. The walls were made of woods of different shades and textures.

Cledor motioned us to sit around the large round table in the middle of the room. Both table and chairs were made from bamboo and reed. Only the top of the table was made of a huge slice of a tree trunk. That tree must have been enormous, as the slice had a diameter of approximately one and a half meters. The surface was smooth and darkened by age. I could see all the growth rings making a beautiful, nearly mesmerizing inward going pattern.

It was noon, the air was hot and moist, but the shade in the house created a gentle air current between all the open windows. To the right I saw a small kitchen and a bedroom. The door to the left opened to another room which looked empty.

Cledor came back from the kitchen carrying a tray with glasses and a big jar. We drank the deliciously cool water that he had flavored with slices of lemon, orange, and leaves of fresh mint.

Cledor sat opposite to me with hundreds of tree rings between us.

"Why have you come?" he asked, without any preamble.

I stared into my beverage where some shreds of mint leaves were floating among tiny pieces of ice.

"I don't know, Michael…" I trailed off, aware that I could not answer the question.

"You don't know!" he stated matter-of-factly.

"Yes, that is true. Apart from Michael telling me he wants to show me another world, that is related to the crazy stuff I have been involved with, since I met Alma in India, I really don't have a clue as to why I'm here."

"I like an honest answer!" Cledor said, "I'm going to tell you why you are here. But be warned, it's a lot more of what you call 'crazy stuff'. Are you sure you want to know?"

This time I managed to look Cledor straight in the eyes.

"Yes! I've come all this way, and to be honest, I like what that 'crazy stuff' is doing to me. I feel much better, and my life got way more exciting!"

"I like your sense of humor, Luke!" Cledor said, laughing, and the tension between us had evaporated.

"As you have come to my house, I'd like to tell you a few things about myself and this place." He leaned back in his reed chair, pointing to the table. "Look at the circles in the wood, how many do you think there are?"

I straightened in my chair and looked at the huge number of concentric circles. They alternated from dark to bright but were too many for me to count.

"I can only estimate," I said, balancing my head from left to right, "there could be several hundred, maybe three hundred?"

"Yes, you are on the right track, there are nearly four hundred, three hundred ninety-seven to be precise. That tree died forty-seven years ago, which means that tree started its life four hundred and forty-four years ago. That was a time when my people, the Caribs were still free and had not yet suffered from being conquered and enslaved."

Something started to itch in my mind, some vague memory of that name.

"I'm sorry to interrupt, but I heard about your people in a documentary I have seen recently."

Undisturbed, Cledor asked: "What was this documentary about?"

As I remembered the details, I immediately regretted my interruption and felt embarrassed.

"I'm sorry to say; it was about cannibalism. I remember somebody saying that the word originates from the name of your people."

Cledor was quiet for a few moments then said very seriously, "Now that you are warned, I guess I can go and tell my friends to take the cauldron off the fire!"

I had not noticed that I had stopped breathing, but

when I heard Michael's loud outburst of laughter, I exhaled with relief and joined in the hearty laughter with Michael and Cledor.

When our merriment had subsided, Cledor continued to speak.

"Yes, my people have unfairly been reported by the Spanish invaders as eaters of human flesh. At that time the Spanish had a decent queen who had prohibited the arrest and capture of the local population whom she wanted to treat as her subjects. The invaders had used some of our old rituals dealing with captured enemies, where practically none of their flesh was touched, to label our people as human flesh eaters. In that way, they could justify the enslavement of our whole population."

Now that I had become wiser, I refrained from asking Cledor what he meant with 'practically none of their flesh'. I was happy to let go of the subject.

"Let's go back to the slice of the old tree we call gommier, a huge tree you can still find in some of our forests. When it was a sapling, nearly half a millennium ago, some of my people found a gateway into another world."

I raised my eyebrows, thinking, *Finally! The other world!* But I said nothing, just nodded, as if he had not just said the most extraordinary thing.

Cledor continued, "It is not the spirit world many traditions talk about, but it is one step nearer to it."

Now as I started to react, beginning to open my mouth, Cledor held up his hand. "Just let that information sink into your mind for a while, we'll soon take time to explore the subject in more depth."

Then, without adding anything else, Cledor stood up and went into the kitchen. After a few minutes, he came back with a big tray loaded with food. There were fresh local fruit, cooked plantain and dried fish in a spicy sauce with some bread. I had been hungry for a long while, and the food came as a welcome break.

After we had finished eating, Cledor went straight to the porch of the house and lay down in one of the hammocks that were suspended between the pillars holding the roof. He stretched like a cat, grunting with pleasure.

"Come, my friends, take a nap!" he called to us, "we can save the world later."

I followed Michael to the porch and saw that there were two more hammocks suspended between the pillars. The porch was facing an opening in the surrounding jungle, through which one could see part of the bay below and a far view over the sea.

Lying down in the hammock, I was welcoming the break from the intensity of the day. I could feel the light breeze on my skin. The sky was a mix of blue and clouds that were carrying one of the quick and intense tropical rains of the day. A colorful bird that looked like a small parrot had landed on one of the outer posts of the porch.

Next thing I know, is that the sky had turned a deep ashen color, and a strong wind was bending trees, threatening to throw them upon the house. The whole porch was shaking, the poles and planks rattling loudly. I jumped out of the hammock, which at once got blown away. Cledor and Michael were gone, nowhere to be seen.

I turned around, but the wind had already blown off the roof of the house. I could only see the big table with the old tree slice, sole remaining furniture in the wrecked house. When I looked out towards the sea, I froze. Everything else halted, like a video on pause. In front of me, coming from the sea was a gigantic dark wall of water, twice as big as the hill I was standing on. It was darker than the sky, a mass of fast-moving water. In a few seconds, it would swallow the hill. My terror exploded in a scream, and everything lit up.

The brightness was the clear sky. Cledor and Michael were half way up from their hammock. It had been a nightmare! A really bad one. I was shivering, cold, and was drenched in sweat. Cledor brought me some water. With a shaking voice, I told them what I had seen in my dream.

Michael put a hand on my back. "Your mind is healing itself. What occurred to you and your family rarely happens in a lifetime."

His friendly gesture and the warm energy of his hand helped me shake the dream away.

Cledor asked: "How real did the dream feel?"

"Totally real! I was there, there was noise, wind, I could feel it. I still remember it vividly."

"Did you see what you saw in the dream with your eyes?"

"No, it all happened inside my head."

"Do you mean your mind?"

"Yes, it was in my mind, but as real as if I had seen it with my eyes."

"I'm sorry to enquire on such an opportunity, but it is a useful subject for us, right now, as it demonstrates, that you can see without your physical eyes."

"Yes, one could say that I was seeing with my mind's eyes."

"Would you say that now, at this moment, you are seeing with your eyes, or with your mind?"

"I know what you're getting at. It raises essential questions, like whether anything exists outside the mind and it also connects to the question whether consciousness exists independently of the brain."

"Yes, exactly," Cledor said enthusiastically, "these are fundamental questions. Are you as a person, the sum total of your memories, located in the frail tissues of your brain, or is who you really are, stored somewhere else? If so, where would that be?"

Michael made eye contact with Cledor, and it was obvious that they had come to a silent agreement.

"Let's go and sit over there, at the fireplace." Cledor motioned us towards a round bench facing a small circle of blackened stones.

When we were seated, Michael said: "Luke, in Paris you witnessed me switching into another body."

"Yes, that was the most shocking experience I ever had in my life, apart from the w..wave." I started to stammer and I looked away, at the distant Caribbean sea that stretched far to the horizon.

Michael continued, unperturbed, "You witnessed something that is quite impossible."

He tapped his chest. "This very body you see now disappeared. There was an instant when it was pure energy, pure potential that had no particular form."

"Yes, that blew my mind! What was that high energy that filled the room?"

"That energy is an expression of the essential creative life force of the universe. It is the energy field that connects, transforms and creates."

Michael said nothing more for a moment, while I felt the sun warm my body. Cledor broke the silence.

"Coming back to our initial question about where our consciousness resides: What happened to Michael's brain cells when his body disappeared?"

My eyes widened, as I started to understand what he was getting at. "The physical brain dematerialized, and everything that was stored as electric charges in the neurons must have been deleted, or at least damaged."

"Exactly, how then, when Michael reappeared into a different human body, with an entirely different brain, could he continue to be his old self?"

"That's impossible!" I exclaimed, looking suspiciously at Michael.

"It is not, if what we are is stored in another dimension than the physical," said Michael.

My mind was spinning, trying to understand and connect all the implications that followed from Cledor's affirmation.

"Let's give your mind a break!" Cledor exclaimed before I could say anything else. "It's time to have some fun!"

He stood up and put an arm around my shoulders, pulling me up and leading me towards the back of the house.

His seriousness had disappeared, as he showed us another clearing behind the house. Surrounded by tropical plants, it was a perfectly cleared area of a hundred square meters, covered by fine gravel.

"Holy cow, Mister Cledor! You have your own boules field!"

I was delighted, as I'm particularly fond of this French game. The 'jeu de boules' is played a lot in the South of France. The game consists of throwing iron balls as near as possible to a smaller wooden one, which also means kicking away the opponent's balls.

"One of the good things brought by French colonization," Cledor said, chuckling.

He went to the house and came back with six pairs of boules, and we set ourselves to play, each of us having four balls to play with. We played for a couple of hours, just focusing on the fun of playing the game. Cledor and Michael turned out to be great opponents. It took me a while to keep up with them, as I had not played for a long time, but it was great fun. It helped me relax and land into the new place, after all the roller-coaster days.

It was a joy to simply be and play with two guys, something I had not done for ages. For these couple of hours, I forgot about the crazy story I had gotten myself into, and it was the best and most healing thing that could have happened. When we finished, we sat on the porch, and had a beer watching the sun slowly travel towards the horizon.

Nothing else happened that evening, apart from having a meal while doing some light conversation. I did not ask any more questions, as I had the feeling I was enjoying my good old world for the last time. I was not going to spoil it.

Chapter Eight

I woke up with a start from an uneasy dream that seemed to continue as I heard a strange noise. It sounded like a far away engine coming closer. I looked out of the window, and saw, coming from the direction of the sea, two black helicopters. They were big ones; I could distinguish a row of windows behind the cockpit. Just as I looked, a side door opened in the first helicopter. There were black figures in it. As the helicopters approached, I saw they were men holding something. Machine guns! And they were heading straight towards the house. They would be here in no time!

I turned around as I saw Michael enter the room, immediately followed by Cledor. They were dressed and carried backpacks.

"Jump into your clothes, Luke, and grab your things," Michael said in a loud, but calm voice.

There was no point asking questions. I swiftly put on my clothes, took my backpack, and followed them to the back of the house. I looked up at the sky, searching for the helicopters, but could only hear the loud rumble of their engines coming closer. Luckily, the house was hiding us from their view. We dove into the nearby dense vegetation, and Cledor led the way on a narrow path going downhill. Behind us, the noise of the helicopters had intensified. I could not see anything through the impenetrable vegetation, but it sounded like the helicopters had started to hover above the house.

A minute later I heard shouts from where we had entered the path. My heart was racing, but my two companions in front of me remained calm and did not even quicken their pace. They seemed to know exactly what to do. This helped me get a grip on my growing panic.

After another long minute, Cledor left the path and stepped right into the dense vegetation. Michael followed without hesitation, but halfway in waited for me to catch up and took my hand. I followed him as best I could, whilst he pushed his way through dense weavings of vegetation. He finally stopped and told me to sit down. Behind us, high-pitched engine noises had started, with a lot of rumbling and cracking. It sounded like they were cutting through the jungle to follow our trail.

"Touch the ground with your hands, Luke. You'll find an opening in the ground just in front of you. Lower your legs into it, and let gravity do the rest. You'll slide down into a cave, where Cledor is already waiting for us."

The voices and noises had intensified behind us, and it was clear that this was the way to go. I hesitated a few seconds, as I have never been an Indiana Jones kind of guy, and hate big spiders and snakes. I took a deep breath and slid into the hole.

'I'm like Alice in Wonderland, following the rabbit into the hole.' I thought as I glided down the shaft. It was dark, and I could feel it's stony sides, around half a meter apart. Then I fell out into a cavity where Cledor was standing with a torch. At first, I could not distinguish anything else through the blinding light. I had to swiftly move away from my landing place, as dirt was already preceding Michael's descent through the shaft.

A few moments later we were reunited in an underground cave. The walls were made of rough stone, and the ground was a mix of wet soil and small stones. There was no trace of any human activity. I could not see any other exit than the one we had come through. The cave was not very big, and I started to feel uneasy.

"Where do we go from here?" I asked with a tight voice.

"Just sit down and wait, all is well!" Michael said, sitting down himself and taking a flashlight out of his backpack.

Cledor stood motionless in front of a wall. I watched him impatiently, as time seemed to stand still.

"What's he doing?" I asked anxiously.

"He is opening the door to where we are going."

I could see nothing happening; no secret doorway was sliding open in the rocks that looked unquestionably solid.

"What…"

Something had started to happen. The wall was faintly

glowing. A very dim red glow at first, rapidly intensifying, but bizarrely not getting brighter. I had to close my eyes, as the strange light made me sick. It felt like a radiation, that pierced my eyelids. Then abruptly it stopped. When I opened my eyes, I saw a perfect rectangular opening in front of Cledor, who was already stepping into it. He motioned us to follow.

Even after having seen Michael's transformation, Cledor's performance left me glued to the ground, unable to move.

"Come, Luke, we're almost there!"

"What kind of magic was that?" I got up, but my legs were shaky.

"Electricity also appeared like magic to the people who first saw it," Michael replied, who was already halfway inside the opening.

"But…"

"Come, no time for discussions now!"

I followed Michael into the dark rectangle. The narrow tunnel had been cut to perfection through every rock layer, and all the surfaces looked perfectly smooth. I could distinguish a dim light a short distance ahead. After a quick walk through what had been solid rock only minutes ago, we arrived at a very different place.

It was a huge, round cave, at least twenty meters wide. Cledor had put his flashlight on the floor, pointing it to the center of the high ceiling. The result was a spectacular multiplication of the light, as a myriad of small reflective glass and ceramic fragments covering the walls glittered with the reflected beam. As I looked up, I saw that the whole room was shaped like a drop, broad at the bottom and narrowing towards the top.

Cledor stood in front of the tunnel we had just come through. It's amazing what one can get used to. This time, as I expected, after a time that seemed much shorter, he reversed his 'magic trick'. The rectangle opening started to glow, before reverting to a smooth patch of the wall covered by the glittering materials. It looked as if nothing had ever happened.

I felt exhilarated by the latest events, and also much safer, far away from helicopters and armed men.

"That was a very nifty trick, Mister Cledor! Any chance you could teach me?" I said jokingly.

"I'm glad you got your sense of humor back, Luke! And yes, one day I might well teach you!"

"Do you mean, I could do what you just did?" I nearly stammered.

"Yes, reality and matter are not at all what they seem. We are going soon to a place where you will experience that first hand."

"Where is that place?" I asked, looking around the cave, as if I could find a clue.

He pointed towards a wide round circular stone bench at the center of the room, right beneath the droplet's narrowest point.

"Let's sit there. I am going to tell you a story." Cledor stepped over the stone ring, and sat down on the bench. When we were all sitting, he made an opening gesture with his arms.

"Like many good stories, this one also starts with 'once upon a time there was…' He paused, and adjusted the way he was sitting on the hard stone.

"What I am going to tell you is part fact and part legend, but as these things go it probably covers much of the truth of what has really happened. So, here we go: Once upon a time, as long as half a millennium ago, there lived a thriving community in this precise area. They were proud people and had a well-functioning society. They had a very close relationship with nature which they considered to be part of themselves. They had learned to understand the many ways the Earth was giving them useful information. They were very attentive to how they felt in various parts of their territory. They observed the behaviors of animals, the development of plants and how the climate behaved. It was all part of a whole in which they felt included. There was no separation. This hill, where my house is built, was already in those days considered as a sacred place connecting this world to the spirit world. It was this closeness and sensitivity to nature that led their shaman to discover this very place where we are now. At that time, it had been accessible through communicating caves."

Cledor paused, gesturing at the circular cave. "In those days it looked very different, just a big ordinary cavern." He took a deep breath and continued.

"The shaman could feel the particular energy of the cave and the effect it had on his body and mind. That is why he started using it for the most sacred rituals of his people, like healing prayers for the sick, coming of age rituals of the young, councils of elders to resolve conflicts. That shaman had a particular talent with instruments that sounded deep Earth tones and also big drums. They helped him reach a trance to access the spirit realm.

One day, he was here with a group of youngsters, performing the introduction to their coming of age ceremony. This was a ritual, where he would go into a deep trance and give each of the young men a special message and a name he received from the spirit world. On that special day the group of youngsters was unusually big. Nine boys were passionately drumming together, while the shaman's big pipes filled the cave with powerful earth tones. At the culmination of all their combined efforts, something unexpected happened. They all lost consciousness."

Cledor paused again, taking a long sip from his water bottle.

"When they woke up, they found themselves in another cave, whose opening led into dense vegetation. At first, they were just crawling on the ground, like worms. They had lost all their memories. Even the faculty of how to stand up. But fortunately, after a long time of complete oblivion, the shaman's sense of self started to come back. He did not understand what had happened, but he made sure they all remained close together. One by one the young men gradually regained their sense of self and their memories.

To cut a long story short, they had no idea where they were. As they had been very familiar with their tribal territory, they knew that they were no longer at home. Everything was different. The air smelled differently, carrying fragrances they had never smelled before. The plants around their location looked familiar from a distance, but when they approached them, they saw that the leaves had different shapes and other colors than the ones they knew. They saw animals they had never seen before. They also noticed that their bodies, as well as things they carried, seemed lighter.

They realized that they were on top of a hill very similar to the one at home. The sea that they saw at a distance, as well as the sky and the plants around them, everything had brighter colors. It must have been weird and disorienting for them. They could have remained there for the rest of their lives, without knowing the truth, had it not been for the Shaman's intelligence.

At some point, he understood that they had to be in a different world. He also guessed that the unique energy in the cave, together with the sounds they had made during the ritual must have been responsible for what happened to them. He imagined that recreating these conditions might take them back home, and he was right.

They started to build shelters from plants they could cut without tools and established a camp on top of the hill. Through trial and error following the Shaman's guidance, they found fruits and roots they could eat. They also found a water spring in the nearby jungle.

After they had met all their vital needs, the shaman set them on building drums and pipes similar to those that they had used during the ceremony. That was a great challenge for them, as they first needed to create tools to work the wood, as well as weapons to hunt animals, whose skins they needed to build the drums. It took them a long time, but, as they were people close to nature with practical aptitudes, they gradually learned and built what they needed.

Finally, they gathered together in the cave, at the exact spot where they had woken up the first day. It did not happen right away, but finally, after many trials, during a particularly intense session, they hit the right sounds, which took them back home.

Unlike at their arrival to the other world, they arrived conscious, with their memories intact. They soon were able to find their way out of the cave. They were shocked at how different their world was from the other they had already gotten used to. Later they described their return as a subdued, depressed homecoming, where they felt exhausted by the sheer weight of their own bodies.

As the group had grown strong ties together, it was easy for the shaman to convince the youths to keep their discovery secret. When they came back to their tribe, the people did not behave towards them as if they had been gone for months. Some of them asked their families, how long they had been absent. To their surprise they were told that only ten days had passed since their departure. Their families had not been worried, as this was nothing unheard of for a coming of age ritual. But it was beyond a doubt for the shaman and the nine youngsters, that they had spent several long months in the other world.

I was mesmerized by the story, and the reality of the incredible cave that amplified Cledor's deep melodious voice. I knew in my gut that the story was true.

"What happened afterward? Did they go back?"
"Yes, I will give you a short summary of a very long story. The shaman initiated a secret brotherhood that developed their knowledge of how to get to the other world and come back safely. They started the process of shap-

ing this cave in a way that concentrates the sound. They gradually built a village on the other side, selecting people they could trust. Fortunately, they managed to keep it all secret until the time the Spanish and other Europeans arrived to colonize the Caribbean islands.

After the wonder of the first contacts, the Europeans rapidly showed their true faces. Their real intention was to conquer, find gold, and at some point, they even started to take slaves from the population they had wrongfully accused of being human flesh eaters.

At that time, safeguarding the secret of the gateway to the other world had become even more important. The nine men who had become the shaman's successors were careful to select the most trustworthy of their people and above all families with many children, to bring them over to the other world where they would be safe.

Because of their frequent passages they soon deduced one of the most important differences between the two worlds. When nine days passed in the new world, only one day went by in the old world."

My mind was racing, immediately fascinated by all the implications arising from what Cledor had just said. "Hey, please stop a minute, Mister Cledor…"

Cledor had a warm smile, his eyes glittering in the reflected torchlight. "Luke, being where we are, I think you can leave the 'Mister' out."

"Cle.. dor, what you just said means that time passes nine times faster in the new world, which means, if the events you are talking about happened more or less five hundred years ago… that would mean that four thousand five hundred years have passed for the people that are…

"My voice trailed away, my mind was spinning, assaulted by visions, ideas, and fantasies, then abruptly stopped.

"That can't be! That's impossible!"

"Yes, it is possible" Cledor said softly, "Michael and I are from that world. I can bend your mind even further by telling you that we come from a future humanity, which still is in the same linear time as yours!"

I could not help but stare at my two companions as if they had changed into green Martians with antennae on their foreheads, which come to think of it would not have startled me more.

"This is totally nuts!" I managed to say.

I was blown away by this new information. Not only was I told there existed another world which I was going to visit shortly, but the society living there had four thousand five hundred years of development. But then I thought, my world also had a few millennia under the hood, and the new one had started with…" I rained in my thoughts and asked:

"Cledor, what happened to the people in your world? How did everything develop, how many people are you, what kind of technology…?"

Cledor laughed, "Now you get going! That is, obviously, a very long story, filling lots of history books. You are going to find out for yourself when you have landed in the New World. I only want to say this: My world had a different starting point and has evolved in its own way, based on other premises. My world had more than four millennia to arrive at its present point of evolution which is very different from the one of Earth."

"Are we going now?" I was feeling goosebumps on my arms, and my stomach was grumbling with excitement and fear.

"Yes, very soon, but before, you need to quiet your mind, and put yourself in touch with your inner self."

"What do you mean by 'inner self', and how do I do that?"

"First, try and relax. Remember our conversation about, the mind and the sense of self a person has. We have questioned whether this sense of self is solely located in the brain or not."

"Yes! You said that who we are is located in another dimension than the physical."

"Exactly! So, now, when we are going to transit to the new world, your brain is going to be temporarily reset, before it gradually reconnects with the non-physical dimension that is the place where you have your true existence."

"Could I lose my memories?" I started to panic. "What if they are not restored? Memories is all I have left from my family!"

Michael sat next to me and put his arm around my shoulders. "I understand what you feel, Luke, but it's going to be ok. You will keep your memories. It's very safe to travel back and forth between the two worlds. We had a long time to perfect the way it works."

"Thank you! I don't think I'm scared for myself. I'm just a bit overwhelmed by the whole thing."

"That's ok, Luke. Try to relax now, Cledor is going to start sounds that will affect your brain in a calming and focusing way.

"I don't see any instruments, nor other devices." I said, looking around the cave.

"It is part of the stone bench, and it uses Earth energies and magnetism. Just lie down, with your head on the stone and let it happen. These sounds have been specifically developed to strengthen the connection with the non-physical dimension of your being, and it will help reduce the length of time before you regain your memories and sense of self."

As I still looked confused and doubtful, Michael, continued with a firmer voice. "Luke, are you ready to come with us to the New World?"

This shook me out of my wobbly state and as I looked at both Michael and Cledor, I felt their undivided strength and clarity. Underneath my fear I felt a lot of excitement for what was about to happen. I cleared my throat and said with as much confidence that I could muster, "Yes, I want to, I trust you, and I'm as ready as I'll ever be!"

As I said that, I stretched out on the hard, circular bench and tried to empty my mind, focusing on the physical sensations of my body touching the cold stone.

At first, nearly imperceptibly, I sensed a vibration coming through the stone. It grew stronger and developed into a deep sound, like uuuuuu. It gradually intensified, and I started to hear the sound inside my head. It vibrated throughout my whole body. After an initial resistance, I let go. The sensation became like floating on water. Then the water disappeared, and it was just a feeling of floating without any body sensations.

There was a shining empty blackness, but an emptiness that was fuller than anything I had felt before. It was spacious, timeless, and much more, I'm short of words to describe it. I have no idea how long it lasted, but when I opened my eyes, I felt very different. The electrical nervousness that had been all over my mind and body was gone. My breath had deepened, and I enjoyed the cold air of the cave. I could sense my body as a whole from feet to the top of my head. My mind was as quiet as the big round cave that was glimmering around me.

My companions were standing in the middle of the stone circle. We looked at each other, sharing the inner calm. The endless internal chatter and monologues of my mind were gone.

"Wow, this feels good!"

"It's possible to be in that state most of the time!" Michael said, touching my shoulder.

"Are you ready for the big journey?" Cledor asked, picking up his backpack.

"What do you call your world?"

"She has several names in our cultures, but my ancestors called her Ke'a and that has become her universal name."

I took a deep breath and grabbed my backpack. "Let's go and see Ke'a!"

Cledor and Michael sat on the floor, right in the middle of the stone circle, back to back without touching each other. Michael motioned me to sit in the same way. As we sat, I was holding my breath, until my heart started to hammer in my ears.

'Relax!' I told myself, and inhaled a long gulp of air. Then it started. A deep humming sound was rising from the ground. It grew more intense until the stone circle around us began to vibrate on what felt like a very high frequency, blending with the deep O sound coming from the ground. I felt the air move around us, like a small whirlwind going up to the apex of the ceiling, which seemed to glow with an inner light through the mosaic of glass and ceramic.

I kept breathing, holding on tightly to my backpack as if it was a lifebuoy. Then the last thing I remember, is being fascinated by the sound and the light becoming one, and for me, the world disappeared.

Chapter Nine

*T*here was the strange gluey sticky vastness. I could sense it around me, like a heavy, nondescript presence, dark and murky. I could observe it, but it felt like a part of me, as I had no sense of what I was. I was just awareness of that gloomy somethingness without being anything else. It/I was darkish, reddish something, barely aware of itself. There was no language, no words, just that omnipresent brownish jelly. No time, not even eternity.

Change. Bubbles. Jelly is foaming, bubbling. Then there was another timeless eternity of jelly blobs. Red blobs. Something. There is something I remember. What is remembering? Curiosity. I want to know. What is I? Questions. What is Curiosity? Nothing. No response ever, forever.

Faces, animals, shapes, out of focus. What is animals? No response, ever. Red jelly. Sticky nothing. Sticky, gluey worm, wiggling inside the jelly. Me, worm?

It was a very long time. There was no memory, just an empty brain. Null, zero. No universe, nothing.

Then there was sound. What is sound? Yes! I know! Sound!

Light! What is light? Is it a sound? Yes! I know! It is light! Light! Light!

Jelly is changing. What is change? It is different. I feel something! Something! I am a body! What is a body? Hands, moving, touching. Legs, moving. Head, moving. Ears, hearing. Hearing? Sounds! Eyes, moving, opening, seeing! Light! Suddenly a thought! Luke? Luke? Luke!

'I am Luke!' I saw a face through my open eyes. An angel? What is an angel? Yes, a being of light, with wings. The light was blinding. Light all around the face, a body, wings? I saw eyes, then a mouth smiling, and it all came back in a flash.

Michael, Cledor, helicopters, Alma, Paris, Guadeloupe, the cave, the other world!

I got up with a start. "Where am I?"

A soft feminine voice answered, "You are here on Ke'a. All is well!"

The face moved out of the light, and I could see her. Long, very curly dark hair. Brown eyes in a light brown face. "I am Jehanne'a, I'm happy you are back!" Her English was well pronounced but had a definite accent that I had never heard.

"Back from where?" I asked, confused, having not yet realized where I was.

"Back from the spirit world, back into your body."

Now I got the disorienting recollection of the alien mind state I had been in.

"It was very bizarre, what I dreamt before I woke up…"

"You were not sleeping, Luke, you remember what your mind felt like when the connection with your inner self was extremely tenuous. Your spirit self was always present; it was your brain that needed to tune itself back to the energy stream of your consciousness, personality, and memories. All your cells have been renewed and changed by the passage."

"How does that…."

She interrupted me, putting a soft finger on my lips. "For now, it's enough to know that this is another realm of reality with slightly different laws of nature."

"Where are Michael and Cledor?" I asked, feeling vulnerable and lonely.

"They are here in this circle, I mean we call a circle, a community of people living together. They are nearby, meeting with other people. We'll go see them soon."

I stretched my back, still feeling confused and disoriented. The woman was sitting next to me on an extension of the kind of couch I was on. She looked like a native from the isles.

"Are you all speaking English here?"

"Some of us, who have a connection with the Earth cultures, speak Earth languages. But we speak our own languages."

"What…"

"Take it easy and slow! You have all the time you need to land and get to know this world. Just know, that things are quite different. Be ready for surprises!"

She had been sitting close to me, and I could feel her

warmth. She obviously was a human being like me. I had been focusing on her face, but as she stood up, I suddenly saw the details of her body, the precise outline of her breasts, of her belly… She was naked! I looked away, feeling awkward. Seeing my reaction, she sat down again, laughing. "I'm sorry, Luke, I forgot, that things are so different in your world!"

"Aren't you wearing any clothes?" I asked, a bit nonplussed.

"I told you to be prepared for surprises! Better take it slowly, but it seems we have to jump right into it. We do wear clothes on Ke'a. But the fashions and customs vary a lot. There is a lot of freedom around it in our societies. These clothes are what most people love to wear at the moment, here on Karuka'e."

"On Karuka'e? I thought the name of this world is Ke'a?

"Karuka'e is the name of this island, corresponding to Earth's Guadeloupe. Here we love to be free and have no concern about our bodies."

To demonstrate what she said, she stood up again. This time I looked at her with a steadier gaze. The middle part of her body had a different color than her face and arms. It was a shade darker than her skin, and completely uniform.

"We Ke'alians are living as a part of the ecosystem of the planet. We live in symbiosis with nature, and in that way we have learned to accept our naturalness. That is why in the warm areas people often choose to appear as natural as possible. This is very much the habit in our Southern Americas, but it can be different in other regions of the planet. Everybody has the freedom to express their individuality through what you call clothing."

As she said that, the dark body wrap abruptly changed color. It was an intense green, then it switched to orange, then blue, before being a patchwork of all colors of the rainbow.

"I think you get the idea," she said, "but do not assume that this is a special fabric stretched over my body. It is what you would call a holographic force field."

To further her demonstration, her body wrapping field transformed into a set of jeans and a rainbow-colored T-shirt.

"I think you are more used to that kind of body coverings!" She said.

I laughed, starting to unwind. I touched the denim on her leg, and it felt exactly like my pants.

"Wow! This is cool!"

"Ok, Luke, I have to leave you alone for a short time. Please lay down and rest a while. Try not to think too much."

She laughed and added, "I'm sorry, but I need to do something now, that will be another shock for your mind. When I leave the house, I'll simply pass through the wall."

"W..what do you mean by p..pass…" I stammered.

She looked at me, some worry in her eyes. "I'm really sorry, Luke, this is a lot to take in. Just try and accept that things are very different here. The house is like my clothes, a holo-construction. It recognizes my personal energy field and lets me through. That is why I ask you not to attempt to do the same, as you would hit a real wall."

As she finished saying that, she walked towards the nearby wall, and did not even slow her pace when she reached it. I was shocked, as she disappeared into what looked like solid matter. From my perspective, she had been sucked right into the wall.

I gulped, releasing my breath.

'*Very simple indeed,…! Welcome to the fifth millennium…!*' I thought, feeling an inner vertigo.

I looked around the room that was a half sphere of about five meters in diameter. Its wall was a deep golden yellow. There was a window stretching all around the sphere, with no apparent support, just connecting the upper and lower part of the sphere. The view to the outside was unobstructed, with no reflections, as if there was just an empty opening. But as I touched both the wall and the transparent part, they were perfectly smooth and solid.

I looked outside and saw tropical vegetation. Lots of big brightly colored flowers. As I was not familiar with the tropical vegetation of Earth, I could not tell if the plants were different. What struck me most was that the colors looked different, as if the overall saturation was higher. Had I seen that picture on my television back home, I would have slightly corrected the saturation settings, as the colors did not look natural to my eyes.

I also noticed that my body felt lighter, and I remembered that detail in Cledor's recounting of the first crossing. The gravity of Ke'a was obviously less than the 1G of Earth.

I continued to look around, with growing curiosity and excitement.

The room was empty, apart from the oval-shaped couch on which I had been lying. The floor looked like hardened earth. It was different shades of brown that produced a natural looking pattern. I wondered if this was also part of the holo-forcefield.

I had seen enough sci-fi movies in my life, to be familiar with potential future technologies. Star Trek, Next Generation had been one of my favorite shows when I was a teenager. They had what they called a holodeck, where you could materialize anything you wanted, landscapes, people, animals, all sort of scenarios. You just had to clearly state your wish to the computer.

As I was starting to feel a natural bodily need, I wondered if the house had the kind of facilities. *'No harm to try.'* I thought.

"Hello! Hello, house! Please, I need something."

Nothing happened.

I tried again, now quoting Star Trek, a smile on my face.

"Computer!"

No characteristic beep and female computer voice answered.

'Ah, well, it can wait.' I thought, *'maybe it's good to take Jehanne'a's advice and get some rest.'*

I lay down on the couch and closed my eyes, but my mind was too active for me to find any peace. It felt like going around on an old carousel, and I was hopping up and down on its old wooden horses, getting dizzy with the speed and all the mirrors. What a ride I had been on since I had met Alma on the beach in India! It was like I had become an entirely different person.

Before my journey to India, I had lived like an automaton, leaving for work in the morning, doing complex computer simulations at the Institute for Climate Studies. I would just disappear inside my job, not think or do anything else. I was not connecting with anybody, apart from job talk.

After a day's work, I always had dinner at the Café Saint Victor, where they had learned to leave me in peace. That had been my secret pleasure, in the warm season, to sit on the terrace, drink my red wine, look at life passing by. Later I would buy two croissants at the boulangerie Kayer on my way home. I would have them for breakfast. At home, I would watch TV for the rest of the evening.

I had done this routine, for all those years, like clockwork. I had managed to hypnotize myself into a numb, emotionless state.

As I looked back at the events of the last week, I wondered if it was really me, the character in that fast-paced movie, packed with more incredible action than everything put together that I had ever lived before.

Lost in my thoughts, I suddenly saw a hand appear on the wall facing me, instantly followed by Jehanne'a's body. She had appeared inside the wall that instantly closed behind her. This time she was wearing a loose yellow tunic. She carried a medium-sized transparent bottle.

"Hey Luke, did you get some rest?"

"Not really," I said, getting up from the couch and noticing how easy it felt.

"I was wondering if the house could adjust the holo-field and create a toilet for me?"

"Of course, I should have thought of that!" She exclaimed, raising her arms.

She briefly closed her eyes, and a walled-off triangle slice appeared to my right. It was the same golden-yellow material as the rest of the room.

"Hmm, I don't see any doors?"

"Oh, I need to think more from your perspective, but it's not for long, soon you are going to have your own holo-field."

"But I want to keep my clothes!" I said, alarmed.

She laughed, bending over, holding her sides. "You guys from Earth are so funny; it's a pity we only rarely get new people visiting."

"How often do people like me come to your side of the universe?"

"Very rarely, not even once a year. The Guadeloupe gate was the first. Nowadays there are lots more, on all the continents. But let's come back to your toilet needs. Can you wait ten more minutes?"

"Yes, I think so. Why?"

"I have prepared your personal info-particles, you would call them quantum information particles. They are a potent mix of elementary particles your science has yet to discover. One of the many properties and functions they have is to act as a bridge, and interface between the most fundamental holographic matrix of the universe and your mind. They are amplifying your mental connection between your reality field and the universal matrix."

"Hmm, I've read a lot of science fiction, but you lost me here."

"Don't worry, Luke, in a nutshell, it is a powerful enhancement that allows you, aside from numerous other things, to create whatever you want, using the energy field that creates the visible universe."

"Ah, it's that simple! Now I understand!" I said laughing. "Why did you not say that before?"

"Luke, you are so funny!" Jehanne'a laughed heartily.

"Believe me, it's a recent acquisition!"

"Now, let's get down to business. Otherwise, you might run out of time… in terms of toilet."

Again, we had a good laugh. I felt my spirits rising, as well as my overall energy. She had a very particular body language, using her arms and certain hand gestures. Her whole body was unusually expressive.

She pointed to the bottle she was carrying. "This is your personal key to all of Ke'a's facilities, including toilets, wherever you need them! When you drink this water, the info-particles that it contains will rapidly get into your bodily systems and your brain. That will set up the connections to the planetary holo-field."

"This sounds a lot like sci-fi technobabble! But seriously, if one day I want to get rid of the stuff?"

"No worries, these particles are extremely intelligent. They can restore everything they have changed and remove themselves if you want them to. They can do much more than connecting you to the holo-field, but again, this is a vast new domain of knowledge that is best taken in gradually while making your own experiences."

She handed me the glass bottle with the transparent liquid.

"It's just simple water that is carrying the mix of info-particles. For now, this is beyond your scientific knowledge to comprehend. Put very simply, Ke'a's universe is in another dimension where matter is lighter, less dense. Your body is now also part of this universe."

"Will I be able to go back to my universe?"

"Yes, that is what has happened during the millennia, where many from our and your cultures have gone back and forth. The special Earth gateways like the one you used in Guadeloupe can focus the mind-image that you are, and translate your physical body, and what you wear and carry to our universe, without losing anything from the information and pattern. That is why you are here with the same body, wearing the clothes you had before. But all the atoms and elementary particles they are made of are now from this universe."

"How is that possible?"

"In time, we have understood that everything in our universe, as well as in yours, is in reality a projection from what we call the Spirit Realm. That is the realm where you truly exist. From there, your vast consciousness trickles down to your human awareness.

Our reality, as well as the reality on Earth, are holographic in nature. They are a projection of consciousness and mind that have their anchor in the Spirit Realm. Without a mind and a consciousness observing, there are no outer universes."

"I have heard about similar theories from our quantum physicists."

"Yes, that is the part of your science that has the most advanced knowledge. For now, Luke, as your scientist's mind wants to know, a simple way to put it is this: During the passage your body information was translated from one lower vibrating illusion that is Earth to the higher vibrating illusion that is Ke'a. Both are holographic in their most fundamental elements. These gateways focus and bridge the pattern that is your holographic body-matter and create another one in the other universe while retaining the Spirit connection which is the origin of it all. We have learned to use the possibilities of this holographic nature of reality."

My head felt dizzy with this new knowledge, which was beginning to make sense. But my need to pee suddenly overpowered everything else, and I did some expressive movements.

"For now, would you please create a door for me to that holographic toilet of yours?"

She laughed. "Ok, but drink that first, as it needs a few minutes to work through your body."

I took the small bottle and drank the water, which tasted heavenly, as I was very thirsty. She briefly stared at the bathroom slice, and an opening appeared. I went inside the newly created room. Behind me, the door had returned to solid wall. There was a toilet. The inner part of it was a deep bowl that had no drain but nonetheless made everything disappear. It was weird to observe. Even the water which kept running from a well in the wall flowed into a big bowl that lacked any drain. The water did not overflow and remained at a constant level.

"Lots of surprises, she said!" I mumbled to myself and went back to the wall that had been an opening a few minutes before.

Jeeezz, what do I do now? Have these few minutes been enough to transform me into a wall passer?'

I carefully touched the wall, and my fingers felt the soft texture of it, a very dense material.

'Maybe she wants me to figure it out myself?'

I remembered that both times she had done something with the holo-field, she seemed to concentrate. The first time she even closed her eyes. So, I thought it might involve thinking. *'I should perhaps just think that I want to pass, and just do it?'*

I tried to visualize passing through the wall. I realized it was hard for me to imagine, as I had no previous experience, and I was scared. I took a deep breath and tried to empty my mind. I reviewed my memory of seeing Jehanne'a passing through the wall. It had looked natural and fluid. I tried again to imagine myself passing through the wall, keeping in mind that the solid looking wall was in reality a holographic field. I released the breath that I was holding, and marched towards the wall.

The sensation was very bizarre. I felt a slight pressure around my body, as my vision blurred for the fraction of a second. Then I saw myself imbedded right inside the wall. I panicked, and fell backwards to the bathroom floor.

"Wow, holy cow!"

My heart was pounding, but I was okay, as much excited as confused. But I had done it, and I knew it worked and how it had felt. I stood up, and this time, after visualizing my passing through the wall, I resolutely marched forward, and a few seconds later I was standing in front of Jehanne'a who was clapping her hands. She had reverted to her naked looking holo-clothes, but this time I barely noticed.

"You've done it, and you figured it out yourself!" Her face was glowing with a big smile.

"Will there be more unexpected tests coming my way today?" I asked more cheerfully than I really felt.

"I guess there will be many, as you are discovering an entirely different world. First, you'll get to know the enhancements the info-particles have brought to your body and mind.

"Can you give me some advance warning? What it will be?"

"Yes, that much I can do, and perhaps it will make it easier for you to recognize things when they happen. The info-particles exist in more dimensions than the four space-time dimensions we are familiar with. That gives them a quasi-infinite processing and storage capacity. All the technology and gadgets you know from your society and much more you have not yet imagined, are now inside your body and connected to your mind. All the technology you will ever need is now inside your body-mind system. The info-field also enhances and safeguards your mental and physical abilities."

I sat down on the couch, as she continued.

"We connect to nature's own info-holo-field that brings into being the visible universe and use our mind to create material things. As human beings, we already have a natural capacity to do so, it's only powerfully enhanced by the info particles."

I was trying to catch my breath, as it got stuck with my spinning mind that was trying to wrap itself around the massive flow of information. I held up my hand.

"Wait! Hold on, Jehanne'a¨ This is all fascinating, but I can't take in anymore!"

She stopped the arm movements she had been making while talking, and closed her eyes for a second.

"Yes, you're right, Luke! The best approach is to take things as they come and it will all make sense to you in its own time."

She took my hand and said, "Let's go now! You have a new world to discover!" We walked together through the wall.

Chapter Ten

Being outside, I instantly knew I was on another planet. If I had any doubts left, they were rapidly dispelled. The air carried complex fragrances I could not identify. The colors felt unnatural to my eyes, just a bit too intense, like the blue of the bright sky, that nearly hurt my eyes. The colors of the vegetation also had an unusual vibrancy I had never seen on Earth.

Around Jehanne'a's house were various kinds of tall trees and big bushes of fern-like plants. The dominant intense green of the vegetation was balanced with much yellow and red, mostly from leaves of low-growing plants. I also noticed a wide variety of flowers, unlike any I had ever seen on Earth. Only one kind of flowers jumped out of the lot, as they reminded me of big sunflowers, but the round middle part of the flower looked different.

When I turned back towards the house, I did not see any trace of it.

"Where is the house? Has it disappeared?"

"I could have made it disappear, but right now it's still there. Look again and focus your gaze. Tell your brain that it's there."

As I focused my eyes, I started to see a glimmer that stood apart from the rest of the scenery. The house was there indeed, and I understood how it was hiding in plain sight. Its walls were simulating the surroundings, filling in the missing picture, thus making it almost invisible. I approached the dome-shape house with my outstretched hands. The outer wall felt like the one I had touched on the inside. When I moved around, I noticed that the images that the wall was generating were adapting to my viewpoint.

"Fascinating!" I said, lifting my eyebrows.

"As I told you, my people have always been very close to nature, but in the last millennium, with the development and mastery of our info-technology, we can have all we need, anywhere, anytime."

She made a sweeping gesture with her arms.

"We want to have a minimal footprint on our planet. We recognize and respect the power and intelligence of nature of which we are part. There were times in the past where our creations left more visible marks. Most of them have been removed and are kept in info-storage."

"Info-storage....?"

"Again, one of the things made possible by our info-science."

I did not enquire further, as most of my mind's bandwidth was already being used to take in the alien surroundings. There was no road, but an obvious path nature seemed to have grown, leaving room for a broad passage the breadth of a country road. It was covered by a kind of dark green moss, which felt smooth and sturdy under my feet.

We went towards an area that had crossroads of these moss-covered pathways. Further away I could see people walking. As we approached, I saw that the moss paths were bordered by many small clearings. As I knew what to look for, I saw that these clearings contained cloaked houses like Jehanne'a's. There was vegetation all around, and the whole area gave the impression of both being virgin, and tamed. There were wild flowers growing everywhere.

I caught sight of a patch of seashore beyond one of the bigger avenues, and realized that we could not be on the equivalent of Cledor's hill.

"When we arrived on Ke'a, did we appear on your side of Cledor's hill?"

"Yes, but as our community circle is located at the foot of the hill, like the first ever Ke'alian village, they took you down to my place."

"Are you related to Cledor?"

"Yes, Cledor is part of my genetic family, he is my great, great, grandfather."

"Your what?"

"Yes, my great-great-grandfather," Jehanne'a repeated with a big smile, "this is easy to understand, when you consider that time passes nine times slower on Earth. Cledor has spent the last fifteen years in Guadeloupe." She paused, allowing me to do the math.

"So, while he was on Earth, 135 years have passed on Ke'a!!" I was baffled.

"Yes, this is a challenge for the guardians and various other agents we have on Earth. When they stay for longer periods, like Cledor, they regularly visit for a few days, so as to keep in touch with their circle and tuned to what is happening on Ke'a."

"This must be very challenging if you have friends and families," I said, imagining seeing my children grow old and die in my lifetime. But then, with a painful pinch in my heart, I reflected that I would have preferred that scenario to losing them at such a young age.

Jehanne'a tore me from my muddy reflections. "The family structure and how we raise children has changed during the millennia of Ke'alian culture. You'll see that for yourself, but basically, the only exclusive relationships we have is with our mate with whom we form a couple and have children, until the time we choose to part. Children are very much taken care of by the whole circle."

As Jehanne'a was talking, we passed a place where a dozen people were sitting around a big round orange table. Next to it was a half-spherical house, like Jehanne'a's, but visible. The walls looked as if they were entirely covered by flowers. The men and women were all young-looking people. They were 'wearing' various bright colors on their bodies. One woman amongst them was wearing the same pretty flowers all over her body, as those displayed on the house. The table was covered with drinks and dishes I could not identify. They were having fun, talking animately and laughing. Some of them waved when we passed by. Some others called out to Jehanne'a's and they exchanged a few words.

"They are celebrating a friend's fiftieth birthday." Jehanne'a explained.

"Hey!" I cried out, "are you are kidding me? I just saw a group of very young people, barely in their twenties, not one of them looked like fifty!"

Jehanna'a rolled her eyes upwards and made a downwards gesture with her arms.

"Luke, I know, that this is a lot to take in so fast, but I cannot hide the fact that these people around the table are all around fifty, as they are friends having grown up together. We Ke'alians do not visibly age until we are way past our nineties."

As my jaw was dropping, she added, "Our average life expectancy is somewhere around two hundred and thirty years."

I stopped walking, my brain drawing a blank. Jehanna'a put her arms around my shoulders and gave me a warm, but firm hug, whispering into my ears.

"This is a very different world, Luke. We are four thousand years apart in our evolution. I told you, that you were in for many surprises. Maybe you should just consider us as aliens, that might make things easier for you."

I shook my head, feeling shivers crawling around my arms. This information had knocked me out.

"But…. How old are you… then…?"

"Hush now, I'm not going to tell you!" Jehanne'a grinned at me.

Then she gently took my hand and we continued walking.

A man and a woman, their arms around each other came out of a side path. Both of them were wearing their naked looking holo-fields. From the neck downwards their bodies showed a bright indigo color. I noticed that the man's genitals were rounded out by the field, as if he were wearing tight bathing pants. The couple was looking intensely at me, particularly at my clothes. Not knowing how to greet them, I just waved my hand. I was still feeling dizzy from the latest revelations.

They exchanged a few words with Jehanne'a in their language. The way they spoke sounded like no other language I had ever heard before. The sonority was pleasant and had a singsong to it. For me it was funny to see how much they accompanied their speech by arm and hand movements.

"Which language did you just speak?"

"This is our local version of standard Ke'alian. A long time ago, we established a common planetary language, but diverging versions exist everywhere on top of the few local languages that have remained. Of course, everybody knows the standard Ke'alian that is used in all the planetary communications."

I don't know how somebody from the Middle Ages might have felt if he had been catapulted into the twenty-first century, but I think that day, and the following ones I got a good taste of it. Ke'alians were clearly human beings, in no way physically different. But they had more than twice as long a history as Earth humans counted from the beginning of the Roman empire. As Jehanne'a had warned me, I was bound to have some big surprises.

And that first day was only the beginning.

Something in the back of my mind was bothering me, as I did not know how it was fitting into the picture I was getting of the Ke'alians. I had to ask.

"Are you all changelings, like Michael?"

She laughed, "Do you mean if we can change our bodies?"

"Yes, I have seen Michael's body switch into the appearance of Alma's."

Jehanne'a laughed, "Unfortunately, not here on Ke'a, otherwise I would love to try it. That would be fun!"

As I looked at her with big puzzled eyes, she continued.

"This is a very complex subject relating to the differences in how matter behaves in both universes. I can try to put it as simply as possible."

She paused, for a moment, her gaze going inward, then said, "Both universes are essentially holographic, but they exist at what could be described as a different matter frequency. Matter transferred from Earth to Ke'a through the planetary gateways is translated into the higher dimensional Ke'alian frequency.

But going from Ke'a back to Earth does not reverse Ke'alian matter to the frequency of Earth particles, as the higher plane of Ke'alian matter already includes all the potential information of particles constituting the elementary matter-energy of Earth. For reasons, we have only recently started to comprehend, it gives Ke'alians the special faculty to change their body image in the Earth environment. Up to now, only a small number of people, including Michael have done it and are experimenting with it."

I had no more questions, I was completely saturated, and felt I needed a break. There was so much I did not know about this world.

We remained quiet for a long time. I tried to feel at ease, just walking, but I had difficulties not staring at the colorful people that crossed our path. Nearly all of them looked very young. A few, like Jehanne'a had distinct racial features, but the majority seemed to be a blend of all human races, they were not distinctly white Caucasians nor Asians nor Africans, or Amerindians. Many had colors on the body field, but some looked as if they were naked, as the color of their holo-clothes nearly matched their skin.

Seeing these people, it struck me that I was seeing a new version of humanity, humanity 2.0, a genetic blend of all human races. I started to feel out of place, not at ease, in my own skin and my clothes. The muscles between my shoulders felt tight, my body heavy despite the lower gravity.

As our path approached the sea, I noticed that the bay was not surrounded by palm trees but by a very different vegetation that looked like huge ferns with very thick trunks growing into many smaller stalks, all covered by a dense growth of narrow long leaves. They looked like a great shielding for the inside of the land.

I also saw a large group of children of mixed ages, sitting in a circle surrounded by the fern trees, not far from the water's edge. Beyond them, on the beach was another group of smaller children that looked very young. Both groups were attended by several adults.

As we reached the sea shore, I realized that its shape was similar to the Guadeloupe beach, but not identical. At the far end of the bay, it featured a similar hill with a rounded top, where not long ago I had spotted the red roof of Cledor's house.

"Is the geography of Ke'a identical to the one of Earth?" I asked, pointing at the landscape.

"Both yes and no," Jehanne'a said, "the general setting of the continents is very similar, but there are big variations in coastal areas and islands. Many islands in the Caribbean have different sizes or do not exist at all on Ke'a. We also have islands that have no corresponding ones on Earth. Luckily for our first ancestors discovering Ke'a, Guadeloupe is a rather good match. Another positive factor for our ancestors is the fact that the Caribbean Islands on Ke'a form an arc of islands much denser and closer to each other, nearly touching the continental coast. That made it easier for them to reach the South American continent and expand from there."

"Are we going to the hill?"

"Yes, it is the most ancient meeting place of our civilization, the localion where we hold our important councils and meetings. Right now, there is an ongoing council of the planetary guardians to review and advise on the latest events on Earth. We are invited to attend."

"I guess Michael and Cledor are there?" I said, already happy and excited at the prospect of meeting the only people I knew on the planet.

As we approached the hill, I was already looking for a

similar path to the one we had recently taken. But now it felt like ages ago.

Jehanna'a took my hand and guided me to a small rocky mound that grew out of the sand, half-way from the hill. I stopped, confused.

"Why are we not walking to the hill?"

Jehanne'a grinned at me mischievously and said, "This is going to be another mind-blower for you, Luke. I now have the honor to introduce you to our transportation system."

"Are we going to teleport to the top of the hill?" I asked sarcastically, thinking I was making a joke.

"Yes, Luke, exactly! We are going to stand on these stones which are infused by info-particles and constitute an anchor point to another anchor point on top of the hill."

My blood pressure rose instantly, and I could only open my mouth and stare at her before I managed to speak. "But, … I'm going to lose my memory again… how..?"

"Relax, Luke, this is very different. We do not transfer from one planetary dimension to another, we stay on Ke'a. The info-particles that have merged with your body have translated your physical body into pure information that is precisely you, at this very moment, including your inner connection to your Spirit Self. As for the info-stones, they are a simple means to transfer the information that is you, to a receiving info-anchor that will instantly anchor the new location of your body. Nothing about you will have changed. Only your info-presence-energy will have been relocated. It is important for you to understand, that the nature of reality is not material. It is energy and information translated through the holographic matrix of the universe."

I was barely listening to what Jehanne'a was saying. I had to sit down and needed to feel something solid. I touched the ground with my open hands, grabbing a handful of sand. I relaxed my grip and watched as a narrow trickle of sand grains were escaping and re-joining the beach. I did that several times before Jehanne'a took me out of my self-induced hypnosis.

"Hey, Luke, what's happening?"

"I can't do it! It does not make sense!" I groaned, still fixating on the sand trickle escaping my hand.

"There is nothing you have to do, Luke. It happens all by itself. You don't even notice anything, as there is no discontinuity."

I heard what she was saying, part of my mind even understood, but somehow my reason was locked away. I was feeling panic, plain panic, my heart was racing, my breath was short. I was stuck in the movement of grabbing sand and letting it flow out between my fingers.

Jehanna'a sat down next to me and waited quietly. Her silent presence by my side eventually helped me to get a grip on my panic. I stopped what I was doing with the sand and took several deep breaths. I felt my naked feet on the warm sand. I looked around the beach, the sea, then turned my gaze to the hill that looked vaguely familiar. Finally, I took another deep breath and said, "Let's do it!"

As we both stood up, she put a friendly hand on my shoulder, and said, "You are doing great, Luke! It's been quite a ride for the first day! Let's go and stand on the stones."

She took my hand and we both stepped onto the rounded boulders. As we stood on the warm rocks, something incredible happened. As if done by an all-powerful picture editing program, the beach landscape we were in was instantly replaced by a big round clearing surrounded by Ke'a's jungle vegetation. I felt dizzy and had to hold on to Jehanne'a before my brain could re-establish my inner balance.

"Wow! This is amazing! I can't believe what just happened!" I exclaimed, hugging Jehanne'a in my newfound enthusiasm.

"This is incredible!" I was reeling on, feeling a kind of drunkenness. I had to sit down on the stones to catch my breath and calm down."

"Your technology is incredible!"

"What you experienced is very simple, nothing much has happened," said Jehanne'a as she sat down next to me, "this is an entirely different scientific paradigm than the one you are familiar with. It uses the very nature of the universe that is holographic and informational. Everything contains everything, everything is connected and exists at the same time, to mention but a few of the principles that are the base of Ke'alian science."

"I have to go back to kindergarten," I said, meaning it seriously.

"Of course not, Luke, you will soon understand how

things work here. The more knowledge approaches the true nature of things, the simpler it gets. Truth is elegant and simple."

"You talk about science as if it's philosophy."

"I see your mind is back online! In a way that is true, as science and the philosophy of the true nature of life have merged in our civilization. But let's continue this conversation later, I think they are waiting for us to continue their council."

Jehanna'a led me to the other side of the circular clearing. There was a spacious, open cavern, with it's roof half covering a stone circle, similar to the one in the gate cave on Earth, where I had last seen Michael and Cledor. Here they were again, sitting on the circular stone bench, together with at least ten other Ke'alians. I had to bite my lip to suppress an outburst of laughter. Cledor and Michael as their fellow Ke'alians were wearing their nakedness beneath the holo-forcefield. I had thought that I had gotten used to it, but seeing Michael and Cledor reminded me how awkward it looked to my Earthen eyes.

Most Ke'alians, sitting in the circle were probably above ninety, as, without looking old, men and women alike did not have the luster of youth anymore. A couple of them even had greying hair. In a weird way that was reassuring and made me feel more at ease.

They all turned towards us, giving me some friendly nods, some exchanged a few incomprehensible words with Jehanne'a. It was Cledor who spoke to me first.

"Hello, Luke, my friend, welcome to our circle! Please come and sit next to me." He gestured to the empty space on his left, and I sat on the stone bench, followed by Jehanne'a who sat at my left.

Michael who was sitting at Cledor's right greeted me with smiling eyes and turned to Jehanne'a. "Please Jehanne'a, instruct our friend in the way to initiate the translation, as we are going to continue our council in Ke'alian."

I looked at Jehanne'a, expecting her to retrieve some hidden device, but instead, she said, "One more new experience for you! The info-particles inside your body-mind system have an incredibly vast potential. Given the proper instructions they can do nearly anything you want. For now, to be able to understand our language, you need to instruct and allow them to translate languages."

I looked at her questioningly, wondering how on Earth I was supposed to do that. But then I realized, 'Now it's *What on Ke'a!*' and smiled inwardly.

Jehanne'a, oblivious of my mind's chatter, continued, "Just close your eyes, and feel the desire to understand what everybody is going to say in this circle. Try to feel, and know that it is so, and say an inner yes to it"

"Yes, just...." I mumbled, but closed my eyes nevertheless. I tried to imagine that all the people around me were going to speak English. My mind had no major doubts, as I had seen what Ke'alian info technology could do, and this was one more kindergarten lesson for me. I relaxed into that inner knowing and said a big inner yes to having everything translated.

I opened my eyes and nodded to Jehanne'a. Immediately I heard the woman who was sitting opposite to me start talking in clear, perfect English, with a tint of Ke'alian sonorities. The incredible thing about all this was that I heard the words as if she was pronouncing them, and the movements of her lips seemed in sync with them.

"Welcome Luke of Earth, to our circle. I am Tane'a, today's speaker for the circle of the planetary guardians. I am going to give you enough information about us, that you may be able to include yourself in our knowledge-finding and seeing what is best for all."

Hearing that complicated paraphrase, I thought that she probably was expressing a Ke'alian concept that had no equivalent in English. I focused on what she was saying, as I felt the importance and solemnity of the moment.

"We are a deciding and inquiring circle of what we call the planetary guardians. The planetary guardians are actively observing and communicating all over both human planets. They have many tasks and purposes, one of which is to watch over the development of the Earth cultures. We do that mainly for our selfish purpose of keeping Ke'a safe from any unwanted intrusions. In all the millennia, we have succeeded in keeping the existence of the Ke'alian civilization secret and to suppress the very rare occurrences where Earth people have stumbled upon us.

Our purpose has also been, with minimal intervention, to guide Earth humanity to an evolution that we consider the most aligned with the true nature of life. We have done that through placing guardian agents into key governments, universities, multi-national companies, and other influential organizations.

Our info-technology that works so well here on Ke'a, only works in a limited way on Earth, due to fundamental differences in the laws of physics of both universes. That is the reason why the higher dimensional info-particles in our bodies have a limited potential on Earth. Our agents must mostly rely on Earth technology to do their work. There have been developments on Ke'a involving the connection between the two worlds that have become a challenge for us. To explain that to you, I give the floor to Lire'a who is one of the Ke'alian population focalizers who is the planetary enquirer for this ongoing issue."

A still young-looking woman, who was a good representative of humanity 2.0 nodded to Tane'a, making an opening gesture with her arms. Her body holo had a dark green color that harmonized well with her tanned skin and long black hair. She started to speak, her eyes blazing with the energy of purpose.

"Greetings to you, Luke. We are happy to have you in our circle. We Ke'alian have had a very long history of peace and social evolution. We have barely known any conflict or health issues in the past thousand years. We have found ways to be in tune with our Spirit Selves, and clear away and forgive anything that hinders that essential connection."

She paused, taking a deep breath as if she was going to say something that required a significant effort on her part. She continued after yet another deep breath.

"This has begun to change, very subtly and nearly imperceptibly around two hundred Ke'alian years ago. All Ke'alians are interconnected through the info high dimensional particles that enhance, protect, and when needed give them access to a huge variety of planetary services. One of the functions of the info-particles is to warn the local population focalizer when a person has been hurt, is physically ill, or has a mental state that is out of balance. These occurrences have been extremely rare in the past, and the affected people could easily get all the help they needed."

She paused again, rolling her shoulders and her neck as if to ease tension.

"Out of a global population of two and a half billion people, the occurrences have risen from an average of seven to more than five hundred a year. The growth has been accelerating in the last ten years, and this year has seen a record number of incidents, as if there was a new speeding up of the phenomenon. The striking characteristic of the geographical distribution of all the cases is that they are concentrated in very specific areas."

She paused, and I could feel the tension in the circle. It was as if most people were holding their breath.

"We have been able to solve all our problems and create a healthy society of individuals in tune with themselves and the whole. There are no more issues around power, money and limited resources on Ke'a. For the first time, we were faced with problems affecting us that were originating outside of Ke'a. We rapidly understood that the regions affected on Ke'a corresponded to areas of heavy conflict or ecological disasters on Earth."

Her long pause allowed me to look around the circle. All the faces were earnest, even tense. I glanced at Michael, feeling the warmth of our connection. He returned the gaze and nodded knowingly.

Lire'a continued. "Recent research has shown, that this process must have started at the time of the first world war on Earth, around nine hundred Ke'alian years ago. For a long time, there were no visible effects on Ke'a, but our researchers have understood, that the effects on Ke'a have intensified due to the cumulative effects of Earth's rising pollution levels and modern warfare. It looks like this has diminished the Earth's own capacity to heal the damage, which is the main reason why the effects have started to trickle through to our dimension in a much stronger way.

It demonstrates that Earth and Ke'a are connected in more ways than we had previously been aware of. Intense wars and massive damages to the Earth have a slow and lasting effect on Ke'a. Our researchers have found that it is not only humans that get affected, but there have also been visible signs of animals as well as plants being touched. It seems that the planetary life force has been weakened in the areas linked to the worst places on Earth.

Of course, we have advised the concerned populations to move away from these areas, and that has partially solved the human problem."

She nodded towards me and made a circular, closing gesture. She then turned to the man sitting on her right. He was the youngest looking in the circle. His black hair contrasted nicely with the orange of his holo-field.

"This is Mane'e, he is one of the focalizers of planetary decisions, he will continue this clarification."

Mane'e turned to me and made an opening gesture towards the whole circle.

"Welcome Luke into this working circle. I have been

given the task to focus and clarify, what we Ke'alians as a whole feel and think about what is happening, and to help arrive at a point of decision in harmony with the whole. For the first time in many centuries, Ke'alian society as a whole has not been able to agree on a clear path.

There are three different avenues that up till now have not been able to converge into a clear decision around what strategy to devise to solve the problem with the negatively touched areas on our planet.

The first and most popular action plan is to keep Ke'a protected by the four millennia old secret, that has served us so well, and allowed us to develop the way we did. They are worried about the long-term unpredictable consequences any disclosure would have. They want us to strengthen and intensify our secret infiltration of governments and influential organizations in order to guide and educate Earth humanity towards new ways of living that respect their fellow humans and the planet. Advocators of this plan have also suggested that we help their scientists make significant breakthroughs towards free unlimited clean energy.

The second, smaller group always had concerns about any interference, wanting the Earth population to be free to follow their own evolutionary path, even if that means to let them make their own mistakes. But now, they have understood that Ke'a is not isolated from Earth, and that the destinies of both planets are linked. This group is the closest that we have to religious people. They are in touch with the circle of shamans who relay the insights and visions they get during their rituals connecting them directly to the planetary consciousness.

We all consider our planet a living, intelligent organism, and include her in all the important decisions. The circle of the shamans has learned through the millennia to fine tune their ways to connect with the huge entity that is Ke'a. She is a sentient being existing on a cosmic scale that has a very different awareness.

The shamans and the people in closer contact with them are focusing on finding ways to heal and clean the disturbed energy fields from the Ke'alian side and hope that it will have the reverse beneficial effect on the affected areas on Earth." He paused and picked up a glass from a tray at the center of the stone circle. After taking a long sip, he continued.

"A third, formerly very small part of our population is rapidly growing these days. They are for openly revealing our existence to Earth and to use our wisdom and superior science to convince Earth humans to change their detrimental behaviors. If they could not be reasoned with, and educated, they suggest the option to threaten to use technologies we possess that can suppress the electrical power. Without electricity, Earth would be forced to return to an agrarian age that would lack the power to continue the damage of the planet."

Mane'e made a closing gesture and nodded to Tane'a, the woman who had opened the round. She, in turn made a circular gesture to the assembled group and said, "We have for now given our friend Luke a lot of information to take in and digest. It is time now to adjourn our council till later in the day and to close this circle in honor of all its gifts."

She reached out towards the people on both sides who

took her hands, imitated by everyone in the group. I felt Cledor's and Jehanne'a's hands taking mine. Everybody in the circle had closed their eyes, and I did likewise.

At first, I only felt the warmth of Cledor's and Jehanne'a's hands. Then I felt a tingling of energy that rapidly increased and became a powerful stream flowing through my body. It extended to the circle of people I was part of, as if my body had grown to include all the bodies in the circle.

I could feel Jehanne'a's and Cledor's particular energies. I had a sense of the texture, the specific color of their minds. I felt the presence of Michael, together with the warmth of our common experiences in Paris, before the colors and presences expanded to include all the people in the circle. Without knowing the men and women holding hands in the circle, I literally dove into a twirling torrent of images, feelings, and information about their individual lives and how it all connected to the common intention of this particular circle. The circle was alive, and I was part of the new energy it had created. I could feel that new energy as an added presence. It was the richest mental and emotional experience I have ever had to that point. And I'm glad to say it would not be the last nor the most amazing.

Chapter Eleven

After we let go of each other's hands, a whole new energy erupted in the group. It seemed that everybody had started to talk at the same time. Small groups formed, laughter could be heard everywhere. The seriousness and solemnity of the council had just evaporated. Michael, smiling brightly, came straight to me and gave me a friendly slap on my back. "And? Didn't I say that you wouldn't regret your decision? How do you like our planet?"

"There was a moment in Paris when I thought you were an alien from another planet!"

We laughed, clapping each other's shoulders.

"Come, let's go and eat something," he said.

"You said the same thing not that long ago," I remarked, with a twinkle in my eyes, "you have spent too much time in France. The only thing you ever think about is food!"

We laughed again, then Michael said, "We can translocate from here to the center of the village. I'll get you there if you hold my hand."

As I just stared at him for a few seconds, he added, "I know, this is very disorienting at first, but soon you'll be able to easily do it on your own. The thing is, that you need to know the place you are going to. Thinking and visualizing that you are there activates the powerful higher-dimensional info-particles in you, that…"

"…simply relocate the info-holo-presence of my body!" I interrupted.

"Jehanna'a has been teaching you well!" he exclaimed, "you'll get used to it faster than you think! This is much better than the Parisian underground!"

We laughed again. It was so good to connect with Michael in such a light way. By then I felt nearly at ease, after having woken up on another planet, and soon going to be instantly teleported to the village.

We stepped onto the stones, and I took Michael's hand. This time there was no more panic attack, just total amazement at the change of location from the hilltop to the center of the village in literally less than the blink of an eye.

I call it a village, but in reality the settlement did not fit any of Earth's categories. It was was practically invisible, apart from the occasional half-spherical holo building, an irregular pattern of moss-covered alleys and clearings, all surrounded by trees, plants, rocks, water springs. Regarding minimal footprint, I cannot imagine what could have been less. I was told that the village had more than seven thousand inhabitants. At that point, I had not been able to distinguish any communal activities, nor shops or services, apart from a big group of children gathering near the beach.

We had appeared on an irregular rocky platform, located in the middle of another big rounded clearing. Big fern-like tree-sized plants were surrounding the place. To one side I could see an opening to the beach. A warm breeze was blowing from it. As we stepped from the stones, I lurched away, as two people had appeared in the place we had just left. This was the first time I saw a person appear out of thin air, and I must say it's not like seeing it in a movie. The physicality of the appearance is very tangible. There is an air displacement all around the sudden and instantaneous full presence of people who had not been there an instant ago. It shook my mind, that had no previous reference to deal with it. The brain tends to fill in missing parts when the perception is incomplete, according to the expected normality. But when something appears that is entirely outside normality the brain tends to suppress the perception. For a few moments, I felt dizzy, disoriented. Michael noticed and put a steadying hand on my shoulder.

"There is so much you need to get used to, Luke. Knowing is one thing, but seeing and experiencing things for real has a strong impact on the mind."

"It felt like my eyes could not believe what they saw," I said, taking a deep breath, looking around, "this world is incredible! On the outside, your village looks like you still are primitive hunter-gatherers, barely touching the environment, but in reality, you are the most advanced society I could ever have imagined!"

"Yes, Luke this is the real beauty of Ke'a, a beauty that

needs to be protected," Michael said, earnestness coming back to his voice. "But, now, let's…"

"…go and eat something!" I finished his sentence, smiling. I wanted to go back to the lightness we had before.

"What kind of food do you have? Is it going to be holographic?" I asked jokingly.

"Luke, I'm not in the mood to take on the teacher role again, but know, that more than seven centuries ago Ke'alian scientists, together with our shamans have discovered the holographic nature of reality. Matter does not exist in the way it appears to exist. Matter is information and energy that is created by a conscious mind that brings its universe into being."

"How can you do these incredible things?"

"I know you are a scientist and want answers. Let me try to sum up in a few simple sentences, that which has developed in hundreds of years: Already a few centuries ago we have found ways to interact with the holo-field that translates our conscious and unconscious mental energy into the reality we perceive as physical."

I still did not understand, and interrupted Michael, "But how does all that work with no visible technology?" As I am from the 21st Earth century, I am used to seeing technical gadgets everywhere."

Michael put a hand on my shoulder, "The big breakthrough was the discovery of these higher dimensional elementary particles which are part of that energy field that underlies everything. We have learned to use their power that is naturally linked to our mind. These info-particles act like amplifiers of our natural abilities. By now it even seems, that as we humans continue to develop, we will at some point not need this amplification any longer. For now, they are crutches we use. But, enough of that! Come now, I'll show you our kitchen!"

Michael pointed to a holo construction on the edge of the clearing, that was barely visible. On the way there, we passed big round multicolored tables. Around them, people from the council were already seated on comfortable chairs that seemed to grow out of the ground.

"I suppose you know how to enter this house," Michael said and went straight through the wall.

I stopped a moment to gather my wits. Things were going a bit too fast, I had barely time to take in new information, before being challenged by some other mind-boggling stuff. I took a deep breath, looked at my bare feet on the sandy ground, before closing my eyes. I imagined passing through the wall and did just that, wondering if I ever would get used to it.

The room was much bigger than Jehanne'a's house and had a long work table making a half-circle on the opposite wall. I was instantly surrounded by delicious food smells that made me salivate. I could not identify any particular dish, but the overall aroma was very appetizing. There were half a dozen Ke'alians working at the table. In the middle of the room was a kind of pantry containing a wide variety of colorful fruits and vegetables and other things I could not put a name to.

Michael waved me to his side. He was standing next to a very tall woman who wore her long brown hair in a ponytail. She had the same Amerindian complexion as

Jehanne'a. Her body was covered by a flowing fabric, of a kind I had never seen before. She was looking at me expectantly.

"I am Sobrine'a, today's cooking focalizer for our special guests."

I had a vague sense that the automatic translation had kicked in again.

"Hi, my name is Luke, I'm curious about the food you are preparing," I said, looking around expectantly.

"We use a lot of local vegetables and fruits that grow near the village." Sobrine'a explained, "some foods are holo-proteins. They are tissues made of cells that are generated by our love, and our desire to eat these particular tastes. They taste like fish and animals that our ancestors have eaten. We can eat similar proteins without the need to hunt or cause animals to suffer. They are sentient beings like us."

"Can you create life with the holo-field?" I asked, fascinated.

"Fundamentally the holo-field is what creates all matter in the universe, and all matter has life energy. But you probably mean sentient life as in humans, animals, and plants. That kind of life can only originate from the Spirit Dimension, and cannot be created by our mental activation of the holo-field."

This information left my mind blank. The Ke'alians had such a different outlook on life! I went around, looking at the various activities the people were engaged in. It was nice to see that half of the cooks were cleaning, peeling and cutting vegetables as well as fruits. At least those were familiar activities!

I also saw one of these running water wells without an outlet. The water kept on running, never overflowing the basin. On the other half of the circular table stood a variety of pots. They looked like they were made of clay. Some of them were steaming, and as I approached, I could smell the distinct flavors of the foods they contained. One of the big ones held a kind of stew, vegetables and something that looked like big beans mixed with pieces of something that looked like meat. I could smell lots of different mysterious aromas and spices. The dish was apparently cooking, but I could not see any stove, nor any device connected to the pot. This time I did not feel like asking, as already guessed that the cooking was done with their info-particle magic that created it's own energy.

All the pots contained deliciously smelling dishes that made my stomach growl in hungry anticipation. I looked expectantly at Michael who was conversing with the woman.

He smiled. "Hey Luke, I see you are hungry. It's been a long time since we had to skip breakfast at Cledor's house. Let's go join the others." This time he took my hand, and we both glided through the wall.

The group of Ke'alians from the council was sitting around three big round tables. They had been joined by other people I had not seen before. Michael and I sat down at a table that had three empty seats. He motioned for me to sit on his right, next to the other empty place. "Somebody is going to join us for the dessert," he said.

As I sat, I felt the seat perfectly adjusting to my body.

"Well, Luke, I don't see any food on the table, would you like a Ke'alian aperitif?" Michael took one of the blue bottles that were distributed around the table and poured the likewise blue liquid into a clay cup.

"This is the favorite local drink. Take a small sip at first," he advised with a smirk.

I took the cup, smelling a strong fragrance that was hard to define, something of the sea, of algae. I took a little sip and immediately felt my head spin. The ground shook, like a boat on a raging sea. My mouth was full of salty seawater, and I heard the wind. In front of me, I saw a huge black wave, and I screamed.

I heard Michael call my name. "Luke, Luke, it's ok, all is well! I'm sorry, I should have known!"

I rapidly regained my balance and countenance. Everybody around the table was looking at me with warm and caring eyes. Michael handed me a cup of water which I gratefully drank. I felt the shivers going up my arms and down my back.

"Luke, I'm so sorry! This is an experiential liquor, which induces feelings and visions, but usually very pleasurable ones. As this one's theme is the sea, it triggered your biggest nightmare. I should have known!"

"It's ok, Michael," I said, "but do you have anything normal on this planet? Even a simple drink can be crazy!"

"Yes, look at the middle of the table, and you'll soon be eating a delicious normal meal."

As I looked, three big pots and half a dozen plates appeared right in the middle of the table.

This was totally crazy. "Is this what you call a normal

meal? Dishes appearing on the table as if we were in a wizard world?" I started to laugh and could not stop for a while. Finally, Michael managed to serve me a plate of steaming stew.

It was delicious, unusual, but it tasted great. The holo-meat was incredible. It was great to eat and be together with people around a table. My over-stimulated nervous system relished in the apparent normality. I was content to listen to the easy conversations going around, which I was hearing in English. Nobody was talking about the subjects discussed at the meeting.

I became aware that the info-particles in my brain were creating a translation of at least three simultaneous conversations involving six people. They each had their individual voice tonalities, and their lips matched what they were saying. I realized the tremendous power of these particles, and also the scary fact that they were influencing my perceptions. I turned to Michael and expressed my concerns.

He took a moment to reflect and said, "I understand that having these powerful particles in your body can at first be frightening. It is true that the particles can change your perceptions, determine what you see, hear and many other things you have yet to experience. When you realize that, it's like giving up part of your freedom."

"Yes, this is exactly what I feel! How can I be sure that I'm not being manipulated and made to believe that I'm here talking to you when in reality I'm kept prisoner somewhere else?"

Michael laughed. "You have seen too many movies, Luke! But basically you are right. That has been of great concern to many people in the first decades when Ke'alian society started to spread the use of the info-particles. That is why safeguards have been built into the core structure of the particles. Only you can activate them, and they obey your desire to clear out of your system if you express it clearly and consistently. The particles know the integrity of your mind and body and are guarding them against any external dangers and influences. Your mind and free will are more endangered on Earth than here. On Earth, you have all the media that constantly try to control your thinking, and on top of it human brains have the bad habit of filling in gaps in your perception."

A man sitting opposite to us who had been listening to our conversation joined in. "The info-particles give your brain greater abilities to see things as they really are, not just see what your mind has been taught to perceive and filter out everything else."

At that moment, I noticed that somebody was standing behind my chair. Then I heard a familiar woman's voice, "What an intense conversation for lunch time! Usually this is a time to connect and relax!"

I could hear the smile behind the serious words, and felt the soft hand of the woman on my shoulder. I turned around.

"Alma!" I exclaimed, "Great to see you!" In my joy, I jumped up and hugged her, before I had time to realize that she was also wearing the simple naked-looking holo-field as clothes. I could feel the contours of her body all too well. But my joy was stronger than my embarrassment, and I lingered in my embrace. For me it was much more than just meeting an old friend. She and Michael were the people I had most connected with in many years.

Alma took the empty seat, and for a few moments, I felt the strangeness of having Michael sitting on one side of me and Alma on the other. But this rapidly faded into the excitement of having Alma next to me. At first, I did not know what to tell her.

Fortunately, she started the conversation, "I'm happy you crossed over to Ke'a, Luke. Right from the start, I had the feeling that you were one of us."

"What do you mean by one of us?" I asked, pleased and confused at the same time.

"We the immigrants," she said smiling.

"Immigrants?" I must say that at that moment I did not realize what she meant by 'we'".

"Yes, immigrants to Ke'a, people from Earth who have crossed to Ke'a and have become part of our society."

"Do you believe I'm going to become part of your society?" I felt a very warm tingle in my body, seeing her so beautiful next to me, and at the same time, I was getting irritated by what she was saying. I added, "compared to you guys, I'm a cave man, what use do you have of me?"

"Come on Luke! You are already part of Ke'a, you are connected to the whole, and I know you are a fast learner."

"Are there more 'immigrants' like me?"

"Many! We have never stopped bringing in Earth people that we knew we could trust, and as soon as they come to Ke'a the integration happens very quickly."

"What if I go back to Earth and reveal your secret, or am forced to do so?"

"That is something that may upset you, but in all fairness, you have to know. In that very unlikely case, which up to now has only happened twice, in a very long time, the info particles would erase any memory and knowledge from Ke'a before withdrawing from your system, leaving you perfectly intact and free to continue your life on Earth."

I grabbed the thickness of the table as if to make sure it really existed.

"Come to think of it, I'm not upset. Similar ideas have crossed my mind when I was listening at the council. It seems like a logical safeguard considering the technology you have."

Alma gave me her mysterious smile, and it made my heart ache.

"You are exactly the kind of person we love to welcome into our society."

I felt a bit ruffled by the impersonal content of her statement and did not manage to hide my irritation.

"But how can you be so sure? You barely know who I am, and I spent the last ten years as a depressed recluse!"

She put her hand on my arm and said very softly, "Now you are getting upset. Let's take it easy and enjoy a tasty dessert. We'll have the rest of the day together, as we have important things to talk about and for you to experience."

I took a deep breath, said nothing, disarmed by my bubbling feelings for her. I was delighted at the prospect of spending more time with her.

Chapter Twelve

I don't remember what kind of desserts we had, as my attention had been entirely focused on Alma's presence. I was very happy, but at the same time I needed to catch up with the fact, that this was the real Alma. My recent adventures with another version of her in Paris were still very present. As we left the table, I followed her to the clearings's opening towards the sea.

"Do you want to go for a walk on the beach?" she asked.

"We've done that before and…"

"…it'll be very different this time!" she finished my sentence, making an embracing gesture towards the incredibly beautiful bay in front of us, "this is another world!"

We passed the tree line and walked on the white sand where a light breeze carried the smells of the see. She walked briskly, and I nearly had to jog to keep up with her.

"This wind is the right thing to clear our minds," she said, taking deep breaths.

"How…" I started, but she immediately cut me off.

"Let's walk and breathe for a while, and then we'll talk!"

We went to the firm sand on the water's edge where the waves of the turquoise sea licked at our feet.

Seabirds were flying high above, as we walked silently, tracing parallel tracks into the sand. The sea wind was carrying an unusually rich fragrance. My speedy mind had slowed, as my focus had gone to my breath and to my naked feet walking the wet sand.

The long bay ended with a ragged stony prominence that reached into the sea. Light blue-green sea-foam was tossed around by the breaking waves. We had to climb over the rocks to access the next beach segment, which was a much smaller bay, enclosed by the same rocky slopes. A narrow strip of sand separated the rocks from the water.

Alma's face looked much more relaxed and shone in the warm glow of the afternoon sun. She stood there, at the water's edge, contemplating the pristine landscape.

"I have missed Ke'a's and her sea! Come, let's go have a swim!" she exclaimed, and without waiting for me, she ran into the water and dove into an oncoming wave. At the last moment, before she hit the wave, her red holo-field vanished and I saw her naked body disappear into the water.

I froze for a second, then realized how clumsy conventional clothes were. Suppressing my tingling anxiety, I quickly undressed and followed her into the water. It was heavenly temperate and very salty.

Alma was swimming straight towards the horizon and was already too far for my comfort. I swam back and forth near the beach and waited for her to come back. Soon I started to worry, as I could not see her anymore.

When she finally reappeared, she waved; her scream carried by the warm breeze.

"Yeeeeaah!!"

She swam like a mermaid and reached me in no time.

"Awesome! Just what I needed after my long stay on Earth!" she exclaimed.

Her wet beaming face and hair reflected the intense sunshine. She was an incredible sight, naked, on the amazingly beautiful Ke'alian beach. At that moment I wished I would always remember it, in connection with the sea and beaches.

I felt a twinge of shyness as we lay in the sand, so close to each other, but it was a pleasurable unease. I had felt drawn to her from the first time we met, and the silent walk on the beach with her had brought back and amplified my feelings.

Without moving, she said, "Now we can talk, this is a perfect place!"

Yes, the place was perfect, but my mind was empty of all the questions I had had before. Fortunately, she continued to speak.

"It has been very intense for me in the last days on Earth. As you probably have guessed, I'm part of the guardian agents. Like you I am an immigrant from Earth. I was selected, tested and introduced to Ke'a by Michael nearly five Earth years ago. That gives us a special connection."

I could not help but had to interrupt her. "Wait a minute! Did you know that he switched his body to yours, when we were in Paris. I spent a few hours with him looking, feeling and sounding exactly like you!"

She smiled, "That must have been interesting, he has not told me!"

"It was crazy, mind-blowing, I'm lucky I did not go nuts!"

Alma pushed herself up on her elbows.

"I can appreciate that, Luke, as he played the same game with me when he was assessing my capacity to take in the Ke'alian reality."

"So, this was mainly a test?"

"Yes, the capacity we have to transform, only exists on Earth. It is due to the fact that when we transit to Earth, we retain the higher dimensional Ke'alian matter creating our body. The repeated transitions to Earth also strengthen our connection to the Spirit Dimension."

I was fascinated, "But how can you make your body disappear and get the body of another person?"

"It's an exceptional skill only a small number of guardians have learned and mastered. With the help of the info particles in our body, we can focus on the spirit, and all we know and have felt about somebody we know very well. You sense the person from the inside, connecting your spirit to her essence, and then it happens."

"Have you done it?"

"Yes, a few times. Honestly, it's something I was scared of. I could not imagine having a body other than my own. But as Michael was my guide for becoming a guardian, he insisted that I do the necessary inner training to overcome my fear and strengthen my connection to the Spirit Dimension. He was right, as it has made me much stronger in my own identity. But it's a mysterious process that even the very advanced Ke'alian science does not fully understand."

Now, my questions came back in a flash.

"Why did I feel that high energy jolt when we hugged at the temple?"

"Exactly for the same reason that enabled Michael to switch his body. In India, my body had a higher energy matter that you reacted to, as you seem to be very sensitive to energy. You pulled me very close, and all this combined made the experience stronger and more vivid. If we hugged now, nothing would happen, apart from the normal human perceptions."

I was thinking, with a big smile on my face, that if we would hug right here, and now, I would very much enjoy these normal human perceptions, but said nothing. She saw my smile and must have read my mind, as she stood up, took my hand and pulled me towards her.

"You Mister scientist, you don't believe that which has not been properly experimented," she said with a big smile, while giving me a full body hug.

She had me completely unprepared, and I have to say, I did not resist. We hugged. Our warm bodies merged in a very natural and sensual way. She started to move as if dancing to a piece of music only she could hear. I moved with her, and we laughed. Finally, we sat at the water's edge, and I took her hand, dizzy with all that just happened.

We looked at each other, smiling. That moment was pure magic, and her smile was an arrow that went straight to my heart.

Then she said, "I think this is the right time to try your holo-clothes!"

"What...?"

"Yes! See how easy it is!"

Instantly her body was dressed in a floating sari, like the one she had worn in India.

"You preferred me before!" she teased.

She looked stunning, her long lustrous hair floating in the wind that blew from the sea.

I was speechless, still not accustomed to all that holo magic.

"You see, you can even have your old clothes if you choose to."

Right there, I was in no mood to be taught something new by her, and I wanted the magic of the moment to last forever.

"Maybe you show me another time," I said picking up my clothes and starting to get dressed.

She did not insist, instead began to walk along the beach. I caught up with her, and we continued for a while.

Suddenly she said, "Would you like to join me in the work as a guardian agent on Earth? We need good people like you," she turned towards me, taking both my hands, "and I would love to have you around!"

"But I barely know your world, not to mention all your holo-tech that looks like magic to me. I have a lot to catch up with! That will take some time!"

"Yes, it will take a bit of time, but the only thing you need to do right now is to decide to do it."

"Do I need to decide here and now?"

"No, you do not have to, but I think you could," she said, her brown eyes boring into me.

"Yes", I said, "my old world is gone…," I inhaled the pure Ke'alian air, and looked at the incredible landscape, "…and I already feel at home on Ke'a," I added.

She looked at me, radiant, her amber skin golden in the late afternoon sun.

"Is that a yes?"

I closed my hands more firmly around hers.

"I think I need more time, but my heart says a big YES. I want to be part of this beautiful world, and part of your life!"

She leaned towards me and kissed me on my lips, then drew back just before I could pull her into a deeper embrace.

She smiled, "This will give us time to let everything unfold."

She leaned towards me and said softly, "I share your feelings, I also know I need to take it slowly."

At that moment, I felt a wave of happiness, my heart welling up, as what she had said, felt like a yes. Part of me was also scared to confront the reality of a new relationship. My heart was still scarred by the loss of my wife, Simone, on another beach of another world. I kissed Alma softly on her lips.

After a long lingering moment of intense eye contact, she let go of my hands and said, "Let's go back to the village, there are things you need to see and know."

The late afternoon sun was warm with intense red colored rays that twinkled over the sea's surface. A flock of big white birds was flying over the bay, making sounds I had never heard before. The white sand was crunchy beneath my feet. The water line was strewn with glittery shells like a necklace of precious gems. As I took a deep gulp of fresh air, I smelled the rich fragrance of the sea enriched by the nearby flowering vegetation. This was a day in paradise, a paradise that needed to be protected.

As we got nearer to the village, there was a big group of people sitting around an area where a game was happening.

As we approached, I saw there were three teams, clad in either yellow, green or red. The ball was thrown in rapid succession between the players, that were both men and women. At the centre of the circular playing field was a high pole ending in what looked like a big bowl. I immediately understood that the aim for the players was to keep the ball long enough to throw it into the bowl.

We joined the outer circle of onlookers and were

greeted by several people. It took me only a few minutes to understand the basics of the game. When a ball disappeared into the bowl on top of the pole it did not reappear from it nor at any place around the pole. Another ball instantly materialized randomly on the periphery of the circle. Part of the strategy for a team was to be present in as many potential re-emergence areas as possible or to guess where it would appear, giving the finder a significant advantage in the game.

More than a hundred people were sitting around the playing area that was about twenty meters in diameter. I noticed that the area was surrounded by a force field that kept the ball inside the circle.

People were laughing and shouting, supporting their teams. It was great fun to watch, as the ball holder was rapidly surrounded by players of the two other teams who tried to grab it. The ball holders had to pass the ball very quickly to their teammates and tried in a rapid succession of passes to approach the center pole and shoot the ball into the bowl. Immediately after a successful shot, all the players would scatter towards the periphery to be first to grab the reappearing ball.

All strategies seemed allowed to get and keep the ball. The only rule, being creative and having fun. There were lots of shouts and laughters from the players and their supporters.

After a while, as we left the noisy crowd, Alma said, "This is a very popular game all over Ke'a, it's great fun to watch, and even more to play."

As we walked, she suddenly reverted her sari holo-clothes to the natural local appearance, choosing a dark green color.

"How do you like the local fashion?" she asked teasingly.

As I only managed to stare at her, she laughed.

"You'll soon get used to it!"

"I thought I had," I said, blushing, "but with you it's different!"

She laughed again, and took my hand, as we headed to a nearby opening in the tree line. There was practically nothing visible of the village apart from individuals and groups of people walking on the moss paths. As we approached the clearing where lunch had taken place, I saw that the tables and chairs had been replaced by a dozen clusters of comfortable armchairs arranged in circles. Each had a round low table at the center, with all sorts of drinks and tapas-like food items. Most sitting groups were occupied, and there was a light, cheerful vibe all around.

Alma went straight to a group on the far edge near the stones where I had appeared with Michael a few hours before. He was sitting with Cledor, Jehanne'a and two men and a woman that were the ones who had spoken at the guardian council.

Cledor stood up and gave us a joined embrace. "You two look radiant, come and bring your light into our circle!"

We sat and were warmly greeted by the whole round.

Jehenne'a pulled at my t-shirt, "I see you still hang on to your old clothes, I must warn you, we have no washing machines on Ke'a!"

I laughed and gave her a quick hug, "Nice to see you too Jehanne'a!"

It felt like a joyous reunion. We drank fruit juices and ate small items of raw and cooked food.

"This is traditionally a late afternoon snack we have with friends," said Alma.

At some point, the conversations died down, and everybody was quiet. I saw that most people were looking expectantly at Alma.

As seemed to be the way on Ke'a she made an opening gesture with her arms.

"You have all got the new information that I have sent into our inner circle, but for the sake of Luke, who has not yet been introduced to our ways of communicating, I will sum up the recent developments on Earth that are of importance to Ke'a."

She straightened her posture, and continued, "Ke'alians use 'Gaia' as the name for Earth, as it represents the Earth as alive and conscious in the same way as we know Ke'a to be a living planet, conscious in its own very particular way. The vision and hopes we have for the future are that Earth people will realize and understand that their lives are intimately connected to their living planet, and that she is not just a commodity to use and to exploit.

The main Ke'alian policy towards Earth is facilitating that Earth-Gaia transition in the consciousness of Earth humans. This is the best way to protect Ke'a from the old world's aggressive and predatory behaviors. It will also ensure Earth humanity's survival.

Earth humanity is confronted by major planetary challenges that are the direct consequences of short-sighted and unwise behaviors. Earth-Gaia, the living planet has her own ways to correct the damage done to her, where the whole balance of the ecosystem is the priority, not just humanity.

Population growth is the second major challenge. The number of Earth humans has tripled in the last sixty years and has yet to be met by intelligent, sustainable solutions to provide a decent living for all.

Criminal rulers have destroyed the economies and ecosystems of their countries, forcing millions of people to live in extreme poverty with short and often brutal lives.

Unfortunately, the majority of people in democratic countries lack the capacity to see beyond the short-term problems of their lives, to elect people that would have the wisdom and capacity to steer their countries into the right directions.

The Middle Eastern and other conflicts as well as the high pollution zones on land and in the oceans are creating energy disruptions in the life energy fields of Gaia. These have rippled into Ke'a.

Right now we are focusing on finding ways to ease the planetary disturbances in the worst Earth zones that correspond to acute and long-term pollution and aggressive destruction of ecosystems. Our strategy has been so far to place our people as near as possible to the most important decision makers. This has been successful so far, and we have even in a few instances been able to get our people on the very top of major corporations. But there have been unfortunate developments that could destroy much of that work.

The guardian agents on Earth have recently been confronted by new challenges coming from the secret services of the most powerful Earth nations. A couple of operations involving our agents that have gone wrong made them suspicious of being infiltrated by competing countries, or even alien invaders.

Another event that happened around the same time gave them the confirmation that made everything much worse. At an American research center for nuclear fusion, the researchers detected the particular high-energy signature of our agents that were present, as they tested the reactor containment field, using extremely powerful magnetic fields and sensors.

Unfortunately, it was an undercover CIA agent, who monitored the unusual readings, and he could trace it to our people. They barely managed to get away before security was called.

The secret services managed to rapidly analyze their findings and figure out ways to program sensor devices that could detect the Ke'alian higher energy signature.

That is why many of our agents have recently been tracked down and in some cases even identified."

She turned to me, "This is what happened to me in India, where they must have used a portable device. The American secret services have also been able to reprogram sensor devices on their military satellites and have detected many of our people's locations around the world. Fortunately, a majority of the guardians and agents were on the move or out on missions. The damage is also limited due to the relatively low resolution data they received.

We were able to quickly determine what had happened and our info-particles research teams could rapidly develop a countermeasure that works on Earth.

This countermeasure is a shielding of the energy sent out by a Ke'alian organism on Earth. Its implementation was broadcast to all our agents and guardians in just a few Earth hours."

I was thinking of my recent adventures and interrupted Alma. "But they were on us at Cledor's place only a day ago!"

Alma turned to me, concern in her eyes, "Unfortunately, they have been able to gather a lot of data in these few hours. Right now, they are systematically raiding all the locations they have been able to identify through their satellite survey. Luckily, they have only been able to pinpoint a minimal number of active sites. We don't yet know which ones and have instructed all our agents to be vigilant and to change their locations and identities. The Central Planetary Council, together with the Guardian Council will meet tomorrow and decide if we are going to put all our operations on hold. Normally that is what we would do, but the increasing disturbances on Ke'a linked to Earth have created an unprecedented urgency that makes it difficult to leave Earth alone for too much time."

Alma made a closing gesture towards the people in the circle, then turned back to me.

"Luke, this is a good opportunity to experience the direct information that is available to you with the info particles. It will be easier, now that you already have a sense of it."

I felt the importance and urgency of the situation, and suppressed my instinctive reluctance towards something I still considered as a break into my personal integrity.

"Ok, how do I do it?"

"Focus on wanting to know the contents of my latest info update into this circle. You are now part of it."

I closed my eyes and took a deep breath. I recalled how it had felt to want, and then successfully pass through the solid walls of the houses. This time I focused on Alma, feeling her presence, her wish to share this communication with me, then I focused on wanting to know the information she had shared.

It happened all by itself, and I felt my mind literally light up. It was as if an unknown inner door had opened and I had stepped inside a vast inner space. There were pictures and sounds, not like a movie, but it was as if I was seeing and hearing them myself. Places, people, amazing live scenes at the research facility, seen with the eyes of the Ke'alian agents that were present. I could feel their emotions during the events. I even relived the scenes involving Alma and me in India, but this time with Alma's background knowledge and worries about the ongoing events. I instantly knew the full content of the phone call she took at the temple. I saw the helicopters at Cledor's place. It was like a high-speed download into my mind of thousands of information and recorded situations, all closely linked together. I must have tensed up pretty badly, as I felt a massaging hand on my back.

My mind expanded into understandings and insights

about the whole situation, at a depth I would never have imagined possible. Then it stopped. The crazy thing is that all that speeded up information was still there, available, like my own memories of events that I had lived.

"Holy shit!" Was all I could say.

Alma handed me a glass of water.

I looked around. Their smiles told me they knew what I had experienced. Nobody talked, giving me time to gather my wits.

"This was incredible! I remember everything!"

Michael, who was sitting opposite to me, said, "It was a direct download into your mind. This is direct seeing, direct hearing, direct knowing, without any distortions."

"Yes," I said, "seeing is really believing. I have now a full picture and understanding of what is happening on Earth."

Tane'a, the first speaker at the council who sat next to Michael said, "Please do not feel overwhelmed by the new knowledge. Right now it is not your responsibility to solve anything. Know also that Alma is your guide into Ke'a and into the circle of guardians if you choose to become part of it. We Ke'alians see much wisdom in sharing and then relax, letting the mind and spirit digest and find the true inspirations that will lead to the best solutions."

With that she stood up, followed by her colleagues from the council. The ones I had started to consider my friends stayed with me.

"We thought we could all go to the hall," said Jehanne'a, her eyes brightening, "tonight there are great musicians, you'll love it! Are you up for it?"

"I love music," I said, "but I'm sure there will be a new unexpected Ke'alian twist to it?"

Jehanne'a laughed, "Yes, but considering what you already discovered today, I promise you're going to enjoy it."

On the way to that hall, I started to see the village with different eyes. There was much going on in the clearings around the houses. People were playing games, creating art, even sitting in small groups with closed eyes. They all looked young and healthy, their multicolored holo-fields adding a very joyful touch to the scenes. Kids were running around; some were playing games involving turning their holo-clothes into bright blinking lights.

I even saw people dressed in clothes that looked like moving spirals going up and down their bodies, changing colors when they ran into each other.

'We're not in Kansas anymore', I told myself, seeing my naked looking friends walking alongside me.

Chapter Thirteen

The concert had definitely been from this world and totally out of my world. It was performed in a big open space, where wooden benches surrounded a platform. The evening sky, free of stray lights, was shining with a myriad of stars.

The string and wind instruments had been accompanied by two bizarre round instruments that were emitting beams of light. As the musicians touched the beams, they changed color and translated the movements into sounds, harmonies, melodies, rhythms. At first, it all sounded strange and incomplete. As I started to relax, I realized that the sounds were coming both from outside as well as inside my head. I started to see colors overlain on my normal vision, then full immersive scenes took over my vision, with explosions of colors, sounds, and amazingly, even fragrances. It was a total sensory overload for me. That is probably why I fell asleep. I must have slept very deeply, exhausted by the incredible first day on Ke'a.

The next thing I knew was waking up in the dim light

of dawn. I felt disoriented, not knowing where I was. Then I recognized the similar setting to the one I had woken up to, the day before. Ke'a! I got up from the couch and looked out of the circular window. Nature around the house looked similar to Jehanne'a's place. I was wondering if I was in her house or if this was another location. I looked around the circular room and could only see the couch on which I had slept.

As I needed to use a toilet, I decided to test my newly acquired skills with the info particles. I visualized the bathroom that had manifested in Jehanne'a's house and focused on wanting it to appear. I started to sense how it had felt, the items it had contained. And it happened! In the twinkling of an eye, the bathroom slice was in the room as if it had always been there.

This gave my confidence a big boost. It was like being a god, or at the very least, a powerful magician who could create things out of thin air. This time I walked straight through the wall, barely thinking that I wanted to enter.

'Wow, this is so cool!' I thought, adrenaline rushing through my body. *'I did it! I can do it!'* It had felt so easy and natural. This was the moment when I started to land and feel at ease with Ke'a and its magic.

It was fun! That morning I was a child discovering the world. Inside the bathroom, I wished for a shower, and it appeared, water running at the perfect temperature. It felt both incredible and natural.

When I finished washing, I wished for a towel, and was delighted to see the exact replica of my favorite towel appear in front of me. The original towel was probably still in my Parisian apartment.

At that point, I understood that the info-particles in my body were intimately linked to my mind which was the directing power. The info-particles used the information stored in it and my consciously focused thoughts directed their creative power.

That morning was info-holo time! I tried to visualize my body, already dressed, wished for my clothes, feeling them on my body. They instantly appeared! I was fully dressed in a holo-version of my old jeans and T-shirt that were still lying in front of me on the couch. The clothes had the same texture and felt familiar to my body. Everything was there, even my underpants!

This was so much fun! I turned part of the wall into a big mirror and played at wearing all sorts of clothing and costumes that I could imagine.

Alma popped into the room and found me gesticulating in full Roman centurion uniform. We both exploded with laughter.

"I see you found the perfect attire for being a guardian agent!"

After I managed to stop laughing, I said, "This is so much fun, and easy!"

"Yes! I played with it like you, the first time, it's amazing how fast you get used to it."

I turned my holo-field back to the safe appearance of my original clothes.

"You look good in these, but now you know you can change any second. Another big advantage of the holo-clothes is that they are fresh every time they appear."

I saw that she had a short light sari draped around her

body. "You also seem to favor your traditional clothes."

"Yes, sometimes. They feel comfortable and safe," she said with a charming smile.

My thoughts went back to the evening, "How did I get here, did someone carry me?"

"There's much more you have not seen, Luke. Here on Ke'a you can always get what you need. The first step is to know what it is you need. The second is to feel it and know it to be there. We just created a floating chair under you and floated you to your bed."

"Just… floating… how?"

"Come now, Luke, let's go, there's still a lot of fun things to discover!"

She took my hand, and we went outside. We walked to the village center that had reconfigured itself into a lively area with low tables and brightly colored cushions on the ground.

"This place is the common area of the village, where people meet for all sorts of reasons. In the morning, it provides breakfast for all the visitors like us."

"Where are you living, when you are on Ke'a?" I asked.

"In an area corresponding to my home city on Earth, south Indian continent. I would like to take you there after breakfast."

"Yeah…. Yes, of course, after breakfast!" I said, my eyes opening wide.

And so, amazingly, after our quick meal, where I even got something resembling coffee, Alma led me towards the rocky platform in the middle of the village plaza.

"Now, let's go to my home! Friends I have there see me all too rarely! Time goes by too fast on Ke'a when you're on Earth. I have been away a lot lately."

Her expression grew more serious, when she added, "There is a remarkable man I want you to meet. Later, I'd like to take you on a tour. It's time for you to get to know Ke'a!"

I stopped in front of the rocks, trying to wrap my mind around the fact that I was going to travel half around the globe in an instant. Even after having transited to Ke'a and teleported twice in a day, there was a part of me that was still lagging behind.

"Come on Luke, what are you waiting for? It's as fun as changing clothes in front of a mirror!"

I laughed, knowing she was right.

I stepped on the stones, took her hand and everything changed instantly. Not even a blur, a ripple, or anything I've seen in the movies, it was merely instant change from one location to the other.

"Holy cow!" The air felt instantly warmer and carried an entirely different mix of odors. There was a jungle on one side of the rocky mound on top of which we had appeared. The trees were taller. I could see a mountain in the distance. Nearby, amid lower vegetation were houses and lights. In the far distance, a diamond-shaped construction radiated light like a distant rainbow. A red glowing evening sun was already low near the tree line. We had jumped nearly ten time zones! The evening colors were vibrant and gave a sense of intense reality.

"Are we really in India?" I asked, completely awed.

"Yes, we are. Here we call it Ary'a. This is Mu'ad, the city where I live, or, more accurately, where I have my base. The first humans known to have crossed to Ke'a were from India in the first millennium. They were a small group, and unlike the Caribs of Guadeloupe, they did not find a way back to Earth. They were stranded on a virgin planet. There are no historical records of the events, but legends tell the story of a group of men, women, and children having appeared on Ke'a after hiding in a cave from pursuing enemies during a long-forgotten war."

"So, they have been even much longer on Ke'a than the Guadeloupe humans. Their society must have been very advanced?" I asked, getting excited.

Alma smiled at me and continued, "Theirs was a different story. Due to the smallness of the initial group, they developed very slowly. They also had no new influx of people. When they were discovered, nearly three thousand Ke'alian years ago, they were merely a population of around a hundred and fifty thousand, mostly concentrated on the southern tip of India. Their technology had basically been the one of an agrarian society."

"It must have been a huge surprise for the Ke'alians to find other humans on the planet!" I said.

"Yes, at first, they thought they were indigenous to Ke'a, until they were able to communicate and share their stories."

"There is so much I don't know about this world!" I said, tasting the bitter-sweet feeling of being a stranger in a strange world. But I did not want to let it overwhelm my joy and eagerness to make this new world my own.

Alma, who had sensed my mood, said, "It's perfectly ok not to know and understand everything, Luke. Think about all the things you don't know about the many different countries and cultures of Earth. Have you ever worried about it?"

"No," I said, conceding her point, "it's just that it's so much to take in, and I still can't believe that I'm here, I would be less surprised if I woke up in my bed in Paris, realizing this was all a very elaborate dream!"

She smiled, "I understand, Luke! This is only your second day, and we are already on a tour around the world. Take in what you can, relax for the rest, and you'll soon know Ke'a better than you have ever known Earth."

Her words lifted my spirits, and as we walked towards a group of people, holding her hand, I realized again how incredibly lucky I was.

She continued, "The diamond shaped construction in the distance is an important shamanic temple. Here lives and works a mighty group of shamans. Their main focus is to be in touch with the Spirit Dimension and to connect with the planetary consciousness of Ke'a. The information and wisdom gained by their spiritual work is an important part of how the planetary council guides Ke'alian society."

We arrived at a plaza that was brightly lit, full of the hustle and bustle of human activity. What was immediately apparent was that there were more people around than on Karuka'e. Local clothing showed a bigger diversity of stiles. The most frequent one seemed to be short togas worn by men as well as by women. Everything was richly colored. Only a few people had the naked-looking style of a colored force field, and even those had it less tight, more loosely floating away from the body.

Unlike the village in Guadeloupe, this one had numerous visible houses and small shops. Some were half sphere domes like the ones I had seen on Karuka'e. But most houses around the plaza were visible and were shaped differently. The whole setting looked very much like a village center with its houses and shops. Many constructions looked like they were made of stone and wood.

"Are these real buildings, or are they holographic?" I asked.

"Here, there are both. As you probably are beginning to understand, there is no fundamental difference between the two. They are made of the same matter. Only the creation process is different. But a significant thing to remember is that a holo-object can only be changed or removed by its creator. The reason is that the object's existence in the universal holo-field is linked to a particular individual consciousness."

My head was spinning again, feeling the depth of the information I was getting. I was literally feeling my brain reconfiguring and rewiring itself to adapt to this new reality.

"Does that mean that the objects created by an individual disappear when that person dies?"

"Yes, Luke! Exactly, that is part of the beauty of it. It keeps clearing the space for the new creations of the next generation."

There was a glow at the center of the plaza. The familiar smell of burning wood floated in the air.

"This village looks much more like Earth, I feel nearly at home," I said.

Alma stopped walking and looked around, "I know what you mean. This helps to ease the intercultural challenges we expats face at the beginning. Through the millennia Ke'a has developed a unified planetary culture that is fully integrated with the planet's natural processes. But the beauty is that it allows each local community to express its unique individuality."

We continued our walk through the plaza. There were stalls offering fruits and vegetables; others were displaying artwork, sculptures, paintings. I looked into a house that was beaming out intense patterns of light. Its inner walls were displaying light shows of colors, patterns, live pictures of nature scenes, animals I had never seen. When I entered the house, I was immediately immersed in loud sounds and music, but it stopped as soon as I stepped outside.

"Wow, it's amazing!" I said. "There's so much on offer! How does it work economically?"

"Ke'a's central government has long ago ended the concept of money. Everything you see is freely given out of the joy of expressing oneself and sharing it. A very important Ke'alian saying is 'giving is receiving', and people live that reality here. There is no lack on Ke'a, as every individual can create whatever they need."

Several people that passed us greeted Alma. Now I understood the few friendly words they exchanged. We continued to walk past the central place. Smaller paths were leading in all possible directions. The place felt organic, like it had grown out of the soil all by itself. Within a few minutes, the sun had set, and lights appeared all over, shining through the low vegetation that was all-around. It was an incredible diversity of lights, in brightness and color, creating a magical, joyful atmosphere. Spicy smells of cooked foods were drifting out of houses.

"Alma! You are back!" A tall woman holding a baby called out to us, as we passed the house. "Come in with your friend and join in our meal."

Alma hugged the woman and took the baby in her arm. "What a lovely baby you have Senia! Last time I saw you, you were still pregnant."

"Her name is Tara; she was born three months ago. We missed you! You've been away for too long!"

"I know," Alma said, handing back the baby, "I am sorry, Luke and I just had breakfast. We are going to shaman Gahala'o, he is expecting us."

"That's a pity," Senia said, then turned to me, "but meeting Gahala'o is a rare treat. He asks the right questions." Then without saying more, her eyes beaming, she went into her house.

I turned to Alma, "Who is that Gahala'o? You have not told me anything! How come he's expecting us?"

"Luke, Gahala'o is the remarkable man I wanted you to know. I have been in contact with him at breakfast, and it suited him very well that we meet him right away."

"But… but how did you contact him? I've been with you all the time…"

Alma laughed, "One more Ke'alian magic trick! On Ke'a you can connect by thought with anybody on the planet as long as you know the person, or have established with her any kind of connection. You just need to want to get in touch, and if the other person allows the connection, you are instantly linked together."

"One more of these 'just'…" I said, "could I then connect with Michael, Cledor or Jehanne'a?"

"Yes, of course, I think you can figure it out by yourself."

Our conversation had distracted me from looking ahead, and I had to catch myself, not to fall over my own feet, when I saw the temple.

It stood there, like an alien starship that had just landed. The honeycomb diamond structure looked as tall as a ten story building. It was partially transparent and glittered in the light of the moon that had just risen.

"Holy crap!" I exclaimed.

"Yes, an impressive sight! It's one of the seven major planetary temples. Gahala'o, the man we are going to meet, is the speaker of the temple's circle. He is also part of the planetary council."

"Is it like meeting the president of a big country on Earth?"

"In a way, yes, but all Ke'alian leaders have their position because of their wisdom and experience. They are easily accessible to all Ke'alians who genuinely want to meet them. There is no hype around them as there is on Earth."

The sight of the temple was mind-boggling, and I

could barely believe what I was seeing. Part of the construction was quasi-invisible. It could only be guessed through the reflections of the moon light. Other areas of the crystalline structure were alight and glowing different shades of light from the inside. But paradoxically, the sight of the massive structure was not intimidating, on the contrary, it radiated a warmth that invited me to come in.

Alma saw my smile, "This is a fantastic place of love and wisdom, You can already feel it, standing outside."

She took my hand and guided me towards an octagonal entrance. "Come, let's look around before we meet Gahala'o."

It was like stepping into Santa's headquarters at the icy north pole. Everywhere were lights of all colors and shapes. The big hall we had entered was like the inside of a huge crystal that was shining with a million lights, and at the same time, it was transparent to the outside world. The ceiling was a live picture of the night sky with the milky way's light amplified so that it's billions of stars seemed to illuminate the hall.

I was a child again, turning around on my axis, looking up, totally taken by the sight.

After a while, I heard Alma whisper in my ear. "Luke! Luke! Ke'a calling Luke!"

I laughed, shaking my head, "This is incredible, wow!" was all I managed to say, my mind was blown away. Finally, Alma took my hand and pulled me along towards the opposite end of the hall. Only then did I notice the crowd around us. Many people were gathered in groups. Some groups were holding hands.

Alma led me to an opening in a transparent wall. It was a circular alcove leading nowhere. She turned around and took my other hand. "There are no elevators on Ke'a!" she said, smiling mischievously.

I instinctively closed my eyes, and when I reopened them, we were standing in a smaller version of the hall, high above the ground. It seemed to be inside one of the upper diamond facets of the temple.

One wall facing outside and upwards instantly drew all my attention. A vast, moving, three-dimensional live picture was covering it as well as floating above. In the middle of the picture, taking up one-third of the space was a big blue sphere, like a planet. I could discern ripples and tiny waves on its liquid surface. The remaining space around the blue planet was filled with watery spheres of diverse shapes, sizes, colors, and textures. They all looked different and moved around in singular ways. Some slow, some very fast, some erratic; not one ball was moving in the same fashion nor at the same pace. Now and then one of these small balls found its way into the big blue planet and was absorbed. Each time it happened, the whole planet radiated a short flash of the same color as the absorbed sphere. It was an amazing dynamic view that radiated it's aliveness into the whole hall that was lit by it's changing lights. I felt goosebumps running up my arms.

A deep, loud voice took me out of my trance. "Welcome to the inner circle of the temple!" I turned around and saw a tall man walking towards us. He was wearing a long kaftan in the same blue color as the big sphere. His short white hair stood out in strong contrast to his dark amber skin. His face and eyes had a shine of energy and warmth.

"I am Gahala'o, shaman, and child of Ke'a."

He opened his arms and touched both Alma and me in an embracing gesture. Then he turned to me, "I see you are fascinated by the temple's 'Bringer of Light'," he pointed to the live picture hovering above us.

"Yes, I have never seen anything like this, it looks alive. Why do you call it 'bringer of light'?"

Gahala'o's eyes bore deep into mine, "What you see is expressing one of the most important insights you can have about your life. That insight brings light."

I looked up again at the picture that was a universe on its own. I already understood that the scene had a very clear statement. The myriad of little spheres symbolized individual beings. They were all different, moving about at different paces, but eventually, they were reabsorbed by the big sphere, representing the 'Oneness of Everything'.

"It's the story of the drop being reabsorbed by the ocean," I said, my eyes still fixated on the picture.

"Yes," said Gahala'o, "who is the drop?"

"I am the drop. Many traditions teach about the individual soul."

"What does the big sphere represent?"

"It symbolizes god, the oneness of all, the infinite."

"What happens when one of the small spheres is absorbed by the big globe?"

"It disappears, it merges with the much bigger sphere."

Alma who was standing next to me took my hand. It warmed my heart and made this extraordinary moment even more powerful.

Gahala'o had a gentle smile when he continued, "What is the flash of light at the moment of absorption?"

Here I was not so sure, but I ventured, "I think it could signify that the whole also absorbs the unique color, the individual qualities, and experiences that the individual had at that moment."

"Yes," said Gahala'o, "the whole gets enriched and expanded by the absorption of the individual."

He remained silent for long seconds before he continued. "What happens from the point of view of the individual consciousness at the moment of merging with the whole?"

As he asked the question, I felt a moment of inner vertigo, sensing the depth of his question. I closed my eyes, trying to imagine. I am conscious of myself, my mind, my feelings, my stories, me! I! Then that little drop of mine touches the big ocean and merges with its immensity. What happens to the water that was the little drop? Does it disappear? When I reopened my eyes, I saw my own understanding in Gahala'o's eyes.

"I'm still there, only my point of view is totally changed. I instantly know myself to be the ocean. The ocean still includes my little drop, together with all the other trillions of drops."

Gahala'o's questions had just led me to a deep insight that literally was illuminating my mind. I am the drop as well as the ocean. The ocean is the oneness that is all there is. Nothing ever gets lost.

The last question Gahala'o asked finished to dissolve my mind. "Who are you as the ocean, here and now?"

The question was like a laser beam that vaporized my mind, leaving only emptiness. An emptiness infinitely pregnant with everything.

I do not know how long that moment lasted, it was timeless, a moment of enlightenment that has changed my outlook on life ever since. I felt Alma's hand and the warmth of her body. As I opened my eyes, I saw Gahala'o's bright smile, loving understanding in his eyes. I turned to Alma for a long embrace. When we let go of each other we were again alone in the room, Gahala'o had left.

Chapter Fourteen

After the short meeting with Gahala'o at the temple, I felt as if I had lost my memory again. We were back in the big temple hall. I felt silent like a tree, between earth and heaven, deeply rooted. It felt like the lights around us were singing inside myself. It was as if an inner veil had lifted in my consciousness, expanding it into new spacious territories, like moving to a beautiful big mansion after having always lived in a cramped single room. From that vast inner space, there was a vibrant connection to everything around me. For the remaining hours of that day, all the boundaries between my small individual self and the world had disappeared.

The only words Alma said after we left the temple were, "I know what you feel, Luke. I'm with you, all is well!"

These words helped me not to fall into the opposite that I was feeling at the edge of my consciousness. It was the fear of losing myself, of completely dissolving into that ocean of oneness.

We went to her home, that was nearby. It was invisible when we arrived and was similar to the other two houses I had been in the previous days, with the big difference that it had a personal touch, and was tastefully decorated.

In the middle of the room was a big painted sculpture of an Indian goddess. When I asked Alma who she was, she said, "She is the goddess Tara, I love her, she is my star that shines when I lose my way."

Alma's place felt homey. Carpets covered the floor, alongside cushions and small furniture. She motioned me to sit on one of the big cushions around a low table and said she would get something to eat. I watched her pass through the wall. In my blissful state of mind, I did not even blink.

After a short time, she came back with a steaming pot of vegetable stew and what looked like a kind of cooked corn. Of course, she made plates appear in front of us, and we ate the deliciously spiced meal.

After we finished eating, I broke the silence.

"This has been the shortest and richest day of my life. It feels like we left Karuka'e ages ago."

She did not answer. Instead, she moved to the pillow next to me. As our shoulders touched, I put my arm around her waist. This felt so good that I did not dare to move for a long while.

"Come, let's be even more comfortable," she finally said.

She led me to her bed, where she lay in my arm, her head on my chest. I caressed her back and could feel her skin through the light fabric of her sari. I felt her body relaxing.

The place was very quiet. I smelled her favorite patchouli perfume floating in the room which was barely illuminated by a few lights shining through the window. I was very content holding her like that till the end of time.

I fell asleep, and woke when she moved against me. She was awake. I kissed her lips. This time I felt her mouth lean on mine, our lips caressing each other for a long time. I slowly pulled her towards me, and her lips parted, joining our tongues. I felt an explosion of sensations as I tasted her for the first time. The dance of our tongues became wilder. As my hands were finding a way under her sari, it suddenly disappeared, opening the beautiful landscape of her body. I had to mentally focus for a couple of seconds to turn off my holo clothes, letting my naked body join her for a long and intense embrace.

I woke up with the sun in my eyes. Alma was still asleep, lying on my chest. I felt her warm, silent breath caressing my skin in a regular rhythm. A beautifully shaped ear emerged from her lustrous dark hair.

Again, I would have remained in that moment, feeling her breath, till the end of the universe. But somebody crossing over from Earth decided otherwise.

I was looking at her sleeping face when she suddenly opened her eyes and was instantly wide awake. She smiled, pulling me towards her.

After a while, she said, "Luke, there's an emergency meeting of the main guardian circle we need to attend."

That morning, at that time, if she had said, 'Luke, the world is going to end tomorrow,' I would have answered, 'great, we have one more day and one more night together,' but she did not say that.

I said, "Great! Can we have breakfast before we go? But… wait a minute, how did you get that information? You have been sleeping… can they…?"

"Yes, a high priority inner message wakes you up, with instant knowing of the full message's content."

"I'm not so sure that I would like the phone ringing in my head."

"It's much subtler than a phone call, and only used for emergencies. This is real one!"

"What happened?"

"As you know, there has been a crisis around the detection of agents on Earth. As a countermeasure, we have been able to shield the energy signature of our agents. But right now, Earth's secret services are working on detection methods and devices that could potentially lead them to gateways between the worlds. The dangerous direction the research is taking recently, cannot be suppressed any longer. The only path left to us is to shield the gateways in a similar way as we have shielded our agents."

"So, there's already a solution to the problem!" I said, eager to go back to my happy bubble.

But Alma continued, "This was easy to do with the info particles inside our people. These can do nearly anything with clear instructions. But with caves and other larger areas on Earth, it's a different ball game. Fortunately, the gateways do not have the same energy signature as the Ke'alian bodies, but they have a distinctive pattern of energy that could be detected by the technology they are developing."

"But...."

"Come, Luke, you'll be able to ask all your questions at the meeting, that will be in half an hour."

"Where...?"

"At one of the three planetary government centers. This one is situated at the south tip of the African continent."

"...Ah, easy, this is just next door, we grab breakfast, and we'll be there in a second." I said, laughing, feeling the tension ease between my shoulders for a second, before the next thought crossed my mind, "but I'm not a guardian, this is not something I can go to."

"Yes, you can. I am your guide, and I can bring you to the meeting as part of your guardian training."

It was warm outside, and smelled of food and flowers. Somewhere music was playing. We walked behind a noisy group of children, towards the majestic structure of the temple that was already visible above the tree line.

Rainbow colored light was reflected from the many facets of the diamond structure. It looked much more real and solid than it had looked the previous evening.

Around the temple were several smaller plazas that extended into the surrounding forest. We had a quick breakfast at a place very much resembling a cozy diner on Earth.

As we left, Alma said, "People on Ke'a can get all the information they want about the Earth cultures. We have a few places like this one, that are directly inspired by what is trendy on Earth, but it remains quite marginal."

"This is good for expats like us," I said, happy to have that in common with Alma.

We entered the temple that was already buzzing with ongoing activities, and went to one of the rooms adjacent to the big hall.

"This is the primary translocating anchor in the temple." Just when she said that, a woman and a child appeared to our left. There was no noise, just a displacement of air. This time I was not as shocked as the previous day when I saw it happen for the first time.

"I guess one can get used to anything," I said, "but what would happen, if space, where you want to appear, is occupied by a person or an object?"

"This cannot happen, as everything is globally connected with the info particles, and everybody's location is always known. If the whole anchor area were occupied or damaged, the translocation simply would not happen."

"Yes, simply..."

"Luke, the beauty of the Ke'alian info technology, is that it is very simple in its core principles. It connects us, our minds, with the power that creates the most fundamental elements of what we perceive as the physical world. In reality, all is energy, information and consciousness. Like you, I have been awed for a time, but then it rapidly felt natural."

"I know what you mean," I said, "it's only my third day here, and it does not shock me anymore. I also very much prefer this way of traveling to waiting in queues at airports, and sitting for hours in huge flying iron cigars."

Alma laughed, "Come now; it's time we go to the gov center."

She took my hand, and everything changed around us. We were in a big open space that was half covered by a round cupola extending from a big spherical building. In front of us was the open vastness of the sea.

"We are at the lowest tip of the African continent," she said, pointing towards the sea, "from here it's straight to the South Pole! But come now, no time for sightseeing."

I saw her expression focus once more, and the majestic sea was replaced by a big round room right under the sky. A second look revealed that we were standing under a huge dome that was perfectly transparent, on the very summit of the sphere. There were three rows of seats around a central part where a big holographic representation of the familiar blue planet was slowly rotating.

"Incredible!" I exclaimed, "is that Earth or Ke'a?"

"It's Ke'a. On that scale, the continents are practically identical, but there's visible difference at the poles."

I looked and saw that both the Ke'alian North and South pole ice caps were noticeably larger than what I very well knew from my work in climate research.

"There evidently is no global warming on Ke'a," I said while being led by Alma to a seat in the middle row.

Numerous people were already in the room. They gathered in small groups or were sitting quietly on their own. They kept arriving, like we just did, at the periphery of the room which was reserved for the translocation.

As I was observing the scene, Michael materialized. Our gazes instantly met. He waved, smiling. A few seconds later Cledor appeared. His earnest face and long white curly hair contrasted with the youthful looks of most people already present. But there were quite a few that were older than they appeared to be. Some men and women had greying temples or even white strands of hair.

I turned to Alma, "How many people are coming?"

"Between two hundred and fifty and two hundred and seventy, all the guardian agents currently on Ke'a. There are many more right now on Earth."

I watched Michael and Cledor's slow progress towards us, as they were greeting and talking to many people.

All of a sudden, a loud, invisible deep gong rang. Instantly, all the chatter stopped, groups dissolved and people took their seats. Michael sat next to Alma, Cledor next to me.

"Hello Luke, great to see you here!" Cledor's face lit up. We grabbed each other's hand in a warm gesture.

The gong rang a second time, and all the remaining conversations died. A red-haired woman, who had been sitting in the front row, went to the central area, right below the rotating holographic planet. Instantly the globe morphed into a holographic image of the woman, from head to waist, including her hands and arms. It was a striking sight.

"Welcome fellow guardians of Ke'a. An urgent matter calls for our rapid action. We need to protect all the interplanetary gateways. Earth technology is still very crude, but an unfortunate chain of events made them aware of new research fields and technologies that are becoming a treat to our gate network. In a rather short time, they could find ways to monitor vast areas, and thus detect the subtle, but distinctive energy signature of an activated gate. Inactive gates have an even subtler energy signature that, given time, they could potentially learn to detect. We cannot take that kind of risk.

Rapid action is required to protect all seventy-three known gateways. The dimensional portals are, with one exception, of three main types: below ground, mountain, and open field."

The woman's holo-image was replaced by the familiar rotating planet. Blue, green and yellow dots appeared all over the globe. The blue dots made out the majority of around two third, the rest mostly green and only half a dozen yellow.

"We have gathered soil and rock samples at some of the gateways and identified the particular low energy signature that could potentially be detected. Our scientists are right now developing a protection that will mask the energy signature at the deepest level of matter. One of the challenges in doing so is to not affect the very nature of these places that enable the passage to and from Earth.

We plan to apply info-particles to these areas that will connect to the slower elementary particles underlying Earth matter and instruct them to implement the needed changes.

Before we can go ahead with our plan, we need to test and fine-tune our procedure. We will also apply it to only half of the gateways at first. That's why this is a time where we must be extremely vigilant and need most of you to be on Earth. We still have a few agents in key positions of major secret services which might be able to give us early warnings. We have also intensified monitoring governmental encrypted communications.

As gate activation has to be kept to a minimum, you need to cross over in groups. One positive side effect of all these challenges is that the info-particle research has made substantial progress to improve the connection between our particles and those of the lower dimension of Earth. From now on you'll be able to activate a protective field around your body. Inner communication and many other capabilities that did not work before are now possible. Please gather in small groups and share any insights and questions in our next session in an hour from now."

Instantly, the hall reverted to its initial noisy and chaotic state. People gravitated towards each other, and soon clusters of around a dozen had formed everywhere. Michael, Cledor, Alma and I stayed together and were rapidly joined by other people. They were four women and three men. They looked so different, regarding their clothes, skin and hair color, that it would take too long to describe them. We connected, exchanging names and origins. Two men and two women were also originally from Earth. I noticed that they were noticeably smaller than the Ke'alian born. At that moment I realized that it had to be because of Ke'a's lower gravity.

Sue, a small black woman from Australia, said, "The Machu Picchu gateway circle just popped into my mind. It's a very inspiring place for insights. Let's go there!"

Everybody agreed, and I instantly felt my excitement and blood pressure rising. 'To Machu Picchu in Peru!"

We all held hands, and for a brief second, the outer space in front of the ocean appeared, then was immediately replaced by a broad round plaza surrounded by mountains. It was quite dark and chilly, but on one side, behind a broad mountaintop, soft light was emerging.

I was confused, "Is this dawn or dusk?"

Sue, who was happily in charge of our relocation said, "It's dawn. Soon the sun is going to rise, a very good time to be here!"

As I looked around, the vista seemed familiar, but I did not recognize anything from the Machu Picchu site I had personally visited several years ago.

"This is a very particular gate, as it's in the open on Ke'a as well as on Gaia," said Xing, an immigrant from China.

Sue turned to him, "And it's the only known one that has never been used."

"Why are we here, then?" I ventured, a bit shy to speak, as I was starting to wonder what I could contribute to that gathering.

"For the beautiful dawn," Sue said, laughing, but then she added more seriously, "this gate will be the most difficult to protect, for the very reason it has never been activated."

Michael joined our conversation, "Yes, I had also been wondering about this one. There is no guardian on the Earth side, as there has never been a necessity for it. When we had the needed science for it, more than five hundred Ke'alian years ago, we searched and probably found all the transition points to Earth on Ke'a. This one was never used as it corresponds to the very busy tourist place that is Machu Picchu on Earth. We will need to travel by conventional means to the gate on Earth to apply the cloaking particles."

Xing turned to me and added, "All the gates function slightly differently, as they are intimately tuned to their specific location. There are no exact rules, as to how they are activated. It has been a long trial and error process to get to know them all."

We had appeared in the middle of a familiar looking stone bench circle. As we silently sat down, everybody joined hands with the person next to them. After a couple of minutes, I could clearly feel the energy of this particular group, it's focus and intent in being there, and the knowing that I was fully part of it.

When we let go of each other's hands, I looked around. These were powerful people, and it felt good to be in their circle.

Cledor made an opening gesture with his arms and said, "We are here together to further the finding of solutions that will help protect Ke'a. If there is anything that is on your minds and hearts, please express it, even if it seems unimportant."

Seeing the mountains all around us, I thought of Machu Picchu on the other side of the interplanetary gate. This was so utterly incredible. A thought popped into my mind, right when Cledor finished talking.

I decided to play my part as newbie of the group. "Are there more planets like Ke'a parallel to Earth?" I asked.

This time a tall Ke'alian man of undefined origins made a gesture with one arm. He was one of the rare people I had seen, having white strains in his thick shock of black hair. He was soft-spoken, and I had to focus to hear him above the wind that had started to blow with the rising sun.

"We have not found any other world up till now. There's an important thing you need to know: Ke'alian science has come to understand, that Ke'a is not a world parallel to Earth in the classical sense."

He stopped, leaving me with a spinning head.

"Not parallel? What is it then?" I blurted out.

"Earth science, and for a long time Ke'alian science have explored the theories of parallel worlds, without knowing that there can be horizontally parallel worlds as well as vertically parallel worlds."

"What's the difference?" I asked, having no clue where this was going.

The man visibly took a deep breath and continued, "Ke'alian physical sciences and in some respects Earth's quantum physics have theorized that parallel worlds are likely to exist. It's like they are strung together in a horizontal line. But according to the models that scientists have developed, traveling from one world to the other would theoretically necessitate an impossible amount of energy. But then there was the fact that Ke'a existed, and that humans could travel to it from Earth. So, we came up with the notion of vertical parallelism. Vertical in a more dimensional, even spiritual sense.

The founders of our civilization believed that there is

a Spirit Realm that is the source of all creation and consciousness in all the universes. As our scientists, together with the shamans found ways to prove its existence, it allowed us to outline a cosmological map of a multidimensional universe. On that map, Ke'a is located in a higher dimension in relation to the Earth plane.

"What do you mean exactly by 'spirit realm'?" I asked, looking around the circle, and feeling everybody fully supportive of my enquiries.

The man continued, "Your question is important, and might be relevant to the present situation. Just imagine, that the Spirit Realm is on a very high plane, where matter is extremely light and sublime, where the essence of all beings is in their truest state. Imagine going down from there, to denser planes, where matter is denser, and consciousness gets trapped in the limiting, dense structures of living organisms. Ke'a and Earth are on that vertical line, Ke'a being in a higher dimension where matter is less dense."

This left me thinking. In the light of my recent experiences it made sense, and what the man just said was probably a very gross simplification. Being on Ke'a, I was on a higher plane of existence, whatever that meant.

Beside me, Alma joined our conversation. "The Spirit Realm is the key to everything, but right now we have to deal with a society who has a limited awareness of all these matters. Their collective paranoia is making it difficult for us to come to the point where we could share with them all the advancements of the Ke'alian civilization. On the positive side, a huge number of individuals on Earth are already capable of making this leap in evolution. We who have come from Earth and have fully integrated on Ke'a are living proof for that."

"Yes!" exclaimed another woman who was also Earthborn, "the evolution of a vast number of individuals on Earth has brought them to the point where they could be easily integrated on Ke'a with its very different outlook on life. But the masses are still bound by fear of anything that is unknown and could threaten their daily habits."

While we were talking, the sun had risen over that part of the Andes, enhancing the already vibrant Ke'alian colors. Misty patches of water vapor were lazily hovering in the air that had a tasty, crispy freshness. I remembered what Alma said the day before, that I would soon know Ke'a better than Earth. Being able to travel all over the globe in an instant creates an incredible connection and intimacy with the planet. I was starting to feel like an integral part of it, not separated, something I had never felt on Earth.

At that moment I felt for the first time an inner reluctance to go back to Earth. Seen from Ke'a, my home planet looked very different. It felt distant, dirty, heavy, complicated, even dangerous.

My reflections had distracted me from the group's conversation. I heard Sue talking, "… accidentally find a way to activate a gate, we are protected, as whoever arrives on Ke'a for the first time will temporarily be helpless as memories get reset for plenty of time for us to arrive on site."

"Yes, Sue, that is reassuring. All gates are constantly monitored through the planetary info layer. But a lot of damage would still be done if such a transition was observed and recorded by the military or secret services."

Another man, joined in, "Absolutely! It's vital for us to hide the Earth gates on the energy level and keep doing our slow work of influence. For now it seems to be the only viable path of action."

A tall blond woman, who had not yet spoken lifted her arm, and said in a high-pitched voice, "I keep wondering why we do not just neutralize all the things on Earth that are a danger to us. Earth governments understand the language of force. They would rapidly adjust when they recognize our superiority."

Everybody in the circle went quiet, then after a few long moments, Michael said, "I understand your reflections, Tulane'a, they also reflect the opinion of a growing minority of our people. I personally think that it would be a dangerous path, and a path that does not reflect the spirit of Ke'a, that is respectful and inclusive. I feel that force should be the very last resort."

At that point, Cledor stood and said, "We have seen force in action when the military raided my Earth home near the Guadeloupe gate. By now the whole area is most probably heavily guarded and monitored. It's very unlikely that they can find the gate cave. Even if the do, they do not know how to activate it. Extra measures are necessary at that gate, to apply the protection. That gate carries a strong symbolic value, as it is the origin of our civilization."

He then made a closing gesture with his arms. "Our time is soon over, let's close this circle and go back." He sat down again, and we all joined hands. I drew a deep breath of the fresh mountain air and closed my eyes. The energy of the group was streaming through my body and mind. I could clearly feel what we had just shared, and the tension that had risen in the last part. But it also felt like a necessary part of the whole. All the parts were allowed to be there.

We all stood up, still holding hands. I gave a last glance at the majestic mountains. A moment later it was replaced by the ocean at the tip of Africa, then, a heartbeat later we were standing in the big hall under a perfect blue sky.

Chapter Fifteen

The session in the hall had resumed as soon as all the groups were back. The red-haired woman, speaker for the guardians, concluded the meeting with a statement that the planetary council was about reconvene to discuss and decide about new policies towards Earth, in the light of the acceleration of the effects on the negatively touched areas on Ke'a. She said that all the group's reflections would be shared with the council.

She concluded that it was time for most of us to transfer to Earth to protect and monitor all the gates. An essential summary of all things of importance, including a coordinated schedule of transfers and locations would soon be accessible to all of us.

Michael, Cledor, Alma and I decided to stick together and go to Karuka'e, Cledor's village where the day had just started.

As Alma and I lingered a while outside on the big platform in front of the ocean, I said, "It's incredible to be able to translocate anywhere on the planet. It's so cool!"

Alma looked at me, smiling, her eyes full of mischief. "And you have seen nothing yet!"

"What is it that I have not seen?" I asked, my curiosity aroused.

She kept laughing, "Sorry, I'm not going to tell you. I won't spoil that moment when I'll be seeing your face.

As I was trying catch and coerce her by force to reveal her ugly secret, she ran away, giggling. I chased her around the place, but she managed to outrun me. We had great fun, even worth the big shock I was going to get with her surprise.

Eventually we left and appeared in the central plaza of Karuka'e where Michael and Cledor were already having breakfast.

"If that's your favorite meal, hopping around as we did, you can have it several times a day," I said, as I sat next to Michael.

He laughed, "There are days like that, where it's difficult to keep track of things."

I chose to have lunch. *'You never know what's coming next!'* I thought, feeling exhilarated after all the jumps around the planet. But a deep tiredness was creeping in on me. It was a mental and emotional exhaustion, a strain that was present at a deeper layer. It felt like part of my mind was slightly out of phase, still trying to catch up.

I was happy, but I felt my nervous system was overloaded. I needed things to slow down. It was good that the Ke'alian custom was to enjoy a meal quietly, or with light conversation. At the end of it, as I got up, my vision suddenly darkened, as everything started to spin around me. I lost my footing and would have fallen, had Alma not grabbed my arm and drawn me towards her.

"I'm sorry," I managed to say, as she was holding me, "I think I need some rest."

"Of course!" she exclaimed, keeping her arm around my waist, "it's been quite a ride in a short time. Now's the time to take a break and relax!" She began massaging my back.

Cledor nodded approvingly, and Michael gave me a friendly punch. "Don't worry! You're doing great. We'll see each other later!"

I sat for a while with my eyes closed, feeling Alma's warm hands. When I looked at her, she smiled. "I think I have just the right thing for you! Come with me!"

We went to an alley, nearby the shore, where the big fern-like trees created a natural shielding from the sea winds. We walked into the surrounding vegetation and found an empty cleared area, like the ones used by the locals for their houses.

"Close your eyes!" she said.

"Why?"

"Give your tired mind a break! Just do it!" she reinforced her demand with a soft touch my forehead.

I surrendered, making a show of putting both hands on my eyes. I felt a sudden displacement of air, heard a door open and some bizarre noises.

'What's she doing?'

"Now you can open your eyes."

"Wow! Incredible! Is this because I'm Canadian?"

In front of us stood a wooden log cabin that might have just jumped out of a Canadian travel catalog. It was totally out of place, near the sea, but it felt so good to see this familiar construction.

"I thought you might like it," she said, beaming her most beautiful smile.

"How did you do that? It must be more difficult than making round houses."

"Now is the time to relax! But to give something to your hungry mind, let's say we also have internet here on Ke'a, but it's more like an innernet," she smiled again, took my hand and walked me inside the log cabin.

"Wow!" It was like being back on Earth, the Canada of my childhood. My father used to take me on long hikes in nature. We sometimes stayed for the night at one of those cabins. They are the best memories I have of my childhood. Those long days of walking with backpacks, cooking meals on the campfire.

"How did you know?"

"Just a woman's intuition," she said and pulled me towards a bed made of round logs and covered with traditional hand-woven blankets.

It was incredible, and it did help me to relax, as it looked like the safest and coziest place that could ever be.

We lay on the bed, holding each other. I fell into a deep sleep.

―――

I was running in a forest, trying to find my father.

Wolves were howling behind me and woke up. Seeing the log cabin's rugged interior, feeling the roughly woven blankets on my body. For a few moments, I had no idea where I was. What on Earth had happened to me? And then I smiled, remembering, it was not 'what on Earth'… it was 'what on Ke'a'. Everything flashed back. I felt rested, and all was well.

I was alone, Alma had gone out, but that was just what I needed, time for some lazy time in bed. It felt good to stare at the cabin's wooden ceiling. I lay like that for a long while, not thinking, just being. Then I stood up and looked around.

The logs were just like I remembered from my childhood, even the stone chimney that majestically took half of a wall. As I was starting to wonder whether I could light a fire, the door opened, and when Alma came in, I burst out laughing. She was dressed like a traditional native American.

"Have you had a good sleep?"

Her amber skin and her broad cheekbones gave her the perfect looks.

"You look great as an Indian woman, but that should be easy for an Indian woman, right?" I teased.

"Yeah, Columbus thought he had reached India, giving people from India that special connection with all the 'Indians' of the Americas!"

She joined me on the bed, and for a long while, I forgot everything, Ke'a and all the Indians.

Hours later, when we finally left the cabin, it was already getting dark.

"I'm a bit out of sync with the clock," I said, "for me, it feels more like starting a new day."

"Then let's go where a new day starts and make plans from there." She led me back to the central place that had the translocation anchor at its center. Night fell rapidly, and lights were coming on all around us.

"Where are we going?" I asked.

"I guess Ke'a's counterpart of New Zealand will be our best chance to start a fresh day. There are some fascinating things to see on that island."

"Great! I've never been that far!"

She laughed, "Like I said yesterday, you have not seen anything yet, but right now we need to take it easy on you, my little surprise can wait."

"What do you mean by 'can wait'?" I caught her, just as she wanted to run away. "I'm feeling great! And don't we have a mission to secure the gates?"

Instead of answering, she laughed again. It melted my heart, and I felt blessed to be with her. At that moment, I became aware of a sting of fear, that it all would turn out to be just a fantastic dream. I held her more firmly, locking my eyes to hers.

"I asked you before, but I keep pinching myself. Are you real? Alma, mysterious Indian woman I just met a few days ago?"

"Yes, Luke, I'm as real and as unreal as everything else. And yes, here and now, on Ke'a I'm as real as it gets, and," she leaned over and whispered in my ear, "I love you, Luke."

If it had been possible, my heart would have exploded as I kissed her. "I love you too," I said, kissing her again.

That moment reconnected me with my experience at the temple, the oneness I had felt. But then I thought, I was very happy to be this tiny Luke droplet for a while, in love with the Alma droplet. I did not want them to dissolve into the ocean. I wanted that moment to last forever.

She must have been in a similar place, as she said, "New Zealand can wait, there's another greater place, where we can start the day. Maybe you are ready for my secret place. You will see Ke'a in all her glory."

After a sparkle of apprehension hollowing my belly, I said with a voice I had wished stronger, "Yes, this is the moment! Bring on the magic!"

"Ok, let's stand on the anchor stones. But brace yourself, this is going to be big!"

I had no idea what was going to happen, but I mentally prepared for a big scare. I took a few deep breaths, looking into her eyes that were sparkling with anticipation. What could be so big, I thought, but then I had no idea what was coming.

"Luke, close your eyes, and keep them closed until I tell you."

"Ok! You really know how to build up the tension!"

I closed my eyes, then immediately felt an unusual lightness in my body, nearly as if I was floating.

'Floating, you're crazy!', I thought, but kept my eyes shut, not daring to open them. This was very strange.

Then Alma said, "I'm holding you, slowly open your eyes."

I felt her grip tighten on my arm, and I opened my eyes… "Holy Jesus!"

There was a blue planet, massive, right in front of me, not a picture, no hologram, but the real one! We were in space! Holy sh..!

We were under a transparent cupola, in a big circular room. The huge globe with its continents, seas and clouds, completely filled one side of the panoramic view. The colors were intensely real. The planet looked like my familiar Earth, but she was Ke'a. Vibrantly real and alive.

Alma was holding a railing that ran all around. There were other people, further away, also holding on to it.

"Wow, wow, wow…! And how's my face, is it like you expected? This is insane! We're in space! I'm weightless! Are we on a space station?"

I think I could not close my mouth for a while; it was just hanging open.

"This is nuts, we've traveled to space in an instant!"

Alma was intensely observing me, looking very pleased. I was a much more interesting sight for her than the planet hovering before us.

It was totally unbelievable to suddenly be in space. In an instant we had left the planet. It is quite a jump for the mind to catch up when you are unprepared. I felt Alma's hand massaging my back. Worry had replaced some of the joy in her eyes.

"Are you going to be ok, Luke?"

She abruptly changed her mind and kissed me, which was the perfect thing to do, as it brought me straight back into my body.

"I'm all right," I finally said, "but that was the mother of all surprises! Where are we?"

"We are on one of the Ke'alian space stations orbiting Ke'a. This one is the oldest, and it's open to all Ke'alians who want to admire their planet. All Ke'alian kids come here as part of their teaching about the living planet."

I was mesmerized, as I watched the slowly rotating planet. She was shining its own light and was amazingly beautiful. In front of me was a full disk, unlike views I had seen from Earth's international space station. Ke'a was two-thirds full. I could see the Australian continent emerging from the night side. All around the planet was the darkness of space, speckled by a myriad of stars. The sun, which was behind us, looked dimmed, as the space station was protecting us from its radiations.

"How far are we from Ke'a? This station is much further away than the ones on Earth."

I saw her eyes focus inwardly, then she said, "Around eleven times further away. The intention was to be far enough to see Ke'a as a full disc."

"It hits me right in my gut and heart to see the real planet in space, this is very powerful!" I said, letting go of the railing I had been holding. Nothing happened, I did not float away, just stayed where I was, feeling no weight from my body on my feet. Then I pushed away from the railing and instantly tumbled around. Alma, who had been watching me and still had a hand on the railing managed to grab my leg.

"Whoah! That is insane!"

She was laughing. "Slowly! You barely need any power to move."

As I stabilized, she held me with one hand above her head.

"See how strong I am!" Then she released her grip, and I stayed, right where I was, two meters above the floor. I started to get a weird feeling in my belly. I closed my eyes, took a deep breath. After a few moments, my stomach had calmed itself. I was starting to enjoy the sensation. No weight, my body had no weight! It was unnatural, and I was thoroughly awed by it. My muscles relaxed, they were out of business. I stretched out my arms and made slow flapping movements and the air in the room propelled me upwards. I was steadily rising towards the ceiling. It did not stop until I reached the transparent cupola that was at least ten meters from the floor.

Alma looked small, down on the floor, but then I saw her give a slight push, and she was in the air, floating towards me.

"Do I need to get you off the ceiling, my dear?" she teased.

I took her arm and pulled her towards me. My gesture was a bit too sudden, and it pulled us both into a wild tumble. This was great fun, we just needed to be careful not to slam into a wall. Finally, our rotation lost its momentum, and I held her in my arm, high up, in the middle of the room! My first kiss in weightlessness!

We grabbed a vertical railing and pulled our bodies back to the floor. I saw that Australia had already entered the daylight zone. The planet looked magnificent, with her blue oceans and white cloud covers.

A sudden displacement of air preceded the appearance of a group of children. They were surely less than ten years old. Judging by their shouts and cries, it was also their first time. My heart went out to them, as we shared this incredible feeling of making a powerful new experience.

"Where do we go from here?" Alma asked, her eyes sparkling.

I said jokingly, "Maybe to the Moon, while we're at it?"

"Ok!" She said and took my hand. An instant later, the room had changed. It was bigger with a very high dome. The sky was still black, full of stars, but high in it was Ke'a, much smaller than before, but still intensely visible. Straight ahead, I saw a grey rocky landscape.

"You are kidding me... we're not...?"

"Yes, we are! This is the Moon base observatory."

Again, I was speechless, I looked outside the circular window and touched it. Yes, it was real, it felt cold, hard, tangible. I was shaken to my deepest core. I did not know any longer what was real or not. All my pre-programmed, pre-conceived ideas about the world and what was possible or not, were shattered. In my world, nobody had gone to the moon since the early seventies, and it had been a huge undertaking. I was in an air-tight room, sensing the lightness of my body in the lower moon gravity. High above in the sky was a big blue planet that looked like Earth, but actually was another world. I took a deep breath, closing my eyes, feeling my body. Yes, my body was a constant, I, Luke, the sense of me was a constant. I felt Alma's arm around my waist.

"Yes, Luke, that is big. That is part of being on Ke'a. The distance between two points is irrelevant when you have an inner connection with it. Even now, Ke'alian scientists argue, whether it's you shifting your location, or whether the whole universe re-centers around you."

I opened my eyes, my scientific curiosity kicking in. "Incredible question! But could one shift if the other location was light years away?"

"Yes, the universe is one vast holographic, energy, information, and consciousness field. All points are connected within that field. Any distance is bridged with the anchor of consciousness."

"Wow! So, you are saying that there's no difference between us translocating from Karuka'e to India or to the Moon?"

"Yes, there is no difference, there also is no energy involved in the translocation."

"Have the Ke'alians gone to other planets and other stars?" I asked, my excitement bubbling up.

Alma looked upwards at the starry darkness of the moon sky and said, "Yes, there is a big base on Mars, that was established several centuries ago."

"And to the stars?" I asked, feeling deeply moved, as this has been one of my big fascinations. I had attended some astronomy courses during my student years when I studied climatology.

"Yes, but only to one star, the nearest neighbor of our sun, Alpha Centauri. The speed of light being faster in this Universe, it only took two hundred years for a Ke'alian mission to reach Alpha Centauri."

"Now hold on! And did they establish anchor points?"

"Yes, that was the whole point of the mission. They found, what we call a living planet orbiting that star. It has a very thriving biosphere, and all the conditions for life are very similar to Ke'a."

"How long ago has that happened?"

"Around one hundred and ten years ago."

"Have they found intelligent beings?"

"Not in the human sense, but there's a huge number of different species on the planet, many similar to Ke'a's fauna, but there's also a whole new category of animals which are very different."

"And, have Ke'alians started to colonize that world?"

"Today there's a small community that is mostly scientists and shamans. They take it very slowly, as they are respecting the alien biosphere. They have taken all possible precautions not to bring in anything that could be a threat to the living planet. First, they want to have a deep understanding of the whole planetary biosphere and connect with the planetary consciousness before starting any bigger projects."

"Wow!" In my enthusiasm, I had lost my connection to the floor. But what would have produced a little hop on Earth, propelled me more than a meter above ground. We both laughed, as I tried to regain my footing on the metal floor of the station.

"Can we go there?"

"Yes, we can, but a special authorization is needed. I can apply for it, if you want."

"You bet! I want to go! How long before we get it?"

"Wait a minute," she turned her gaze inside for a few seconds, then she said, "it can take a few weeks, as particular precautions need to be taken before departure, and we need to have a person on Kai'ila, to guide us."

"Kai'ila?"

"That's the name of the planet."

I felt lightheaded. I was making a technological leap of at least a thousand years in an instant. I guess I was better prepared for it than a man from the middle ages, who would suddenly have had to board a plane. My scientific training, together with my fertile imagination, as well as all the sci-fi books and movies, had paved the way very well. But for an instant, my mind had gone blank again, unable to conceive something that had solely been for me in the realm of fantasy.

Alma's kiss on my forehead brought me back to reality.

"Can we at least go to Mars?" I asked, grinning broadly.

"I thought you'd never asked," said Alma, and took my hand.

I looked upwards, and in the twinkling of an eye, the blackness of space changed to a bizarre light orange. We were on Mars.

Chapter Sixteen

Mars! We were on Mars! Not under a dome, in an airtight station, but being outside, breathing Martian air. We had appeared right in the middle of what looked very much like an oasis. I could see a small lake at the center of a green zone. There were lots of fern-like tall plants, similar to the ones I had seen on Karuka'e. The ground had some sparse grass coming out of a dusty red soil that was littered with reddish stones and rocks. The air was a bit on the cool side, but still pleasant. What struck me most was that the air smelled very different than the air I had breathed on Earth or Ke'a. It felt dry and had a mineral taste. The sky was a mixture of light cream orange and even some patches of very light blue.

I sat on my heels and grabbed a handful of Martian soil. Its color was on the red side of brown. It felt sandy and dusty. In my hand, among the soil, was a tiny leaf of grass. Its small roots were holding softer soil that looked dark and fertile.

"This is incredible! There's life on Mars!"

"Mars has been terraformed as an ongoing process that has already taken more than four hundred years," Alma said. She was looking at me happily, observing all my reactions.

"Is this not the perfect place to start a new day? Come, let's have breakfast!" She began to walk towards a group of low buildings along the lake's edge.

"Breakfast on Mars! Who would believe me if I would tell my story?"

"Any Ke'alian would believe you," she said, smiling.

"Are there many Ke'alians on Mars?"

"Yes, Mars has been opened for all Ke'alians for nearly a hundred years. Ke'alians love their home planet and are generally reluctant to leave her. But there are already almost two million Ke'alians who have established their main home on Mars. The fact that you can instantly travel back and forth to Ke'a has made that much easier."

We arrived at the edge of a settlement built inside a big orchard with small, organic looking constructions beautifully integrated among the trees. Some trees were bearing big red fruits, others had small black berries hanging in grapes. I also saw gardens that had flowers and vegetables of different kinds. The area smelled of moist soil and flowers.

Alma waved towards the gardens and the people working in them, "This is a botanical and agricultural research facility that is adapting Ke'alian trees and plants to the energy of Oko'a."

"What is Oko'a?"

"Ah, sorry, I keep forgetting! That's the Ke'alian name

of the planet."

"I see people who are wearing clothes that are the same blue as Gahala'o's at the temple. Are these shamans?"

"Yes, shamans have been working hand in hand with the scientists. Oko'a has been alive, millions of years ago. They have focused on reconnecting with the old life force of Oko'a. It's like the life energy of the planet had been in deep hibernation.

Lots of things have happened since Ke'alians arrived. The creation of an atmosphere, the import, and cultivation of massive quantities of bacteria and plants have started a new life for the planet, that is in many ways alien to her. It's like the planet has slowly been waking up, but has a whole new outer layer of her body. The shamans are assisting her in establishing all these new physical and non-physical connections with the Spirit World that have slowly been creating a healthy biosphere."

"That's fantastic, and there are already so many visible results." I said enthusiastically, "I'm in awe of your society. Since I've been here, I've discovered one wonderful thing after another. Coming from Earth, I'm somehow waiting for the next problem or bad news to strike. Are there no real problems? Ke'a looks like a real utopia from my point of view."

"Come, let's sit at the edge of the lake. There's a place where we can have our Martian breakfast and talk."

We passed several men and women that were walking in front of carts loaded with fruits and plants. The vehicles were moving by themselves, hovering above the ground. My eyes must have popped out of their sockets, as the group stopped. They looked intently at me.

"Hello, friend, is something wrong with us?"

I heard Alma laugh next to me, but she said nothing.

"No, nothing's wrong," I stammered, "it's just I have never seen such a device hovering above the ground. I'm from Earth, and arrived only a few days ago."

The man who had spoken laughed, "Ah! Welcome to Oko'a my friend, this must also be a first time."

"Yes, one of the many first times of the last days. You have an incredible society."

A woman, in front of the other cart, said, "Yes, we are happy and grateful to be Ke'alians. It's a fortunate and good life we all have."

They waved and were on their way.

As we continued to walk towards the lake, I saw that the shore was lower than the surrounding land. A path went down a slope towards the water. A wide wooden decking had been built around the water's edge on that side of the lake. About one hundred meters away, the opposite shore of the lake was rocky, except for a small stretch of what looked like a sandy beach. Through the clear water, I could see a darker shade of the reddish Martian ground. The dark water was brightened by the mirroring of the orange and soft blue of the sky.

"Let's sit there!" Alma pointed further along the decking where I could see an outdoor café with tables on the water's edge.

The place was busy and alive with conversations and children playing. When we approached, some people greeted us, and I saw that they were looking at my clothes that still were the holo version of my Earth clothes. I made a mental note to change them.

The place was ablaze with the colors that people were wearing. With some exceptions, it seemed the local fashion was similar to the nude holo-field, but a little looser on the body, and brightly colored.

We went inside the café's round building. There were lots of different foods and drinks all around its circular wall. We filled a tray and went to sit at a table on the water's edge.

We ate silently, enjoying the fresh food that came straight from the gardens. It was an incredible feeling to be on another planet, hundreds of millions of kilometers away. In the Martian sky, the sun looked much smaller and was noticeably cooler than on Ke'a. I had just had my first breakfast on Mars!

"It's wonderful to sit here with you," I said, taking her hand. This life, the Ke'alians have is incredible."

"It's also your life now, Luke, you are now living on Ke'a."

"But I'm not a Ke'alian, they all live much longer than what I can expect."

"That is not necessarily true. When you transferred to Ke'a, all your cells, up to the level of elementary particles, and beyond have transmuted into the matter of this universe. One could say, that you, and me, having been Earth humans, have truly become Ke'alian humans."

"Do you mean that my life expectancy is also over two hundred years?"

"Yes, if you don't do stupid things that get you killed."

"What are you saying? I can't believe that! Do you mean I've become an alien myself?"

"No, not an alien, a Ke'alian human!"

My head was spinning again, and something in me went on overload, another voice inside, that I knew all too well kicked in, and I could not stop it.

"But it can't just all be positive! Everything is great, free, unlimited, freedom of everything, endless abundance. All these great things, don't they have a price tag? Is there no polar opposite of all that paradise stuff? Don't people have any problems? Is there no darkness in Ke'alian society?"

Alma took her hand away from my arm and straightened in her chair.

"I have asked myself these same questions during the first weeks I was on Ke'a. I have now been integrated in Ke'alian society for a long time. In a way, it has never entirely left me to observe with my Earth eyes, and I honestly have never found, seen nor heard about truly bad things, people, dark forces of evil here on Ke'a."

"What is so different here?" I asked, putting my hand on her leg, needing to feel her warmth.

"The difference is that Ke'a had a much longer history, had much more time to solve all the petty problems with which Earth people still struggle. There is no money, no real property on Ke'a, because everybody can have everything they want. There is no need to have power over others, as everybody is equally connected in the planetary info-holo-field. There are no wars over limited resources, as the resources are recognized and lived as unlimited.

I also have come to understand that above all this physical cornucopia, it's the Ke'alian's innate connection with and respect for the planet, and a direct knowledge and inner connection with the Spirit World that is the key to Ke'alian harmony and happiness. The Ke'alians have an inner knowing of their essential existence in the Spirit World. That gives their physical lives an entirely different meaning."

"But there still are teenagers on Ke'a? And what about conflicts within families?" I asked, still not satisfied.

"There is a culture of forgiveness and responsibility on Ke'a that prevents all these smaller conflicts from blowing themselves up and get out of hand."

"What do they do when someone is hurt and gets really mad?"

"As I said, there is an ancient habit, ingrained in Ke'alian culture, that is two-fold. First, an acceptance, an awareness that we are creators. We are essentially creating our lives, whether consciously or unconsciously. Everything that we are, the thoughts and feelings we have, our decisions and actions, our beliefs and expectations steer and shape our lives."

"Can we be responsible for something happening to us?"

Alma looked around at the playing children, then said, "We are not blank slates when we are born. Remember, the Ke'alians have a direct inner knowing that the essence of who they are is in the Spirit World."

"But," I interrupted, "what is this spirit world? Is it not like the promises of heaven and afterlife all the Earth religions talk about? There's never been any proof!"

Alma retook my hand, and I loved the feel of her warm skin. She said, "I'm not sure about that proof thing. Words are too limited to talk about that plane of existence. It's much easier when you actually experience it."

"Have you experienced it?"

"Yes, many times, and it's that direct experience which helps so much with conflicts, it's seeing the underlying oneness of everything."

Alma took a long sip of her purple colored fruit juice and continued, "The second ancient habit the Ke'alians have is the practice of forgiveness. Forgiving yourself and others while taking responsibility for your own lives is very powerful. It cleans away lots of rubbish, all the stuff that usually is fertile ground for conflicts and suffering."

We remained silent for a few minutes. What Alma had said was starting to make sense to me.

"Can I also make this direct experience with the Spirit World?"

Alma took my other hand. "Yes you can. There are known ways to get there and see it with your own inner eyes. Shamans are good guides for a first experience; we can arrange a session whenever you want."

I looked at her, at the people and kids around us, at the small Martian Sun in the alien sky, thinking that life could not be better. But then, it seemed that the nature of life was an endless expansion.

"I'd like it very much," I said and kissed her.

As we walked out of the café area, two little girls holding hands passed us by. They both looked at us with shining eyes. I could feel their happiness and how good their life was.

But then, it was as if a very long knife had slowly stabbed me right into my heart. I stood there, frozen, looking at the little girls walking away. These could have been my daughters, Camille and Noémie. I remembered their curly hair that was in my face, how wonderful they smelled and felt. At that moment I felt a horrible pain and sadness.

"I miss Noémie, and I miss Camille, I miss them so much. I'm so sorry that they could not grow up and have such a happy life."

Alma put her arms strongly around me. "I know, I feel your pain. I love you. Life goes on, and nothing gets really lost. I'm with you, a new life. I love you."

Her words helped me come back to the present moment. Her love removed the knife from my heart. Yes, life goes on. I put my arm around her waist, and we silently took a path leading out of the gardens area, towards a rocky mound. Up there the view was breath-taking. It looked like the planet I had seen on NASA pictures. A vast red rocky expanse and a huge alien looking mountain range on the horizon.

"This is your new life! In case you doubted it, we really are on Mars!" said Alma and dug herself deeper into my arm.

A cold wind was blowing around us, and I shivered.

There was still some way to go before Mars would be fully habitable. I suddenly yearned to go back to my new home planet and its warmth.

"How about the mission to secure the gates on Earth?" I asked.

"There have been delays, as the tests have not been entirely conclusive. They are very careful not to damage the gates while trying to protect them. Most gates are monitored by guardian agents on Earth. Even on Guadeloupe, where one of our agents reported that there is a heavy military presence around Cledor's house and the hill. But there is no way that gate can be found, as it has been sealed inside solid rock. Right now, if we only use the most remote and secure gates for communication purposes, the risk of detection is very low."

"So, are we going to go back to Earth in the coming days? I cannot say that I fancy that very much," I said, feeling my energy drop at the prospect.

"Don't worry, Luke, you are not yet ready to go back to Earth. If you still want to become a guardian, you need some training and education into the ways of Ke'a."

"Yes, I would like to, I'm starting to love this crazy Ke'alian world. Right now, the thought of going back to Earth with all her problems is not a happy one."

"Yes, you need some time to land here, before making new choices."

I could feel the feeble heat of the Martian sun high in the sky. *'There are no birds in the sky.'* I thought.

"But, what is important for me right now, is that I want to be with you!" I said, holding her tightly.

She smiled, "Me too, I'm sure we're going to find ways to be together as much as possible."

I kissed her.

"Come let's go back to Ke'a, we can come here whenever we want," she said as we started to go down the mound towards the settlement.

Chapter Seventeen

Alma wanted us to go to Bo'ad, one of Ke'a's three planetary capitals, which is representing Ke'a's mountain regions. The other two capital-cities represent the plains and the oceanic regions. Bo'ad is situated on the Tibetan high plateau, surrounded by massive mountain ranges. When we arrived, the high white peaks were aflame with the red evening light. They looked like the glimmering jewels of a gigantic crown.

We had appeared on a high bridge that was connecting two enormous buildings. They looked like smaller versions of the surrounding mountains, glittering crystal shapes, reflecting the red evening light.

Under the bridge was a sea of lights, thousands of lit constructions and alleys going off in all directions. The whole setting looked organic, mimicking mountains, lower slopes, and boulders, all being made up by individual buildings that were radiating light from the inside.

The unusually warm air carried a multitude of smells

that told stories of foods, spices, and mysterious perfumes. It looked like a big city, but from the height of the bridge, I heard no noises. There was a flow of walking people in the alleys that were winding like ancient roots moving around the big buildings. These looked like crystal mountains that were lit from the inside. The whole setting looked alien to me, nothing that I ever could have imagined.

As we stood there, several people had popped into existence not far from us and swiftly walked towards one of the buildings. We followed the last one inside the tall mountain-building. The inner hall was worthy of the building's exterior. The walls were a mountain dwarf's dream, made of precious looking gems and crystals. After my recent experiences, I was more able to take in this level of beauty.

We walked towards the center of the hall, where a big group of people had gathered. They were all clad in red robes, holding hands and dancing to a slow tune they were alone to hear. I had to stop, something about this group felt odd.

Alma, seeing my reaction, said, "Let's have a look, it's good for your education."

"Education?" I asked, but Alma did not respond. As we approached I started to hear the music. It was mostly drums, gongs, and deep pipe sounds. Suddenly my vision was augmented by images of a radiant Ke'a, hovering in space, and then bang, the image zoomed into several areas where the radiance was absent, all was grey and bland. Then I felt a strong inner incentive to protect the beloved planet. The image shifted again to the whole world, zooming down again. I realized that this time it was Earth. The message was clear, images of wars, hunger, illness, pollution and the destruction of nature assaulted all my senses, together with the words, "We can protect Ke'a by protecting Earth people from themselves. They need our guidance."

The group was continuing their slow circle dance to the deep, hypnotic sounds.

"Incredible!" I said, "they know how to present their message, that is powerful stuff!"

"Yes," said Alma, "they are representing the growing minority of Ke'alians who want to intervene directly on Earth. They argue that we must save our brothers and sisters from the mess of Earth society."

"I can understand that point of view," I said, still under the powerful spell of the message.

"I also understand," said Alma, "but that's the real danger. At the moment that position is gaining more and more adherents, because of the affected zones and the gate crises. The planetary council has been together for nearly two days, and a decision about the Earth policy is going to be announced soon."

"What are we going to do now?" I asked, eager to move to a quieter place.

"Let's go to the accommodation that I have booked for us, and take it from there," she said, leading me towards a room adjacent to the hall.

I already knew that it was an anchor place to translocate locally. We appeared on a plaza that was teeming with people. There was also an art exhibition all over the area. I could see a lot of classical artwork, like paintings and sculptures, but there was even more unusual stuff for me. Light structures, live holo pictures that drew the on-looker inside using the info particle augmentation that makes things visible or audible, as soon as you approach.

I was rapidly getting dizzy with all the input; my head had started to ache. There were people everywhere. Intensely diverse in their clothing, colors, even lights moving around them. I could not distinguish any particular fashion; it was as if each person tried to be as different as possible from all the others. The effect was disconcerting, and it seemed to me that everything was disconnected. I was starting to feel lonely and lost in this alien place.

"This is an incredible place, but I don't know how I fit in, it's way too much for me!" I started to complain.

Alma took both my hands and pulled me towards her. "This is because you see everything from the outside. It's much easier as soon as you use more of the information and augmentation that your info-particles can provide."

"But how do I do that? I have no idea!" I felt quite stressed.

"Take a deep breath, and try to relax. Then imagine that everything here on Bo'ad makes sense, that you are part of the big energy field of the city. Feel that you want to be part of it."

I closed my eyes and took a few deep breaths. I remembered how wonderful everything had been until that moment. I had expanded my range of experiences in an incredible way. This city was intense and utterly incomprehensible to me, but I focused on the thought: '*I want to be part of it!*'. I concentrated on wanting it all to make sense, to know what it was, that the people were doing. What was this inner dimension of which Alma had spoken? I wanted to experience it.

Then, suddenly, I felt my inner stress subside. My head emptied itself and then gradually filled with knowing. Knowing the history, the people, the politics, the architecture, the city council plans, the exhibitions. There were plays that were recorded on the Innernet and were regularly performed in the big hall of arts. The great variety of jobs people were doing, in creating an exchange between other cities. There were news about from all over Ke'a. Everything was connected. Suddenly I knew a lot about what was specific for Bo'ad, what role it was playing in the planetary network, what energies it expressed.

Bo'ad has an endless number of art galleries, concert halls and theaters where the latest creations are displayed and performed. There are holo-memory vaults that contain all the necessary information to visualize or even recreate most major Ke'alian creations in all domains of art and science. People are free to express their talents, in art, scientific research, and also spiritual exploration. The cuisine of Bo'ad is a unique art form that is exceptionally creative and inspires cooks all over Ke'a.

As I reopened my eyes, my perception of what was going on around me had completely changed. My mind, together with my breath, had calmed. I had an inner feeling of knowing, of being connected to what was going on. I looked at a holographic scene that was being projected a few meters away and immediately knew that it was a new art form to portray specific animals in their natural habitat, and showing their significant role in that specific ecosystem. As I approached, I opened up to the holo show that was much more than visual. That particular animal was an enormous feline. It looked like a bigger version of Earth tigers, but with large saber teeth protruding from each side of its massive jaws. The fur was dark red with a pattern of yellow stripes. I could smell it, and as I did, part of me wanted to run away, it was just too real. But then came the cherry on the cake: I sensed its thoughts, felt it's feelings, I could sense how proud and confident the animal was. Its whole mental aura was like, *'I am strong, I am the protector, I look, and I see, I am who I am.'* It was uncompromising, regal, something I have never felt before.

"This is unbelievable! It's like being in the animal's mind!"

"As I've said, you have seen nothing yet, Ke'alians communicate with many animal species."

"How, do they do that? Are Ke'alian animals more evolved?"

"No, not really, it's the info-particles which create a translation between us and the animals, much in the same way as you can understand Ke'alian languages."

"I feel much better now," I said, "but I think it would be wise to take a break. This is a crazy place!"

We went to the outer edge of the plaza and walked up a narrow street that was winding through a maze of small crystalline constructions. These looked like they had grown out of each other and were creating a layered effect that remotely reminded me of a diamond-shaped honeycomb structure.

We stopped in front of one of the modular constructions that were at least half a dozen modules high. The whole thing looked organic, like eggs spawned by some huge alien dragon who had forgotten about them eons ago. Alma took my hand, and bang, we were in a big room, part round and part square, but empty.

"Is this the budget version? Do we need to sleep on the floor?"

Alma smiled. "Remember, we're on Ke'a! Maybe you know what would be nice for us?"

I gulped, thinking I should have kept my big mouth shut. "Ahh, you mean… yeah, it's holo-world. I've only done a bathroom thing… you mean I should create a nice room for us?"

"Yes, come on, you can do it!" she nudged me in my ribs.

"Ok! I'll try…" I closed my eyes. I don't know what I did, but when I looked, the room had transformed into a quite boring looking hotel room suite.

Alma was giggling, "Come on, Luke, you can do better than that!"

"Oops, sorry," I closed my eyes again, then tried to imagine a room I would love. It was hard, and I was drawing a blank. I thought about the Canadian cabin, discarded it immediately. Then I tried to remember what I had seen in magazines, in movies, some pictures came, yes! A big jacuzzi with warm scented water, carpets, and beautiful pillows all around, and a huge bed made of bamboo, the whole place lit by candles. I was starting to look forward to it, happily, anticipate, feel it. The vibrant colors, the very smooth fabrics. Could I conjure up all that stuff? I did not dare open my eyes, but I heard Alma whistle appreciatively. When I looked, the room was exactly as I had imagined it, even better, as it was now real, tangible. Delicious fragrances were floating in the air, water was bubbling in the jacuzzi.

"Holy shit!" I blurted out.

"That's more like it!" Alma exclaimed, grinning broadly, "the jacuzzi is a brilliant idea."

She went straight into the bubbling water, her clothes magically vanishing before she touched it. I imitated her, taking a deep self-satisfied inhale. Alma's green eyes were shining like freshly polished emeralds.

A couple of hours later, her green eyes shining even more brightly, Alma said, "It's still early in the day for our biological clock, and this city never sleeps!"

"Meaning we should go out and get a taste of the renowned Bo'adian cuisine." I ventured, my stomach growling approvingly.

She smiled, everything about her radiant. I had one of those mind zaps, where every thought disappeared, replaced by the entire presence of everything at that very moment. We both felt that magical moment and did not move, needing nothing else.

Finally, we got up from the bed. "What kind of clothes are you going to choose for our evening?" Alma asked, a mischievous little twinkle in her eyes.

I had been holding onto my jeans as long as I could, but now was the time to surrender.

"I guess my favorite Roman centurion outfit would not do?" I said, trying to ease my tension with a joke.

"Nope, you guessed right!" she said firmly.

'*Ok*', I thought, '*be a man!*' I took a deep breath, closed my eyes and dug into the deepest recesses of my mind. What were the clothes I liked and would fit this place and this evening? I have never been into clothes. I am the kind of guy who would shop for clothes once a year, and buy three identical pieces of something I felt comfortable with. Sweat was gathering on my forehead. Nothing! I opened my eyes to a tiny slit and stole a glance at Alma. She looked like she was biting her lip to keep herself from laughing. I opened my eyes, and we both burst out laughing.

"You can also stay naked, nobody would mind here on Ke'a!" she finally said, which brought my laughing to an abrupt stop. Strengthened by that ultimate threat, I closed my eyes again but reopened them immediately. "Maybe you go first, and I'll match your style."

"Ok!" She probably had already decided all along, as her body was instantaneously wrapped in dark red silk that shimmered in the candlelight. It looked like a sari, but was shorter, ending above her knees. Her left shoulder remained tantalizingly bare.

"Wow, you look stunning! But is it not too cold outside for these clothes?"

"No, Bo'ad has a localized climate control. But no more stalling! Now's your turn!"

I closed my eyes and took her cue with the Indian style. I had an immediate inspiration for one of the long coats Indian men wear at festive occasions, matched with loose Indian pants, the whole thing made of silk, the color, a safe bet with black, et voilà! I felt the clothes manifest on my body, and opened my eyes, looking expectantly at Alma.

"Yes! Not bad for a first try, you look like a magician!"

I laughed, "Is that not what we are, conjuring stuff like that out of thin air!"

Without any warning, she took my hand, and we were outside, in the small alley.

"Hey! More magic! Am I ever going to get used to this?" I exclaimed.

"Never!" she said and grabbed my hand even more firmly. We walked towards the moving lights of the plaza that was down the alley.

The air was very mild. I felt great with the loose silk clothes on my body, walking next to a stunning woman. We went straight to a famous food place on the plaza. It was one of those typical Ke'alian restaurants where you have a seemingly endless selection of foods and drinks placed around a circular room.

This one was a culinary dream. A tapestry of dishes covered all the walls. The dishes could have been mistaken for art work rather than food, were it not for the fabulous aromas they exuded. They were arranged on several levels of circular tables and shelves. The place was full of people, who, like me seemed to have a hard time making their choice. I stood there for a while, dizzy with all the delicious smells calling out to my starving belly.

We finally sat outside, at a table along the edge of the plaza that was still teeming with spectacular activities. I had filled my tray with half a dozen small plates containing different dishes. It was a culinary adventure, as I went from one amazing taste to another. Some of the spices went straight to my brain, creating a firework of sensations. It perfectly fitted the sights and performances happening on the plaza. It was one of those moments when I needed to pinch myself to be sure I was not dreaming.

Barely a few days had passed on Earth since I collapsed on the Tamil Nadu beach and I got my first scent of the incredible woman who was sitting next to me. Her light amber skin, her long black, slightly curly hair, her almond shaped green eyes that always seemed to be on the edge of a smile. I realized again that I did not know very much about her life.

"I would very much like to hear about your former life on Earth, and of how you got in touch with Ke'a," I said, putting my hand on her forearm.

"There's not very much to tell," she said, "I was born in a town near Madras. My father works for a foreign software company and makes good money for his family. My mother is a high school teacher, and is very engaged in furthering the study opportunities for girls. That's why I could go and study psychology in England. I came back home the year of the big tsunami. None of my family got hurt."

She took a sip from her drink, and continued. "I was part of a team of psychologists who gave support to many traumatized people. Michael, as part of his guardian mission, had come to Tamil Nadu with a Ke'alian team to give assistance. Officially they were a French NGO and were cooperating with my team. That is how we met."

And that was the exact moment when I got my first 'innercall'. All of a sudden I saw Michael's face at the edge of my vision, waving. He seemed to be calling me. At first, as Alma had just spoken about him, I attributed the sensations to a strange mental association. But Michael's face and the sense of being called by him did not go away.

Alma had noticed that my attention had gone inward. "Are you seeing somebody on the edge of your vision?" she asked.

"Yes, it's Michael, he seems to call me. What should I do?"

"Just mentally welcome his call..."

"Yeah, just..." I grumbled, but closed my eyes, focusing on Michael's call and inwardly saying yes to it, '*ok, bring it on!*' I instantly heard Michael's warm voice as if he were standing next to me, which was very disconcerting. I had to control my impulse to turn around and look for him.

"Bonjour Luke! It seems to be your first innercall. Good I called you!"

I did not know how to respond, feeling a bit stupid, '*should I just talk, or should I only mentally respond?*' That was awkward. Michael seemed to have heard my thoughts, and continued, "You can respond however you like, talk, or just think, it will make no difference on my side."

I spontaneously went along with talk, as that felt more natural to me, "Hi Michael, that is quite confusing, but I'm happy to hear you."

"Likewise, Luke, you're doing great! I just wanted to tell you, that I'll soon be at your location. We'll talk about the planetary council decisions just finalized."

"You know where we are?"

"Of course! There are no secrets on Ke'a!" I had the feeling that Michael was subtly pushing my buttons.

"No secrets? Really?"

"Not within a circle you are part of. Guardians always know everything about each other."

I started to blush, suddenly feeling uncomfortable. "Everything?" I stammered.

"Come on Luke, nobody's interested in your romantic life, if you're not sleeping with a CIA agent."

"Ok, Michael, I got it! When are you coming?"

"I'll be with you in a few minutes."

The inner connection was cut off abruptly, giving me yet another jolt of unease. It was like being suddenly left by someone you have a very intimate connection with, like feeling left in the cold.

Alma's eyes were on me, hesitating between earnest and humorous.

"That was intense!" I exclaimed, feeling as if my head was hollowed out by the experience.

"It's one of the things your brain needs to get used to," she said, kissing me softly and caressing my head.

Chapter Eighteen

I kept looking at the central area of the plaza where Alma and I had appeared hours earlier. The bustle around us was still a mind-boggling kaleidoscope of light shows, performers, people in incredible outfits, but the overall intensity had diminished by a few notches. As I was looking, I tried to breathe deeply, calming myself, telling my poor overloaded senses that all was well, and that this was indeed a whole different society, living an entirely different paradigm than the one on which my world was based.

Here, material objects could be created by the focus of your mind. Here, you could travel from one side of the world to the other, as fast and easily as blinking an eye. Only hours ago, I had been on Mars, hundreds of millions of kilometers away, and someday I would as easily travel to another star. It surprised me how natural it all felt, but then I reflected, it was because it was consistently based on different premises of how the universe works. Ke'alians had discovered the holographic nature of the universe. For them, it was common sense that matter was energy created by a focused conscious mind. As I was enjoying my musings, I saw a tall figure appear on the anchor space in the middle of the plaza. It was Michael.

As if he already knew where we were, he walked straight towards us. He looked great in his turquoise African style clothes. After a quick embrace, he went to get food and drink before taking a seat next to us.

"This food is fantastic!" he said after a few hungry bites.

"I guess Bo'ad has the best cuisine on the planet," Alma said, nibbling at what was left on her tray.

"As soon as Michael's around, there's talk about food!" I said teasingly.

He laughed, and I enjoyed the warmth and ease of our friendship.

"I was just told that you also introduced Alma to Ke'a. So you are the master for both of us," I continued to tease.

"Yes," he said, then opened his arms towards Alma and me, "that makes you both my padawans!"

I bowed to him, speaking in a mock reverential tone, "May the force be with you, master."

We had a good laugh, but the joke had some truth. Michael had introduced both Alma and me to an amazing universe, and an incredible new life.

"You have probably taken in the planetary council proceedings and the decisions?" Michael asked expectantly.

"Yes, I have," said Alma, then turned to me, "but I

guess you have not done it, Luke. Maybe you could take a moment and do it now?"

I had a quick 'mental in-breath' and straightened on my seat, then said, "I need to take it easy for now, my mind needs a break from becoming a hard drive," then I turned to Michael, "you have been there, Michael, could you please summarize the essential for me?"

"Yes, Luke, I guess it's wise to give your brain a little time to adjust. But if you trust the info-particles they'll give your brain just what it needs."

"I'm sure about that, but it's more like I can't fully let go and trust, at least not yet, I'm getting there…"

"Ok, I understand, so let's do the summary." Michael put down the piece of pastry he was holding and made a small symbolic opening gesture.

"The Planetary Council, together with the Guardian Council took in and reviewed all the events on Earth, all the developments in the Ke'alian affected areas, as well as the various global positions of the planetary population. They then explored all the known possible action courses and their foreseeable consequences before agreeing on decisions. They opted for the soft course, which is to continue the quiet infiltration. No direct intervention, but the indirect influence is going to be intensified."

"How are they going to do that?" I asked.

"Through more use of social media to disseminate Ke'alian values, through the production of literature that will seed new concepts and scientific ideas that will have the potential to inspire researchers and scientists. Some of our own infiltrated scientists will also make some important discoveries. We will strengthen existing foundations which finance research that goes into the right direction."

"What about the war zones and the damaged areas of Earth?" I was getting excited.

"It has been decided to send a group of shamans that will connect with the planetary energy field of Gaia and see if they can do their healing work. They will also try to better understand how Gaia and Ke'a are connected and how the traumatized areas are affecting their counterparts on Ke'a." Michael paused and took a long sip of his drink.

"What about the gate crises?"

This time, Alma answered, putting her hand on my arm, "The procedure of shielding the vibrational signature of the gates can go ahead, as the last tests were conclusive. The most critical gates, about half of them are going to be treated first, then nine Ke'alian months later the remaining ones minus three. These will remain as a last resort if anything unforeseen goes wrong."

"Are they afraid to lose all connection with Earth?"

"Yes, this is a concern, as it's not yet fully understood how these inter-dimensional gateways really work. Right now it has become one of the most important areas of Ke'alian research."

Michael added, "It is now urgent to protect the gates that would be the most vulnerable if Earth secret services find a way to detect them. That's why all available guardians are going to transfer to Earth as soon as possible. We are going to use as few gates as possible for the dimensional transfer."

I looked at Alma, my chest tightening, "Are you going to go?"

"Yes, of course, Luke."

"But I'm not yet ready…, I mean, not ready to go back to Earth…" I took her hands and held them firmly, "not ready to be alone on Ke'a."

She gave my hands a healthy squeeze and said, "We are going to work something out."

My thoughts were circling around. I was not even sure that it was in the cards for me to go back to Earth, but even then I dreaded leaving magical Ke'a for old, problematic Earth, with secret services on my tail. It was quite a scary thought.

Seeing my distress, Michael said, "We are going to use a gate located at the center of Western Europe, from there all the European guardians will easily travel to their assigned destinations. Two gates in France need to be treated. Alma and I are going to take care of them. Why don't you come along with us and tie all your loose ends with your old life in Paris?"

I took a deep breath, trying to make room in a chest that had become tighter. "I have been thinking about it, as I have some friends and my parents in Canada. It would be a good way to avoid people getting worried about me…" I felt my heart pounding, and my breath was getting shorter, "but, honestly, I'm scared to go back. I love Ke'a, this is such a better world!"

Michael put a friendly hand on my shoulder, "Don't worry Luke, your feelings are perfectly natural, we don't need to leave right away. The departure is planned in around seventeen hours."

Alma said, "Let's use this time to do whatever we both need to come to a good and clear decision."

"Yes, do that, here is the right place for clarity," Michael said, getting up, "I leave you both to do what you need. Maybe we see each other tomorrow?" With these final words, he left..

Alma and I walked towards a big avenue that was beginning from the plaza. It was already the middle of the night, but there were still lots of people going about. We remained silent for a while. I held my arm around her and felt her warm body and vibrant energy. I could not imagine being on Ke'a without her. We only had a couple of days together, but they were already filled with more experiences than most people had in a lifetime. Going back to Earth, my world, felt wrong. Everything in me rebelled against that thought. When I had known I would cross to another world, I had been excited. Now, the idea of going back to my old world, my old places, was depressing. I had utterly failed that old life, and it had failed me.

"I am confused," I said.

"I know," said Alma, "just let it be, allow yourself to be confused."

"Easy to say."

"Yes, maybe, but let's go back to our place and rest for a few hours, I think that will suit our bio clock. And, a rested mind makes wiser decisions."

"I guess you're right, let's go back!"

Seven hours later, I sat upright in bed and looked at the room I had magically created. Alma was still sleeping, her chest moving slowly with her breath. I felt rested and sensed an inner strength that had eluded me before. The thoughts of dread I had felt at the prospect of going back to Earth were still lingering in my mind, but I was able to see them for what they were: The pain from my old life, the death of my family, the brutal destruction of my home in Paris, the fear of potential violence. But my passage to Ke'a had transformed my body, and I was in the process of healing my mind. Alma and Michael would be there with me.

"I'm coming with you," I said, as soon as Alma opened her eyes.

"I knew you would," Alma kissed me, but immediately started to tickle me. I'm very ticklish, and that was a very nasty attack. When she finally listened to my desperate implorations, she said, "ok, I also thought about it a long time, and my verdict is…"

I looked at her expectantly, but then she started to tickle me again, "No, please!"

"You may come…, if you complete an intensive course first."

"What course?"

"A course that will teach you all the updated essential functions the info-particles provide on Earth."

"There's no time for a course! How could I possibly do that in the next ten hours before we leave?"

"I think you'll be able to squeeze in two minutes for

it."

"Ah, that brain-washing stuff," I said, my instinctive reluctance kicking in again.

"You're hopeless!" she started to attack me again.

"Ok, ok! It's not brain-washing! It's just scary having stuff downloaded straight into my mind. What if there's a virus?"

Now her tickling got really hard, and I had to defend myself. I managed to pin her under me and hold her hands. Finally, we both had a good laugh, and the whole tension evaporated.

"I understand your concerns, Luke, but if there were any problem, I would know by now."

"Maybe you don't know because your mind is already altered…"

Now Alma looked hurt, and her expression started to tense up. Luckily, I immediately managed to defuse the whole thing.

"Sorry, I was teasing you! Sort of… I actually did not mean it that way! I've been in France much too long, that's what they do, they tease each other all the time. I'm fine with the mind download, and I trust you when you say it's safe."

She got up, still ruffled, "Ok, fine! Let's go and have some breakfast first. I think our brains need some food."

This time we translocated to a whole different part of Bo'ad. We had appeared halfway up the nearest mountain, on a broad ledge growing out of its side. I could see the sprawling growth of the city stretching in the distant winding valleys and the plateau at the center of the majestic mountain chain. The whole city with its organic shapes looked like an outgrowth of the local natural environment.

"Wow! What a view!"

"No time for sightseeing now!" Alma said and walked right into the big opening that was leading inside the mountain. The huge rounded tunnel cut through the rock was lit by a fluorescent surface that was emitting light, while the rock underneath remained visible in all its shades of grey and washed out yellow. The walls looked alive. The end of the tunnel opened into a vast circular cave, as high as two cathedrals on top of each other. But it was the width that was mindboggling. It was hard to estimate, but it could have been four or five hundred meters wide.

"Wow!"

"Can't you say anything else than 'wow'?" Alma grumbled.

I swiftly put my arms around her, hugging her gently, "I'm sorry about before, I've been stupid. Please forgive me."

I felt her relax, and I kissed her, "Ke'a is an incredible world, I am so happy you found me on that beach!"

Her face lit up with a smile, "Me too, you terrible French man!"

"Canadian! Not even from the French part," I said, keeping my tone very soft.

"It's all right," she said and returned my kiss, "let's go, I'm starving."

The periphery of the enormous cave was hollowed out like Swiss cheese. There were art galleries, shows, food counters and lots more that I could not identify. Some of the restaurants had tables and chairs outside. I could also see several broad tunnels going off to other locations inside the mountain.

One of the eating places had a particular shine. Its lights were brighter, more colorful than all the others. As we approached, an invisible and irresistible cloud of heady, spicy smells and incredibly rich bakery odors assaulted my nose, made my mouth water and my stomach growl like a hungry lion. It was like a powerful spell calling us, and I noticed that we both had sped our walking. We ended jogging the last meters past the entrance.

Had my mind still been able to function, it could not have foreseen what I saw. It was like the dragon's den, but that dragon had a sweet tooth instead of a golden one. The whole space was dug into the mountain, creating tables, shelves, and niches that were piled high with pastry, fruits, fountains of fresh juices. Some cakes looked like miniature mountains with snowy peaks made of sugar. There were smells of spicy teas and other beverages hot and cold. The place was packed full with people, and there was a joyous stampeding and looting going on. The real magic was that everything kept filling up. As soon as an item was taken another appeared in its place only seconds later.

"Sorry, but I have no other word left… WOW!" I laughed, not believing my eyes.

"Come, get a tray and let's go fill it with lots of delicious stuff!" said Alma, pushing me onwards through the hungry crowd.

There were no queues, no waiting; everything was full all the time, no one was worried he would not get what he wanted. It was a sight of pure joyful abundance. Many of the customers were children of all ages who walked around with big shining eyes. I guess I was one of them.

When we finally sat at a table, outside with the sight of the enormous cave, eating all the goodies we had gathered, I felt like I had stepped into yet another dimension: The land of milk and honey.

I was smiling blissfully, everything forgotten, but the present moment.

Alma pulled a plate with the remaining pastry away from me and said, "Maybe try and grow up a bit. We have a mission starting soon."

"Yes, Ma'am! But, please promise me one thing, bring me back to Ke'a, and to this place."

"Ok, I promise, but now's a good time for our little speed course, all this sugar has surely eased your brain."

"Ah, that's why you brought me here!" I exclaimed with mock suspicion, then smiled, "ok, how do I do it?"

"I'm going to send you a mental cue, and when you accept it, it will give you access to the information."

I closed my eyes, tried to tune down my restless mind. This time I felt positive about whatever alien mechanism that was active on the elementary level of my brain. I welcomed it's support and the enhancements it gave me. I felt my mind clear rapidly, then I sensed Alma's presence, like a gentle inner waving. Then came a knowing that I was getting that cue from her. Did I accept it or not? Yes,

I accepted it. Should the linked information be revealed? Yes, do that. Then came the strange feeling of knowing, a lot of new data flowed into my conscious awareness. It felt like a very fast review of something I already knew, then more things, in rapid succession, and then suddenly everything stopped and the knowing stabilized.

I knew how to communicate with fellow guardians on Earth, and I knew how to turn on a force field that could protect me from bullets. I knew how to access information on a limited Earth version of the Innernet. I had a full map of Earth's gates, the ones that were planned to be treated, and much more. I had all the needed intel about Earth's secret services and armies that were involved in hunting us. I also had all the details of the mission I was joining with Alma and Michael.

When I opened my eyes, I said, "I'm not going to repeat the word, but that's the kind of speed learning I would have appreciated in my student days. Is this also used for kid's education?"

"Yes, in big parts, mostly for factual learning. But Ke'alian Education is focused on educating the inner values of children, their connection to spirit and the whole. How to find their place and role within it. They learn to find and develop their talents, find what they want to express in their lives, what contribution they want to make to themselves and society."

"I guess somebody made a great contribution to society in creating this place," I said, looking at the glimmering food mecca behind us.

"Yes, everybody can create their own food through the holo-field, but not that many actually do. It's so much more fun to go to places that are run by people who have incredible talents and love sharing them."

At that very moment, something happened in the middle of the cave. The light had dimmed all around, and a massive holographic planet floated half way from the top of the cave. It was Ke'a, that I had learned to recognize, mainly because of the bigger polar icecaps. I thought it was one more light show and was waiting expectantly for something else to happen. Then I remembered the political group at the big arrival hall.

"Is this another show from the interventionists?"

"Chances are," said Alma, then pointed at the planet, "look, something is happening."

The image of the globe had dimmed, and bright red areas were highlighted in Africa and Asia, as well as the Middle East. The red color was radiating outwards towards the surrounding areas. Then a voice said, "The planetary council has decided against a direct intervention on Earth. We acknowledge the decision but warn against the long-term consequences. Who is going to stop Earth wars, Earth pollution and destruction of biospheres that have been affecting Ke'a for much too long. Citizens of Ke'a, you have a responsibility for our future. We must heal Gaia to protect Ke'a." The image changed back to a radiant Ke'a that was slowly rotating. It remained there for a few long moments and disappeared.

"They are worried and not happy with the council's decision," I said. "What if the majority of Ke'alians get convinced and want to intervene on Earth? It would have an enormous impact on everything. Probably for the best, but there are great risks involved for both societies."

Alma did not respond immediately. I could see that she was also worried, then she said, "On Ke'a, things of that level of importance are not done only because a majority decides to do it. The planetary council takes the concerns and wishes of the majority to heart, but then, the shamans are involved and get insights directly from the planetary consciousness. There is a lot of talking and direct sharing, but also a lot of silence where the Spirit Dimension is included. Such an important decision comes out of that whole complex process. There are no votes like on Earth. The decision will reflect the whole of Ke'a, not just the human side of the equation."

"But…"

"Come, let's go," she cut me off, "we still have some time, and there's something I want you to see here." She took my hand and guided me towards one of the bigger tunnels leading deeper into the mountain.

After a few minutes walk, we arrived at another cave, smaller than the main one. It was dome-shaped and was at least as wide and high as a cathedral. The walls were entirely coated by small crystal marbles of mustiple sizes. There must have been hundreds of millions of them covering the walls up to the apex of the dome. At the center of the cave was a gigantic sculpture that was at least ten meters high. It looked like an enormous bouquet of flowers. The whole crystalline structure was luminescent, and the flowers were radiating light beams that spanned the entire array of the rainbow. All that light was multiplied and reflected by the millions of crystal balls that covered the cave. The result was stunning and kept changing as the flowers moved as if touched by a gentle breeze.

"Wow!"

As I approached a wall, I could see that each marble looked different regarding size, color, texture and the streaks it contained. It immediately reminded me of the "Bringer of Light" at the temple in India.

A thought struck me, "Are these connected to people who died?" I asked, my low voice expressing the awe I was feeling.

Alma took my hand. "Yes, they are. Since the enormous possibilities of the info particles were discovered, a tradition has developed on Ke'a to preserve creations and memories of those who have died. This is one of the three memory vaults of Bo'ad."

"Are they containing memories of all the Ke'alians who have died?"

"No, only those who wished some events and memories of their lives or of their creations and discoveries to be remembered. Many are on a more spiritual level, as they contain insights and pearls of wisdom that can only be gained by a long life experience. They are preserved to help the new generations to attain them more rapidly and help stop circles of recurring mistakes.

There is no value scale in what is preserved. It can be an amazing artistic creation, scientific discovery, the deepest spiritual truth or the most mundane stories of an individual's life. They are all together next to each other."

I was filled with wonder by the sight of this galaxy of crystal balls giving out their individual lights. All these different lives, millions of them, here in this space. I could feel the power of what was stored. I remained speechless for a long while. We held an arm around each other. The place was powerfully silent despite the crowd that was present.

Finally, my mind came back online, and I whispered, "How is this working? How are these balls put in, and how long do they stay?"

"It's a holo-construction entirely managed by one of the rare artificial intelligence based on info particle intelligence. Of course, there also is a whole administration and procedure about how things are done."

"Who can access the memories, how does it work?" I felt hair rising on the back of my neck. It was the most amazing thing I had ever seen.

Alma, seeing my excitement, smiled.

"Everybody, including you can access any memory. They belong to all Ke'alians. You need to inner-connect with a particular person or in your case access the directory with the help of your info particles."

"Maybe you could help me connect to the memories of people that inspired you?"

"That's a very good idea, let me think who you could connect to," Alma said, her focus turning inward, then after a few moments she said, "I'm also relatively new to Ke'a. What I have done when I've come here, was to randomly connect to one of the info-memories, and feel the life that person has lived. People create these info-memories at the end of their lives and usually focus on the most essential."

She paused for a moment, her gaze focusing on the crystal balls in front of us.

"It has helped me very much to understand Ke'alian culture. Most people are very long-lived and have rich lives. That is why many change their life trajectory once or even several times during their lives. Why don't you do as I did, access one Ke'alian life randomly, let the info-particles choose for you? I have come to believe that their choices are wise."

I looked at the cave. It was like a galaxy of its own, millions of crystal gems connected by the light they were shining at each other. I was getting dizzy, trying to see everything, trying to understand. I closed my eyes as a way to regain my balance, and then I thought to myself, *'my dear info particle friends, I'm still a total newbie, but as you're inside my mind, you already know, so why don't you get the spiel going and show me the content of one of these magic balls?'* I barely had time to smile at my own humor, before it started.

"I am Rose'a, daughter of Kale'o and Marti'a from the Chabra'ne circle." For a few moments, standing in front of me, in an exquisite flower garden, I saw a middle-aged woman with black hair, which contained long streaks of grey. She had a strong jaw and a prominent nose. I had the impulse to tighten my closed eyes, as I saw the whole scene as if my eyes were open. I took a deep breath, as the scene suddenly shifted from seeing the woman to actually being the woman, seeing the garden with her eyes. I felt the love she had for the place, her home, her circle. When she spoke, I heard her voice and felt her strong emotions.

"I have lived a good life in Chabra'ne and been who I wanted to be. I feel the Spirit Realm calling me back. I know that it is the place I come from and where I'll soon return, and I feel peace and love in my heart. Here are the parts of my life I like to be remembered."

The scene shifted to a big round room, with a circle of tables and chairs. A dozen people were sitting in that circle. They had their eyes closed and were holding hands. I instantly knew it was a group of scientists specialized in info particle research. I could feel the powerful field of their linked minds enhanced by the info particles.

The room was replaced by an incomprehensible vision of matter on the elementary level. But bizarrely it made sense in a limited way. I could sense the depth of knowledge and eagerness to discover that was the focus of the group. Ideas came, like the info particles being the DNA of matter, the key to creation in the universal holo-field. The breakthrough in understanding that the elementary info particles had more than four dimensions and that a way had been found to access the particles from our dimension. I could sense the excitement of the scientist exploring the possibilities and potential applications that felt limitless. The group had come to an understanding that the way that power could be harnessed was safe, it was intimately linked to the natural unfolding energy of the universe. I felt a lot of satisfaction and pride in my work.

The vision shifted to her family. A warm feeling of love in a relationship with her partner and two children. I could feel her love seeing them grow up. There was the moment they were released to the world, the boy becoming an animal communication researcher and the daughter being a skilled musician very appreciated by the bigger community. As if it were my own feelings, I felt the happiness and love she felt for her kids.

Everything became quiet. I felt an inner light grow in my mind and heart. There was nothing else, emptiness and a sense of love and connection to everything. I felt a vertical energy in my head, a subtle and yet powerful pull upwards, then I felt more than heard her final statement. "I am grateful for all the love and joy in my life, and I am ready to re-join my spirit home." And then the connection gradually faded away.

I opened my tear-filled eyes, still in that quiet space of love and inner connection. When I looked into Alma's eyes, that love and connection were reflected back to me. I took a deep breath, reluctant to return to the cave. Alma took my hands.

"It's like I was that woman, looking back at the most important things of my life. So many feelings that words can't describe. She was in me, alive!" I said, enjoying the warmth of her hands. "This is really amazing stuff, and I've only touched upon one out of millions! What a treasure!"

"Yes," said Alma, "it's a profound way to connect to a person and get the feel of the life she lived."

I had a moment of inner vertigo, realizing the sheer number of personal lives and destinies that were inside these magic crystals. It was beautiful, but all the twinkles of lights shining from the crystals reminded me of what I had lost. I felt relief when we walked out of the memory cave.

Chapter Nineteen

We silently walked back to the ledge outside the mountain. The new day was dawning, carrying scents of the ancient world and a promise of a new life. The beauty of the snow-capped mountains in the red morning light was breath-taking. The city's highest constructions were barely sticking out of a sea of mist that still lay in the valley.

Today was the day I would transfer back to Earth. I felt my gut tighten, my breath caught in my chest at the thought of going back to Earth. I could not believe that I had barely been five days on Ke'a, not even a day, from Earth's perspective. Much about Ke'a was still a mystery to me, but I had started to feel at home.

Everything was so different here. Ke'alians were free from problems concerning the distribution of resources, energy, wealth and money. This tremendously increased the possibilities for them to develop and express their full potential in their long lives. I had barely touched upon the huge variety of individual life expressions that were possible in Ke'alian society.

Alma was standing next to me, her face glowing in the first rays of the sun that were slowly rising above the mountains. It was one more of these moments that I would have allowed to last forever. But then the god of personal movies pushed the play button, and my life events continued their unfolding towards their mysterious ends.

"We can translocate from here to the place near the gate we are going to use to go to Earth," Alma said.

I felt a strong resistance to leaving the beautiful mountains. "Where is that place? What's the plan?" I asked despite knowing all the mission details that had been downloaded into my mind.

Alma smiled, she was going along with stalling our departure.

"The gate on Earth is below the ground of Luxembourg-City. It's right in the middle of Western Europe. Ten other guardians will cross with us and travel from there to their destinations. The gate is connected to an ancient tunnel network that runs under the old city. Luxembourg is a small country and thus has less surveillance and secret service activity, making it a perfect transfer point to Europe.

"Yes, I've been there in my old life, before my girls were born…" I trailed off, my mind filling with images of a carefree romantic trip with a very young looking Simone, her long blond hair blowing in the wind, as we stood on the ramparts of the old city fortress.

As Alma remained quiet, I continued, "So many lives,

included in mine, I wish she had recorded one of those memory crystals." I felt my eyes burn, as tears flowed down my cheeks.

"Yes, life is a mystery," she said taking my hand, "nothing lasts forever, but one thing is eternal."

I took her into my arms, kissing her softly on the forehead. "And what would that eternal thing be?"

She stared intensely into my eyes, and I felt the power of her presence as she said, "The one thing that is eternal is the present moment. It's the only time that ever exists and the real gateway to eternity."

"Wow!" I exclaimed, my spirits rising again, "yes! I know a truth when I hear one! Let's have an eternal kiss!" and that's what we did, on the mountain ledge, bathed in the warm light of the new day rising around us.

I was shocked by the sudden darkness. As we translocated, the dawning sun had instantly transformed into a nearly full moon that hovered above a grey landscape. We had appeared on a plateau overlooking a narrow valley that looked as if it had been carved by a giant knife. The dominant color was grey and dark green. We were surrounded by trees, high grass, even the rocks were covered with moss. A lazy drizzle of rain was leaking out of the gloomy greyness of the sky.

"Yuck! not a good change, "I exclaimed, "can we go back? The day had just begun!"

"Come now!" she said, starting to walk towards the only visible lights in that whole murky landscape. The air carried smells of moist soil and plant life. The ground was muddy and stuck to my shoes that I luckily had included in my outfit.

"Where are we? There's nothing here!" I complained.

"There is a big virgin forest at this location on Ke'a," said Alma, moving through low shrubs and hanging branches.

"This gate is one of the last ones having been discovered. It is very far from any settlement and has rarely been used. That gives us an added security until we are sure that the gates remain undetectable. It's also one of those that will remain unchanged."

As we approached the lit area, I saw only three rather dim globes of light on the ground in an empty clearing. Then I realized that the place could be invisible, or even below the surface.

"Is the gate below ground?" I asked, squinting my eyes and trying to see something.

"Yes, it is, but there's a holo-house on top, right here," she stretched out her hands, touching an invisible wall, and then disappeared.

After just a second of fright, I realized, *'Oh well, time to play wall passing again'*, and I tentatively walked straight ahead, with outstretched arms, *'ok, passing the wall, passing the wall…'* and, bang I was inside a big brightly lit half-spherical room.

I had my arms still outstretched when I heard laughter. "You're becoming a real expert!" It was Michael standing there with Alma and a few other people I had never seen.

I joined in the laughter, and we had a few moments of hugging and shoulder clapping. There were obviously distinct groups, as the other men and women barely greeted me and continued to keep to themselves.

"Is Cledor not coming?" I asked.

"No," said Michael, "he has surely been flagged since his house was stormed in Guadeloupe. We will need to create a new identity for him if he returns to Earth."

"He's been a long time on Earth. Maybe it's time for him to catch up with his grand-grand-children." I said, smiling.

Michael nodded, and said, "We are going to cross in an hour," then pointed to backpacks lying on the ground.

"I have brought non-holo clothes for the two of you."

"Ah," I said, realizing, "our Ke'alian holo-clothes can't make the transition to Earth?"

"They could transfer," Michael said, "but the Earth's holographic matrix is on a different dimensional frequency than the one of our universe, your clothes would instantly disappear."

"Yeah, good to know," I said, "otherwise we would arrive on Earth like a time traveling terminator!" I grinned, expecting everybody to understand my joke, but it was only Michael who reacted, smiling "You have been watching a lot of movies, Luke!"

"Yes, that was part of my sad old life, the last ten years in Paris! I can't say I'm happy to be going back now."

"You're not going back to stay, Luke," said Michael, "you're going to sort out your stuff, and we'll be back very soon."

Alma was already putting on clothes. As I joined her, I saw that Michael had brought the backpack I had left in Karuka'e. There were my good old jeans, t-shirt, underpants, socks, plus a sweatshirt, jacket, and shoes. Even my wallet with my papers. It all felt strange.

Now the clothes! I had already gotten so used to the ease of the holo-clothes that it felt weird to manually put on all these pieces of fabric. It was tedious, and the clothes felt like they did not fit.

'There's definitely no going away from Ke'a, no going back!' I told myself, as I stood there, feeling my misaligned underpants beneath the hard fabric of my jeans.

More people had entered the room in the meantime. They all looked focussed and kept to themselves. They sat on big cushions on the floor, in pairs or groups of three, talking quietly.

I sat between Michael and Alma, silently stroking her back. Her outfit was out of character, at least I had never seen her dressed in black pants, dark green blouse and beige raincoat. It looked boring, but her eyes were blazing with energy. Her body language and the small hand movements she made told me she was nervous. At least I was not alone being nervous. I was wondering what would happen during the transfer to the lower plane of Earth. I was the newbie of the group and needed to know.

"What is going to happen at the gate? Are there going to be sounds again? What am I going to feel?" I asked, trying to sound confident.

Michael said, "It's going to be very similar to the time when we transferred from Guadeloupe. First, we are going to relax and connect to the spirit dimension, and then without pause, the sound vibrations are going to shift to sounds that activate the interdimentional gateway. It's going to be faster. You will not lose consciousness nor any memories stored in your brain, but are only going to have a few moments of disorientation, as it's your first passage from Ke'a. We are going to be right next to you."

"Ok, that sounds good, but as I understand, my body is not going to be changed back into the matter structure of my old universe?"

"Exactly, that's part of the reasons why your memories stay intact."

"Will I also be able to change into somebody else, like you did?"

"Yes, potentially you could, but you first need a lot of training to be able to do it without endangering yourself."

"Wow! So I'm like superman who has special powers on Earth. But superman can be hurt by kryptonite, matter from his home planet?"

"Ah, movies again!" Michael laughed, "no, we have nothing that could have an adverse effect on us. The matter, atoms, elementary particles of our bodies are in a special way more complex and include the information matrix of Earth. That's why we can exist in that universe."

"But then, why not our clothes?"

"These are complicated scientific questions, but a simple answer is that they are generated by our mind in connection with the info particles that are tuned to Ke'a's universal field."

"I understand, thank you Mister Spock." I laughed with Michael, enjoying my joke.

Alma gave me a little push, saying, "When you two boys are finished, I think it's getting time to prepare and go down to the gate."

The other guardians were already getting ready, putting on coats and getting their backpacks ready. We all cleared away from the central part of the room. All of a sudden it transformed into a round opening with a wide spiral staircase that was descending into the rocky ground.

A short time later we were on our way down. The smooth walls radiated light in the same way I had seen in Bo'ad. After going down the equivalent of three to four floors, the space opened into a broad cavern, and there was the already familiar-looking stone circle. The cavern's walls had been fully glazed over by a shiny crystalline layer that had a subtle bluish tint. The cavern was at least ten meters wide and was otherwise empty.

We all sat on the circular stone bench. I counted thirteen, including me. We all carried backpacks and were fully dressed. Nobody spoke, everybody looked earnest, which made me feel uneasy. There was no happy anticipation to travel to another world; there were only serious looking faces of people who were on an important and potentially dangerous mission.

Luckily, I did not have to wait long, as I felt a vibration in the stones and a slow humming started to be audible in the cave. I saw that everybody closed their eyes. I took

Alma's hand who was sitting next to me, but she turned to me and said, "Better not touch with this transfer."

I felt nervous, but managed to slow my breath. The humming uuu-sound had intensified, and I felt my mind becoming quiet, empty. I felt a vertical energy coming down through the top of my head, running through my spine and connecting me to the ground. The sound changed and the vibrations intensified. There was a sudden bright flash in my mind that rippled out like an electric shock throughout my body. And then I blanked out.

Apparently, it was only for a short moment, as I felt Alma holding me. I opened my eyes and saw her smiling face moving bizarrely in front of me. My head was spinning, and my body was also catching up with some inner movement as if I had turned around my axis for too long. I closed my eyes again, feeling safe in Alma's arms. After a couple of minutes, I felt better. I opened my eyes and, saw another cave. That one looked like a natural vaulting cave with irregular walls made of light and dark brown sandy stone. There even were small stalactites hanging like icicles that were dripping water from the ceiling.

"This looks like the low-tech gate model," was the first thing I said.

Michael who was nearby said, "Yes, it has not been improved, it is in the exact state as when it was discovered. It is also hard to travel back to Ke'a from here. It has only been used as a one-way gate and is going to remain like that."

"So we'll have to go back from another gate?"

"Yes, we'll use one of the two gates we are going to secure in France."

I tried to stand up but instantly came back down on the sandy ground, my leg muscles aching.

"I feel so heavy, what's wrong with my legs?"

"The lighter gravity is one of the things you adapted to very quickly on Ke'a. Here you are around one quarter heavier. It will take a few hours for your muscles to get used to it."

One quarter less was great, and I had quickly forgotten about it, but here, getting more than twenty kilos back on, felt awful. I put my backpack on the ground and tried again. My legs felt like lead, but I managed to stand up.

The whole group was doing some movements and stretching exercise. Alma and Michael had also started to bend and stretch, and I was happy to join in. After a couple of minutes, my legs felt already stronger.

"We are under an old tunnel system that was part of the old Luxembourg City fortress. Part of it is being visited as a tourist attraction. Fortunately, the gate is under an older and unused part of that network," said Michael.

As we had started to follow the other guardians into a climbing and very irregular tunnel, I saw an intense red glow ahead of us. I stopped in alarm, but Alma who was walking behind me nudged me onwards, "That was the opening of the connection with the old network."

"Ah, Cledor's magical trick!"

"What trick?" asked Alma.

"Cledor opened an access tunnel in Guadeloupe."

"Ah, I see," she said, "it does look like magic, as these info particles are specially designed for a particular gate and can only be activated by a guardian that knows the needed mental key. Earth's matter is much denser and therefore gives out energy when tampered with."

We entered a very ancient looking tunnel that was only about one-and-a-half-meter high, so that we all had to bend our backs. It was hard climbing upwards in a body that felt too heavy. Finally, we reached an iron door that had already been opened. It led outside, behind densely growing bushes. Strangely, it was daylight.

"How come it's not night here, as it was on Ke'a?" I asked Alma who was standing in front of me, looking up into a cloudy sky.

"This is one of the mysteries of the connection between Earth and Ke'a. Locations are synchronous, but not time, as you know, time is nine times slower on Earth."

"Yeah, I understand the time thing, but I had not thought about the location. As both planets rotate around their axis they must also be at different spatial locations."

"I guess the gates are anchored together in a way that links them through space and time."

"Yes," I said, "maybe it's good not to worry about all these mysterious details, the important thing is that they are linked and that we can go back!" I was already thinking about going back, not feeling at ease with the beginning of our journey, hiding behind bushes. We were standing at the bottom of a rocky canyon that looked nearly one hundred meters deep, probably the narrow valley I had seen on Ke'a.

"Why don't we go out of the bushes?" I asked as the

whole group had halted.

"We wait our turn, as we don't want to be thirteen people coming out at the same time. Each group waits a few minutes and goes out when getting the all clear signal from the previous one."

"Ah, now we can communicate with inner call! I know from my 'intensive course', that this is a significant improvement for missions on Earth."

"Yes, it's a great improvement." said Alma, smiling at me.

We had to wait a little while longer, but after Michael got the signal, we walked out of the dense vegetation, and I could see that the valley was, in fact, a well-kept park with a narrow road alongside a small water stream that was running in the middle of it.

We walked over a bridge and came to stairs that were leading upwards out of the valley. It was quite a climb, and I had to stop several times. The gravity of my home planet was getting at me. We finally reached the top and had to stop again for me to catch my breath.

Alma and Michael had fewer difficulties and were urging me onwards.

"I'm sorry, I'm a bit out of shape," I muttered with a raspy voice.

"No problem, Luke," said Michael, "it's just that we need to catch the next high-speed train for Paris that leaves in half an hour, and we must buy the tickets."

"How far is the station?"

"Fifteen minutes from here, let's go."

"I'll carry your backpack," said Alma.

"No, I'm all right, let's go!"

We walked towards the main avenue that was going straight down to the railway station. The noise and the smell of the intense traffic were another blow to my system. I was feeling noxious, my head was aching, but I bit my lip and pushed onwards. I did not want to slow us down again. This was the worst walk of my life. I was overwhelmed by everything, people on the walkway, buses, trucks, noisy motorbikes. I was walking like a robot, one step after the other, behind Michael, next to Alma, who was shooting worried glances at me, but did not say anything. She took my hand, and I was grateful for the little support it gave.

We finally reached the station, and I collapsed onto a waiting room bench while Michael bought the tickets.

I don't know how I got down and up the stairs to the platform and the TGV, but I ended up in the train's lavatory, puking out my guts.

After that, I felt a bit better, and went to my seat, as the train was already moving out of Luxembourg station.

Alma looked worried and helped me sit down.

"I'm really sorry," I said, feeling self-conscious, "that was awful, I don't know what happened to me."

Alma put her arm around me, "Don't worry, at one time or another this has happened to most of us. Coming to Earth can hit you like that."

Michael handed me a bottle of water, and I eagerly drank.

"But I was here only days ago!" I protested.

"Looks like your body is very content to be Ke'alian." Michael said, and gave me a friendly slap on the back.

The TGV had arrived in another station, where a big crowd got onto the train, and soon was nearly full.

"I much prefer the way we travel on Ke'a," I said.

"You can't beat that," said Alma, sinking deeper into her seat.

After another stop, the train started to accelerate to its maximum speed. The landscape was flying by. Alma and I had moved close, and my contact with her warmth helped me to relax. I closed my eyes and fell asleep.

I woke up feeling better. We were was approaching Paris, its suburbs already rolling past the train that had slowed.

After the TGV had stopped at its end station, gare de l'Est in north-east Paris, we got out and walked alongside the very long train. As we approached the end of the platform, a large queue had formed towards its exit. Soldiers with machine guns, together with police officers were standing there, letting people through one by one, while selecting a few for paper checks. I immediately felt bile coming up my throat.

"Oh, shit!" I exclaimed.

Alma took my hand, "It's probably only routine checks, after the recent terrorist attacks in Paris, relax!"

We were now waiting alongside a couple of hundred other people. I tried to calm myself, taking deep breaths, but my heart was still pounding in my throat.

Suddenly I heard Michael's voice in my head. "There is most probably no danger for us here, but better be cautious. Let's separate and go through individually and stay in touch with inner-talk."

Yeah, probably...,' I thought and immediately heard Michael. "Relax, Luke, it's going to be ok, this has nothing to do with us. But better not look stressed and worried, as these guys are trained to look for that."

"I'll do my best." I thought back.

Alma had squeezed my hand, giving me an encouraging look, before she moved sideways away from me. Then I heard her, "It's ok to be scared, it feels we could be trapped here, but my intuition tells me that we are going to be fine."

I trusted Alma's feelings and her statement helped me get a grip on my growing panic. The queue was slowly moving forward. I felt my wallet in my jacket and took it out to see that it contained my papers. All was there.

I was slowly approaching the checkpoint. The soldiers were waving most people through, only stopping very few, of which they asked id papers. I did not manage to suppress images of the military helicopters flying towards Cledor's house, and my panic was starting to well up again.

Having a sudden idea, I asked in my head, "Can my info particles help me calm down?"

I heard Alma's voice, "Yes, Luke, great idea. Connect with the knowing that they are inside you, and imagine that they calm your nerves, slow your heart rate, quieten your thoughts." As she was talking, I was going along with what she said and started to feel calmer. "It works! Thank you!"

I saw that Alma was in front of me and would soon be at the checkpoint. I was relieved to see that she was waved to pass, alongside an elderly couple. The line in front of me was thinning rapidly, and I was urging whatever alien tech inside my brain to do its job, but I could feel my blood pressure going up again, my heart thumping in my ears.

I barely heard the policeman talking to me.

"Vos papers s'il vous plaît!"

I had a moment of complete confusion, as, despite all my fears, I had not expected to be checked. The policeman looked at me suspiciously, repeating.

"Vos papiers!"

"Ah, oui, pardon," I said in a strangled voice, "excusez-moi, je suis fatigué."

"Vous allez bien, Monsieur, vous êtes très pâle." He remarked on me looking pale.

"J'étais malade dans le train, une indigestion." I pointed at my belly, not even needing to lie that I was feeling sick.

The policeman was checking my papers, while the armed soldier next to him was staring at me. It was awful; my body had started to shudder with growing panic.

"Ok, Monsieur, vous êtes en règle, vous pouvez passer," said the policeman, handing back my id.

My legs felt like foam about to disintegrate, but I managed to pick up my backpack and walk straight ahead, away from the soldiers and their machine-guns.

I heard Alma's voice in my head, "Well done Luke! All is well! Walk straight down through the main hall and straight outside across the street. Chul is waiting for us with a car."

I felt relief, like a cool shower on a hot day wash over my stressed nervous system. Chul! The fact that he was there, after what had happened on Guadeloupe felt reassuring. There was a sense of getting back to normality.

I easily found Michael's dark red Peugeot. My friends were already in the car. It felt great to sit in the back, next to Alma, smelling the familiar fine leather interior.

"Hello Mister Luke, I'm glad you're back," said Chul.

"I'm not so sure about being happy to be back, but great to see you Chul!" I said as the car started to smoothly enter the Parisian traffic.

"That was intense!" I exclaimed, "I'm sorry that I have endangered our mission, I did not manage to look normal."

"That's not easy, Luke," said Michael, "I don't think one can ever get used to such situations. Having a sick belly does not help."

"Thanks! You just want me to feel better, but I'm not sure I'm made for this kind of stuff."

As the car drove through Paris, I was struck by how different things were on Earth. On Ke'a, even in a big city like Bo'ad, the reality of nature was omnipresent, and everything else was respectfully connected to it. In Paris, nature was covered by endless concrete and buildings, and had practically disappeared. There were only a few sad looking trees along some avenues. The city looked weird and alien through my newly grown Ke'alian eyes. The streets were artificial canals for the endless metallic flow of smelly vehicles. People's body language spoke about stress and worries. They looked isolated from each other and their world.

As we passed into the inner courtyard of Michael's Parisian mansion, I felt like a time traveler coming back to a very distant past. It was crazy to think that I had been there only a couple of days ago. In the meantime, I had been on Ke'a, Earth's sister planet in a higher dimension, gone to the Moon, and to Mars!

Who would I see and talk to, now that I was in Paris, and that I might never come back? What would I tell my parents? *'Hey mom, I've found a much better planet, and a new girlfriend, maybe you could visit one of these days?'* I smiled at the thought, but then also felt sad, that I could not share this with anybody. Then I thought that I should try and tell my parents. They had always been open to new ideas and very supportive whenever I needed them. Maybe if I told them, they would understand and stop worrying about me.

The opening and closing of the car doors tore me from my navel-gazing. I saw Michael walk towards the house.

"Come, Luke, Chul has prepared a great dinner for us!" Michael said, looking pleased to be back home.

"How come this house is in your family when you are a born Ke'alian?" I asked when I caught up with him.

"My father was an immigrant like you," he said, holding the big main door for me, "this is the house of his parents, who were old French nobility that had survived the French revolution."

"Cool, that makes you a nobleman! But where is your Scottish accent from?"

"My mom was a Scottish immigrant and met my dad shortly after arriving on Ke'a. She liked to speak English with me."

"You say 'was', is she not alive?"

"Unfortunately not, I've spent too many extended periods here on Earth, and I lost my parents to the Ke'alian faster time," he said, regret showing on his face.

As he entered the big dining room, he continued, "In my childhood, I had a strong fascination for Earth, as it felt special that my parents had come from another planet. That's why I became a guardian and very much enjoyed coming here. Luckily, my parents had kept their ties to Earth, had registered their marriage and even my birth with the local authorities. For that reason, I still have legal ownership of my family house, and I have loved taking care of it." He gestured at the old walls that were covered by paintings.

Chul came in, calling out, "Ladies and gentlemen, dinner will be ready in thirty minutes. Mister Luke and Alma, you know your way to you room?" His broad smile showed how very pleased he was to be playing his butler character again.

We went to the suite that I had only briefly occupied, not even an Earth day ago. We both went straight to the huge bed and stretched out with pleasure grunts.

"You stayed here before?" I asked.

"Yes, I've been here a few times," she said, putting her head on my shoulder.

"I'm glad that this time we're here together." I said, caressing her arm.

She pushed herself up on an elbow and kissed me. I was starting to finally land, and felt much better.

Chapter Twenty

I woke up from the warm touch of light on my face. As I opened my eyes, squinting, I saw the ray of light that had found a way through an opening in the heavy curtains. Dust particles were having joy rides inside the light beam.

Alma was asleep, still in the shadow, untouched by the light of the new day. Her head was lying inside a crown of her dark shiny hair. Her beautiful face was fully relaxed. I could hear the soft breath of her deep sleep.

A wave of happiness washed over me. I felt grateful for how incredibly rich my life had become. The previous evening, we had dinner in an easy, relaxed atmosphere of warm friendship. There had been much laughing and appreciating the gifts of life together. Later, going to bed early with Alma, and sleeping much later. My heart and body were still aflame with the feel of these hours. That morning, I felt like life could not be better. Even being back on Earth was good, and I was eager to do what needed to be done.

I saw that Alma's eyes were moving behind her eyelids and wondered if she was dreaming. Her breath had become more rapid, and it reminded me of when she was woken up by an inner call. The room looking out into the courtyard was very quiet. Then, all of a sudden, she opened her eyes.

"You've been watching me!"

"Yes, I did… but stop!" I rapidly surrendered to the superior might that had pinned me on my back.

"Let's go and have a great French breakfast with croissants and coffee!" she whispered, biting my earlobe.

"Yes!" I exclaimed, trying to free myself from her grip. "Coffee is the only thing I missed from here."

"Really?" she smiled, tightening her grip.

When we finally came to the big dining room, Michael was already sitting at the table. Chul was serving him, beaming a broad happy smile.

"Good morning Chul. You are the real changeling here!" I said, clapping him on the back. He laughed, just bowing to me in his perfect butler stile.

As we were sitting together having our French breakfast, the conversation started to turn towards the more pressing subject of our mission. I tensed up at the thoughts of what I needed to do, but here I was, and there was no way around it.

"We are flexible as to when we go back to Ke'a." said Michael, "We are going to use the Paris gate that we'll have secured. The other thing we need to do is secure a second gate that is situated in the Massive Central which is a mountain region in the middle of southern France.

That gate is in a very remote area, only accessible on foot. It will take two days to complete that mission."

"As we can now be in touch with inner-call, we do not need to physically connect with our agents in France any longer," said Alma, "that frees me of part of my tasks, so I can stay with Luke and support him in what he needs to do."

"Yes, we can fix the Paris gate together, and I'll be fine on my own applying the info-particles to the southern gate. You're my backup team if anything goes wrong." said Michael, nibbling on his last croissant.

"What could go wrong?" I asked anxiously.

"Right now? Anything is possible since the secret services have become aware that there are aliens around. The cat is out of the bag, and they are delighted to use all their toys to try and catch us."

"Can they succeed?"

"Not really, if we are careful. And, even in the worst case scenario, the info particles will change your memories if you are caught, so there's no real way they can gain useful information."

"That's very reassuring!" I exclaimed, shuddering.

"Ok, boys," Alma, interrupted, "this is all speculation. We need to get the show on the road!"

She turned to me, "Luke, you can start making your phone calls while Michael and I go to the local gate. We'll probably be back in a few hours."

"And Chul can help you if you need anything," Michael added, getting up.

Ten minutes later they were gone, leaving me alone in the vast dining room. I did not know where to start and poured myself more coffee in the hope it would clear my mind, which had lost its initial eagerness and positivity.

I took a sheet of paper and tried to outline what I had intended in coming back to my old world. On top of the list came my parents, who I cared about, and who had been the only authentic contact I had had during my long years of depression. In terms of friends, it was easy, as my contacts had dwindled to non-existence. For my work, I would just send a resignation letter that would be easily accepted.

So, I was left with my apartment. I decided to sell it. I would instruct a former acquaintance who is a lawyer to represent me in the insurance matter, sell it, and send the money to my parents, who were just getting by with their small pensions. Yes! I had a plan! *'Now, just do it!'* I told myself.

It was still night at my parent's place, so I had to wait. I called the police inspector and told him that I was not pressing charges and that I had decided to sell and move abroad. I also called the lawyer's office and made an appointment for the afternoon.

A flow of fresh air smelling of spring flowers drifted from a window that Chul had opened. I could see a slice of blue sky peeking inside the mansion's courtyard. Spring was calling me, and I had to go outside. I took my jacket and my wallet that still had credit cards and money. I might as well enjoy my last days on Earth. I smiled at the thought.

As I left the mansion, I was reflecting on the whole

guardian thing. I had big doubts that I had what it takes to become a guardian. But then there was Alma, and if that was the only way to be with her… But I decided to drop the worries, what did I know would happen in the next days or weeks? *'Let's take one day at the time!'* My whole life had become a big surprise since I met Alma.

I was lost in these thoughts when I started to walk towards the Place des Voges, the oldest square in Paris, that has vaulted arcades all around. As I passed cafés and galleries, I was surprised how much I enjoyed the walk in the narrow streets of the ancient district. The sky was clear, and the early spring temperature was mild. There is a park right in the middle of the square, and I saw a green shine on the trees from the tiny newly growing leaves.

The people I crossed on the walkway reflected my peaceful state of mind. They strolled and looked at shop windows, or were sitting on terraces sipping coffee and chatting with friends. I thought that life could be good everywhere, so much depended on the color of my mindset.

My life had been a happy one here in Paris. I remembered the day I met Simone at the university. It was a lecture in one of Sorbonne's basement halls, on the geologic ages of Earth. We had literally crashed together as the old bench we were sitting on had broken. We both agreed it was destiny. A year later as I finished my Ph.D. in climatology, I remember the day I decided to stay in Paris. That same day I asked her if she wanted to marry me.

Walking the arcades of the place des Voges, I saw her again, with me, right there, looking at paintings in the vaulted shop of one of the art galleries. We had so many great times in the years before the kids came. Life had also been good with Noémie and Camille in our life. We had managed to keep the flames as a couple burning, as we had regular romantic dates without the kids. That morning in Paris, I felt grateful and happy for the time we had. It was all coming back; I felt I could embrace it again, feel it being alive within me, a very precious part of who I was.

My life had been in constant flux. I had been a true changeling, transforming from student to boyfriend, to husband, to researcher, to father, and to depressed wreck for such an incredibly long time. And now, who was I now, I wondered. Maybe inter-planetary adventurer?

Who was the real me in all these roles I had been playing? Who was the being that was looking through my eyes and witnessing all the stories of that particular individual called Luke? I did not know, but I felt in my heart that the question was the key to everything.

Having all these reflections, I continued to walk the streets of the old Marais district. My nose had rapidly readapted to the stink of the big city, and I even found it strangely pleasing. I could smell the freshly baked bread from a bakery. The pedestrians, the delivery vans blocking the street with honking cars behind, all this was so incredibly familiar, but it also felt like I was seeing it for the first time.

The truth was, I was an alien from another planet, my body was made of matter of another universe. I had powerful elementary particles in my body that could do things beyond anything Earth science could comprehend. But, here I was walking through the rue des Rosiers, the

Jewish street with its kosher food shops and restaurants, knowing it all as any old Parisian. I was an alien in a familiar world.

My steps had brought me to the busy rue de Rivoli. I looked at the hundreds of cars and smelly buses trying noisily to crawl up and down the broad boulevard and felt sorry for the people trapped in their moving metal boxes. The smell of exhaust fumes was overwhelming, and I decided to walk back to the small streets of the Marais district.

Just as I was well inside rue de Sévigné, a perpendicular street to the busy boulevard, I saw a big black SUV car parked less than fifty meters in front of me. Instantly, my heart rate went up as four men emerged from it, and started to walk towards me. They were dressed in plain black suits, and their body language showed military training.

Terror froze me on the spot. My panicked mind was racing. I was trapped! This was the end! I would soon lose all my memories of Ke'a, forget Alma, everything. I could not bear that thought. I managed to take a step towards the window of a clothes shop and stood shakily in front of it. My knees felt like rubber that could not support my shaking body.

From the corner of my eyes, I could see that the men were approaching fast. What could I do? Put up my energy shield? Try and transform? I had no idea how to do that. And what good would it do, if they saw it? I could not think straight, my whole body becoming a knot, my bowels threatening to empty. And then the men were nearly upon me, only a few meters away. I could see the hard expressions on their faces. Their eyes were actively scanning everything. Then, the only scenario my panicked mind had not imagined, played out. They passed me by, ignoring me, then entered a house some distance away.

"Holy crap!" I exclaimed, feeling bile rise from my stomach. I could not believe what just happened. What kind of God with a wicked sense of humor had set up such a scene? Just to scare the living daylights out of me? The only thing I managed to do was to walk across the street to a café and collapse on one of its terrace chairs.

The waiter came, looking worried, asking me how I was doing.

"Tout va bien Monsieur ?"

"Oui, tout va bien, juste une petite faiblesse. Apportez-moi une bière s'il vous plaît." I reassured him and asked for a beer.

I took a few deep breaths, closing my eyes. I felt the warm late morning sun rays on my face. The waiter brought the beer, and I took a few long gulps. *'I don't have what it takes for that kind of dangerous life'*, I thought, feeling sad and defeated.

I had been utterly unprepared to face that sort of situation on my own. In India and on Guadeloupe, I had been with people I trusted. They had known what to do and had acted confidently and fast. I felt my legs still weak from the retroactive fear. What was the worst that could have happened? Taken in by secret services, being interrogated, being at the mercy of ruthless people? Then probably having my memories reconfigured by the info particles inside my brain.

At my darkest times of depression my shrink would ask me, what the worst case scenario could be, and helped me to face that idea straight on, letting in the pain and the fear. But here, the worst case was too much for me to face, it felt worse than death.

I asked for a sandwich and another beer, the bright sky and warm sun slowly melting my inner chill. I finally realized that all was well. I could celebrate that nothing had happened, that the men in black had not come for me. The worst had not happened! But my insides were still tied in a knot. I left the terrace and walked back with a newfound clarity and resolve: Take care of my loose ends and go back to Ke'a.

As Chul opened the door, I asked, "I would like to call my mom in Canada, and I want to tell her the truth about what happened to me. Is there a way I can do that and not risk being recorded or listened to by big brother's big ears?"

"Yes, Mister Luke," he said pointing to Michael's office, "I can instruct the info particles to set up the phone for a secure line. The phone will ring at your mom's, but leave no record, and the call cannot be tapped."

"Great, thanks! It's still in the middle of the night at her place. I'll do it tonight."

I went to my room, filled the lavish bathtub, and tried to relax in the steaming hot water. My relaxation must have been successful as I dozed off, suddenly woken by a noise in the room. Alma came into the bathroom.

"That's where you are! All well?"

"Yes, I went out for a walk."

I instantly decided not to share my imagined flirtation with disaster. No more complaining, no more being the weak link in the chain. My return to Ke'a depended on the success of our mission.

"How did it go with the gate? What did you do?"

Alma started to take off her clothes, "Now, work's finished! Before talking I have to reach the same level of relaxation as you," she smiled mischievously, sliding into the steaming water, and lay next to me in the huge bathtub.

In the early afternoon, we took the metro to another part of Paris where I had the appointment with the lawyer.

When we passed a newspaper stall near the station, I could see pictures of destroyed cities in Syria on many front pages. A major battle involving several nations was raging. It sharply reminded me of how my planet was connected to Ke'a and how that war was affecting a world that nobody knew anything about.

When we arrived at the lawyer's place, Alma waited for me at the terrace of a nearby café.

As I knew the guy, we could expedite the whole thing in a short time. When I came back to Alma, she had her eyes closed, head leaning backward, enjoying the warm afternoon sun that shone on the terrace. It hit me, that not long ago I had seen another version of her in a similar posture. I approached noiselessly and kissed her.

"Did I take long?"

"I felt you coming, I can see you with my eyes closed."

"Another info particles upgrade?"

"No, just love."

I laughed and kissed her again.

Michael was already on his way to the South, and would probably be back late the next day.

"We have nearly two days just on our own, 'en amoureux' in Paris!" I said, putting my arm around her waist.

"Yes, let's enjoy it, who knows when we get another opportunity."

We decided to walk back to Michael's mansion and take it from there. I thoroughly enjoyed the simple pleasure of strolling back with Alma in this beautiful city. It was like a peaceful dream of normality. Unfortunately, the quiet often precedes the storm.

As we approached Michael's street, I froze. The same SUV that had given me the big scare was parked very near the entrance leading to the inner yard.

"What is it, Luke? What happened? You look pale!"

After taking a deep breath, trying to quieten my pounding heart, I told her what had happened in the morning.

"As they had passed me, I was sure it had nothing to do with us," I said, my voice strangled with emotion.

"It's because they don't know you, but this looks like they are searching for something. Maybe it's not us, but let's not take any chances. I'm contacting Chul." Her attention went inside, and after half a minute she turned back to me, alarm in her eyes.

"They just entered the house, Chul had to let them in. It seems they do not really know what to look for. They are going through the whole house. They have asked about our room, as they saw that somebody had been staying there. Fortunately, Chul had already tidied it and could say that it was a while ago and that Michael's friends had left their things. Do you have your papers with you?"

I touched my wallet in my jacket, "Yes, I have them, but why are they looking for us? How do they know?"

"They are still acting on the initial coordinates they got from the satellite scans before we could apply the first countermeasure. Fortunately, the data was low in resolution, making it imprecise. In a big city like Paris, an error margin of a few hundred meters means hundreds of houses to search. These are thorough people, and they don't give up easily."

"What do we do now?" I was trying to get my inner shaking under control.

"Let's just turn into that other street and continue to walk naturally, they might have someone posted outside. I'm not sure I want them to see me, as they might have flagged me as an Indian woman when they came after us in Tamil Nadu."

We continued to walk, this time in the opposite direction towards the place de la Bastille. Alma was doing some inner talk. I was barely registering the surroundings, walking on auto-pilot. As we stood to wait at a crossing, Alma said, "I've been talking with Michael, he'll be arriving soon in Clermont-Ferrand. He advised us to take the next train and meet him at the station. Then we'll go together to the gate, secure it and transfer back to Ke'a from there."

That sounded easy and safe, and I felt relieved. "What about Chul? Is he going to be all right?"

"The men have already left the house, and they do not seem to have found anything, but Michael needs to be very cautious for a while. There is no absolute necessity to give up the house yet, as Michael's wealth is a big asset for our guardian operations in Europe."

I was eager to leave Paris. "Let's walk to Gare de Bercy, it's the station to Clermont-Ferrand, and it's not far from here."

We had nearly reached the huge place de la Bastille, and I could already hear the roar of the traffic on its immense roundabout.

"Let's take a taxi!" Alma pointed at a station on the edge of the plaza.

It took us only five minutes to get to the railway station. As Alma needed to go to the toilet, I waited for her in the big station hall. I was walking around and felt relief at not seeing any military presence.

As I was approaching the ticket office, I saw that next to it was an area enclosed by panels. Without thinking, I went around the panels and came face to face with a soldier who was sitting in a kind of military field office.

My heart stopped for a second, and I literally gasped for air. I probably looked as if I had seen the devil in person. The soldier stared at me very suspiciously, standing up.

"Vous avez un problème Monsieur?" He was asking

me if I had a problem, and yes, I had a big one, I was scared stiff. I managed to choke up some words.

"Excusez-moi, vous m'avez effrayé, je ne m'attendais pas…"

He asked me for my papers, still staring at me. I gave him my French foreigner id. He told me to sit while he would check it.

As he took his phone, I saw there were pictures of wanted terrorists on the panels forming the walls. Among many tough-looking bearded characters I saw a picture that made my heart stop again. Alma! It was Alma's face, very recognizable, and it looked like the picture had been taken at the checkpoint when we arrived the day before. How could that be? I tried to calm my heart that was threatening to explode in my chest. I looked at all the other pictures, but could not identify anybody else.

At that moment, I heard Alma trying to contact me by inner-call. In front of me, the soldier was transmitting my name and id number to his interlocutor. I took a deep breath and managed to connect to Alma's call.

"Leave the railway station immediately, the military have your picture. I'm being checked, but I'll probably be ok. I'll connect with you as soon as I can leave."

I could feel Alma's inner gasp. "Ok, understood, good luck, see you soon."

She cut the connection, which was good, as the soldier was handing me back my document. The connection with Alma had given me strength and helped me regain my ground. I managed to look the soldier in his eyes when he spoke. My voice was calm when I answered his questions.

He said my papers were in order and asked me what my business was at the station. I told him I was going on an unplanned short personal vacation to the South. He finally said that the army was protecting me, and that I should not to be afraid of him. I said I was sorry, and thanked him for doing his job.

I left the makeshift office with wobbly knees and walked towards the station's exit. I tried to connect with Alma, calling her with my thoughts. She responded instantly.

"Yes, Luke, are you ok?"

"Yes, but we have a big problem," I told her that her face was on a poster with wanted terrorists.

"How is that possible? We passed a checkpoint only yesterday!"

"The picture was taken at that very checkpoint." I thought back to her.

"I don't know how they did it, but they must have pieced things together after that moment. I cannot show my face anymore. With all the surveillance cameras and the facial recognition technology, it's a miracle the area is not already crawling with the military."

"What are we going to do?"

"I have already been in touch with Michael, and we decided against Chul picking us up. He might be under surveillance too. I'm at the nearby 'bistro du métro'.

At that moment I received the inner knowing of its exact location.

"Great! I'm on my way!"

"Try and get a taxi when you're in front of the bistro, I'll come out and jump in when you've got one. Then we'll go to a safe house the guardians have in Paris, and take it from there."

"Why not use the already treated Paris gate to go back to Ke'a?"

"After everything that has happened, that gate, or its vicinity might not be safe any longer. It has been decided that we won't use it for a while."

I had already arrived in front of the "bistro du métro" and stood one foot into the street. Being a seasoned Parisian, I had a cab stop in front of me in no time. I opened the door, just in time for Alma to get in.

She gave the address, and we were on our way. For the driver, we looked like silent passengers, but we were intensely conversing with the newly operational inner-talk.

"That's crazy, how are we going to get to the southern gate?"

"I have an idea I'm trying to wrap my mind around. You're not going to like it," she said.

"What…?"

"Just relax now, I'm not yet sure about it. We'll be there soon."

The taxi dropped us at rue de Vaugirard in the Montparnasse district. I could see the famous "Tour Montparnasse" looming over the area. It is the only skyscraper within the city limits of Paris. We walked towards the tower into a smaller perpendicular street. After a short distance, we turned into a narrow alley that was wedged between two buildings. It led to an inner yard at the bottom of which stood a small, ancient looking house that seemed to have been forgotten by modern times. Its stony walls were dark and worn.

Alma pushed a stone near the door, and it slid aside revealing a keyboard where she punched in a sequence of numbers. The door opened with a deep metallic clank. Going inside, I was surprised to see brightly lit, modern looking rooms. Everything was spotless and smelled fresh. Nothing one would have expected from a house probably built several hundred years ago.

"It seems the house is being used regularly," I said, looking appreciatively at a very cozy looking sofa.

"Some of our agents have been using it as a base and for occasional meetings, but right now everything is on hold."

I took off my shoes and stretched out on the sofa.

"So what are we going to do now? What is the thing I'm not going to like?" I asked.

"I'm not sure I'm going to like it myself!" she said, sitting next to my head and spreading her fingers in my hair.

I sat up and put my arm around her waist. "So what is it that we both are not going to like?"

She shook long curls out of her face and looked straight into my eyes.

"I need to switch my body into another one. It's too risky with my face on those posters, by now it's probably known by all the police of France."

"But that's a great idea! Why would I not like it?"

"My training has been limited, and I can only change into somebody I'm very close to."

"You surely have some candidates?" I said, wondering where this was going.

"Up till now, I have just been able to change into Michael, as he has been my teacher."

"I would not mind that, and it would be a fair return of things, as he had changed into you," I said, trying to feel some humor about it.

"The problem is that he might also have been flagged, at least as suspicious, after the search of his house. It's even possible that he was spotted at the station checkpoint. We cannot take that kind of risk right now, one Michael around is enough."

I shook my head, not understanding.

"So, then you can't do it, we'll find some other way. Why can't you wear a wig, or dye your hair, and wear sunglasses, like they do in the movies?"

"That's too obvious, too risky. The guys potentially on our trail have recently developed advanced scanning beams that easily penetrate that kind of disguise. Chances of being found are small, but why take any risks?"

I looked helplessly around the room, "Are we going to be stuck here? What else can we do?"

"Recently there is one more person I could change into, somebody I got very close to…" she said, looking intensely at me.

"No, wait a minute, now we're getting nearer to the thing we both might not like… Do you mean, you could change into me?"

"Yes, exactly, you are the only person I have this kind of connection with."

"No way…"

"Yes, I know, but that's the only way I can have another appearance."

"But you'll be me! You'll even feel like me! I remember how it was when Michael was you!"

"Yes, I agree, it'll be awkward, but maybe it could be an interesting experience for both of us. Who could slip into her partner's skin and experience him from the inside?"

"Scary thought," I said, standing up and starting to pace up and down the room. "What if you don't like it?"

Alma laughed. "Come on, where's your spirit of adventure? Remember, you've been on Mars!"

"That was easy!"

"Let's have a break now, we can decide later," Alma said and went to the adjoining kitchen.

I took a moment to look around; everything in the living area was furnished and decorated with the intention of creating a feeling of ease and relaxation. On the walls were huge photographs of nature scenes. Big leafy plants were placed around the sitting room area.

Alma came back with two bottles of Belgian beer.

"That's what Ke'alian agents drink when they're on Earth! There are a few good things that can only be found here!" I said teasingly.

We sat on the sofa, silently sipping our beer. It was unusually quiet for an old house. I could barely hear any noise from the busy Parisian district.

"I'm for doing it!" Alma said abruptly, looking at me expectantly. "What's your decision?"

I turned around in the sofa, facing her directly.

"As if I have any say in it."

"Of course, you have, it's going to be your decision as well as mine. You seem to have been tagging along with Michael and me up till now. It's about time you find out what you really want!"

I looked at her, taken aback by the sharpness and the truth of her words. I straightened my back and put down my beer.

"I guess you're right, I did tag along with you guys, as I had nowhere else to go. I felt like an empty shell, badly needing to be filled."

Alma put her hands on my shoulders, giving me a little shake.

"But has that not already changed? This is your new life! Time to be the captain of your own boat, the director of your own movie. Personally, I love strong captains who know what they want."

I felt a sharp pang of pain. What she had said really hit home because she was right. What was it that I wanted? Yes, I wanted to be with Alma, I wanted to go back to Ke'a, and stay there for a while, maybe forever. What else did I want? It was not clear at all. I was a highly trained researcher, but what good would that do me on Ke'a? I was an experienced family man who had lost his wife and children to a cruel climatic event that I had been incapable to predict despite my PhD in climatology. Even that was an ironic failure. I realized that I had mostly felt a failure since that wave took my family. But what now?

Alma remained quiet; she was well aware what was going on in me. She kindly waited for me to come out of my ruminations.

"Yes, Alma, it's time for me to get my life back! Let's do the transformation mumbo jumbo! I definitely need to have a look at myself! Who gets this kind of opportunity?" I did not laugh, and I was well aware of the seriousness of the moment.

"Great! How should we proceed?" She asked.

I smiled; I knew and loved what she was doing.

"I guess I'll go out and do some clothes shopping for my twin brother. We don't want the kind of attention we would get if he wears your clothes."

She laughed. "Yes, but get me nice ones, I'm a woman after all!"

"I'll make sure you look different than me."

I left the house, and headed towards the towering skyscraper around which I knew to find a lively shopping area.

An hour later I was walking back, carrying bags with a complete new outfit. Green jeans, orange sweatshirt, brown jacket, a pair of Adidas sneakers, including underpants and socks. I even bought a black cap and broad sunglasses. I had accomplished my mission successfully, and felt happy and relaxed when I rang the doorbell. Looking back on it, I know I could not have been prepared for what awaited me at the house.

The door opened, but Alma had managed to hide behind it when I entered. As the door closed, a naked man stood in front of me. It was me!

I had somehow been ready for it intellectually, as I knew she would switch her body to mine. I had gone shopping clothes, just for the purpose of dressing that naked man. But seeing myself, naked, the full reality of it was an entirely different ballgame. I had to hold onto the wall, as my head had gone on a spin.

"Ho, my friend! You know what happened! It's me, Alma!"

"Of course, I know that, but, jeez… this is crazy! You look like me! You are me!"

I heard my voice, saw my face, my eyes looking at me. This was stranger than I could have foreseen, had I had more time to prepare. The man standing in front of me, naked, was me in every detail, and much more than I had ever seen of myself in a mirror. It was unsettling to see myself in flesh and blood, all my intimate bodily details, but outside of myself, as another person. It gave me an uncanny sensation of being outside my own body.

"You have a healthy and strong body, I like it," he said. I could see Alma's mischievous smile on his face and in his eyes, and that was reassuring.

"Now, here you are!" I managed to say, "maybe you put on some clothes; I'm not so much into looking at naked men."

"I see, you prefer naked women," she said, punching me in my side.

I struck back, which led to a playful wrestling on the floor. A few minutes later I was pinned on my back, a naked me on top of me.

"You know, when I was a teenager, I often wished I could be a boy. Life was so much easier for them." he said, out of breath.

He stood up and started to put on the clothes I had bought.

"Good job, Luke, I like these clothes, very comfortable," he said when he had finished.

"Let's decide what to do," I said, feeling impatient to get going, then added, "I think renting a car and driving to the South would be better than taking the train."

"Yes, I agree, let's take a taxi to a car rental. But first, let's eat something. There's food in the kitchen, so we can prepare a quick bite. I have a big hungry male body to feed."

"Yeah, me too, now that you mention it!"

After the meal, we took a taxi to a rental station. Alma looked great wearing my body, a cap, and sunglasses. My hair was reasonably long, and she had managed to tie it backward in a small pony tail. I was surprised how different we looked.

We could easily pass for twin brothers or even just brothers. For me, the thought was a warming one. I imagined how different my childhood would have been with a brother. I was an only child. We lived in a small town near Winnipeg, Manitoba. My father did quite a good job in going out hiking with me into the wilderness. When I was old enough, we did that several times a year. But a brother would have been something entirely different.

As I was finally driving the rental on the A10 towards Orléans, my new brother sitting in the passenger seat, I broke the silence.

"It's strange to feel like a criminal on the run."

My own voice answered, "Are you a criminal? What crime have you committed?"

I looked at the figure next to me, it was hard getting used to hearing my own voice.

"No, I'm not a criminal, but I'm associated with alien invaders from another universe."

"Ha, ha! Is that the way you see us?"

"No, I'm only half joking, but you must admit, it's not easy to see us for what we really are."

Brother Alma banged me on the leg, making me push the accelerator, producing a surge in speed.

"That is the important question, right here and now. Who are you, Luke, and don't say you don't know. I want to know who you are, Luke of Earth."

I swallowed first, trying to sound confident, which I wasn't. "I'm a human being, born on Earth, having lived a life in Paris with a family and a successful professional career. That life was destroyed by a big wave. It nearly destroyed me as well, but I was rescued by aliens from another universe."

Alma interrupted, "That's already an old story, who are you right here and now, Luke? What do you want in your life?"

I turned to her, but could only see myself staring at me. There was no escape.

"I want to return to Ke'a and build a life with you. I want us to be together and have a home. I want to find my new calling on Ke'a. I don't know yet what it will be, but I have talents, and I want to find a way to use them for my own happiness and contribute something valuable to others. I guess I'm more drawn to scientific work rather than this secret agent job we're performing right now. I'm sure I'll find my way!"

This time I felt a gentle hand on my leg.

"I love that! I also want us to be together. Maybe what just happened is a hidden blessing, as I probably will not be able to return to Earth for a while."

The four-hour drive on the motorway turned out to be restful. I kept to the speed limit. No police controls. I finally relaxed and enjoyed driving the inconspicuous French car. I was aware it could be the last time for a long while. Maybe there would come a time when I would miss that kind of hardcore traveling?

During these hours, we both shared stories about our childhoods and families. At the time when she had been recruited by Michael, Alma had been in a relationship with an English man. When it had become clear that she could not share her secret with him, let alone bring him over to Ke'a, she had to end the relationship. That had been one of the hardest decisions of her life.

"We both loved each other," she said, "but I could not be with someone and keep secret what had become such an important part of my life."

We also talked about the guardians, and how Alma became part of them. She told me her own fears when she had first been in dangerous situations. It also became clear, that the acute crisis we were in was an unprecedented challenge for most guardians who were unprepared for it, as they had always been hidden and had never directly been hunted nor attacked. Hearing all of this made me feel better about my own panic attacks.

As we arrived in Clermont-Ferrand we drove to the place where Michael was waiting.

"Hello, you two lovely brothers!" he exclaimed, staring at us, adding, "well done!"

"Hey, Michael, sorry you had to wait," I said, hugging him, then I added, "But I guess waiting in a fancy restaurant was not too hard for you!"

He laughed, "Yes, I do have a soft spot for French food. Fortunately, on Ke'a we have Bo'ad's cuisine which is superior to anything I have tasted on Earth. You could have a little snack here before we continue. Right now, there's no hurry, we're only on our way back to Ke'a."

"Bless heavens for that," I said.

"You don't like your old world anymore?"

"No, that's not the case, but I know my new life is on Ke'a," I said, clapping my twin brother on the back.

He smiled, and said, "You told me about calling mom. This is your last chance, as we need a landline." He pointed at a phone booth on the other side of the road.

"Can you secure that line?"

"Yes, I can even make it toll-free."

I took a deep breath, caught unprepared. I considered it for a few moments.

"Yes, it's good to do it, I'll keep it short."

He put his arm around my neck, directing me to the phone booth. "Come, brother, take whatever time you need, this is important. Don't forget to say hi from me!"

He touched the phone and closed his eyes. "Tell me the number."

I told him, and he immediately handed me the handset. It was already ringing. A familiar voice answered. "Hello?"

"Hi, mom. It's Luke."

"Hi, nice of you to call. How are you? It's been a while since you called. You are back from India?"

"Yes, and since then lots of good things have happened in my life."

"Did you meet someone?"

I laughed. "Yes mom, that's one of the good things."

"I'm happy for you! It was time to move on."

"Yes, it was much too long, but the wait was worth it. I have lived an incredible adventure I want to tell you about. I know that you are open-minded, and it's important for me that you know the truth."

"That sounds a bit scary, you have not gotten yourself into any trouble, do you?"

"No, mom, not really, but listen, I'll tell you a short version of what happened to me since I went to India."

I told her everything, meeting Alma in India, returning

to Paris, my apartment destroyed, Michael. As I did not want to challenge my mom's open-mindedness too much, I did not tell her about him transforming into Alma. Then Guadeloupe, and transferring to Ke'a. I described Ke'a as well as I could, it's info particles and holo magic, the ease, and beauty of the society. Here again, I skipped the part of the Moon and Mars. In the end, I told her about my intention to go back and stay on Ke'a.

"Are you never going to come back?"

"I am going to come back, mom, I promise, it's actually not so difficult. Maybe I'll bring Alma when I visit next time."

I felt her beam of happiness through the phone.

"I would love that, and so would your dad", she said, "unfortunately he's gone shopping, can you call him later?"

"No, mom, I'm on my way back to Ke'a."

I told her also about the selling of the apartment, and them getting the money.

"That's wonderful! Thank you, son, but don't you need some money?"

"There's no need of money on Ke'a, as you probably understood."

"Yes, what a wonderful world that is, maybe we could come and visit?"

"That would be wonderful, but, please understand that you cannot tell anybody about it. I'm not even sure you can tell dad."

"I understand what you mean, son."

"But, do you believe me? What I told you is quite an incredible story."

"I know you, I can feel you. I'm your mom, and I know when you're telling the truth. I'm happy for you. And don't worry, your secret is safe with me. I'll tell your dad a more localized version, like you live in India and can live there with little money."

I laughed, "That version is mostly true. Thanks mom! It means a lot to me that you believe me."

When I hung up the phone I felt happy. It was like I had reconciled Earth with Ke'a. The most important person on Earth knew where I was, and a deep split in me was resolved.

After returning the car to the local rental station, we hired a taxi to drive us to a place outside a small town called Le Mont-Dore. An hour later, we arrived at the end of a small local road and headed on a rocky path into the wilderness.

Chapter Twenty-One

The long walk to the gate location felt already like being back on Ke'a. Nature was incredibly beautiful. We went up and down hills that were gradually getting higher. The spring vegetation was full of new energy. The colors of the fresh leaves and mountain flowers were much more like the vibrant colors of Ke'a. The air was carrying a gorgeous bouquet of fragrances. We had entered the central highlands of France, with its ancient mountains, many of which had been volcanos thousands of years ago.

We walked for several hours until we reached the foot of one of those very ancient volcanoes. From there, Michael led us halfway up the slow rising incline to an opening that was hiding behind a cluster of huge boulders. It looked like a small cave that was going nowhere. But this time I was prepared for the holo mumbo jumbo. Michael went to the furthest wall and stood there until the red glow transformed solid rock into a neat passage.

On the other side was a small gate room, but of the

upgraded kind, with a round dome of glittering crystals and the circular stone bench.

"Ok, boys," brother Alma exclaimed, "I need a few minutes of privacy. Can you go outside and take a last look at beautiful Earth?"

We sat on a boulder near the cave entrance.

"Switching the body, is that your standard procedure to test candidates for Ke'a?" I asked.

Michael laughed, "Not at all, I have used it very rarely. In your case, it seemed like a good way to assess your mental strength and see how you could cope with such an incredible situation, before taking you to Ke'a where we translocate and pass through walls."

"I guess that makes sense." I conceded.

At that moment Alma came out of the cave. My Alma, in her own beautiful body! I was very happy to see her again. What would we have done if she had gotten stuck in my body?

We hugged a long time, caressing each other's backs, it was so good to feel her again.

"What are we going to do to secure the gate?" I finally asked, eager to go back to Ke'a.

"Not much visible action, the info particles have already spread from our bodies to the elementary matter layer of the cave. They are reconfiguring the matter structure, so as to prevent any particular energy signature to emanate from it when the gate is at rest or in use."

"What are these info particles? I'm starting to get a feel for it, but much of it remains a mystery."

Michael said, "It's the same for many people on Ke'a. Think about how few people here on Earth know how electricity really works, let alone how electronic devices function. I would say it's a similar percentage on Ke'a for the info-particles. In a way, the only weakness that the info-particles have is that people take them for granted and totally rely on them."

"But, what do you understand of it, Michael?"

He put down his backpack and sat on the circular bench.

"Info particles are elementary particles that are so small that they are on the edge of the non-physical, the realm of spirit. They are the deepest level of matter. In a way, they are an interface, a bridge between a physical universe and the Spirit Dimension. They are called info as they are the layer directly linked to the minds of conscious beings. The information they continuously receive and update is what creates the reality we see, from the deepest layer of matter to the environment that we perceive through our senses."

"But how can one connect to such a dimension?" I asked, still not getting it.

"The information link between minds and that elementary layer is mostly unconscious. Ke'alian science has found ways to make part of that relationship conscious and enhance it with various technologies that were developed, allowing us to tap directly into that creation field that is the basis of our reality."

I sat next to Michael, my head feeling hollow with a new space of possibilities that was still empty, but I was sure would slowly be filled. But then a thought struck me.

"What if something would happen that destroyed all the info-particles, or made them inoperative? That would be a disaster for Ke'alian society which relies on them everywhere."

Michael tapped me on the shoulder. "Come on Luke! This is your disaster-oriented Earth mind-set! Of course, nothing is impossible, but the info-particles are part of the fabric of what we perceive as reality. That reality would also need to turn itself off for that to happen."

"But it still feels scary for me to rely so much on something nobody completely understands."

Michael gave me a friendly punch on my arm.

"Just relax with it! In time your deeper understanding, as well as your experience, will create trust."

"It's just that I trained as a scientist; It makes me want to understand how things work."

"Maybe you'll be joining a team of Ke'alian researchers?"

"Yes, that thought has crossed my mind. It's probably more in line with my abilities, than being an agent chased by the secret services of a whole world."

Michael laughed. "No pressure! You have time to find out what's best for you!"

I looked at Alma who had been listening. She sat next to me and gave me a very sweet kiss. "Yes, no pressure, I know we'll find a way that's right for us. Ke'alian society has at its core the wish that everyone finds his unique calling."

"How long does the gate reconfiguration process take?

I look forward to going back."

"The info particles have flowed into the cave the moment we stepped in; it's going to take a bit more than an hour for the process to complete," she said.

"Can we be sure that it's going to work?"

Michael turned to me and patted the stone circle. "Nothing is a hundred percent sure when it involves Earth technology, but when it comes to Ke'alian info-science, that in this case has been thoroughly tested, it comes pretty close. So, save having an earthquake shattering the cave in the next half hour, you can be pretty sure that we'll soon be on Ke'a."

Michael's reassurance helped me turn off my busy mind. I was happy to sit and relax after the long walk. It was again a different feeling, transiting to another world that I knew and loved. I looked forward to feeling the lighter gravity of Ke'a, see her vibrant colors. We also would be safe again. I had only been on Ke'a a few days, and it already felt like going back home.

I touched Alma's feet, who had stretched out on the bench, her eyes closed. She was smiling.

"We're going home, Luke."

"Yeah, I was just thinking about it. What an incredible journey!"

Shortly after the time had elapsed, Michael got a transmission from the info particles that meant the gate's energy signature had been successfully modified, and could be safely used.

This time I was conscious during the transition. It felt like being sucked upwards into a whirling energy tunnel.

It left me dizzy and disoriented for a few seconds. I protected my eyes from the blinding light in front of me. I smelled fresh, fragrant air. Alma, next to me, took my hand.

"We're back, Luke!"

"Yes, home, my new home!"

"Yes, come, let's go out!"

As my eyes got used to the light, I saw that the cave was open to the outside. We were greeted by lush vegetation and bright sunlight. I took my backpack and stood up, nearly toppling over with my effort.

"Hallelujah! Everything's lighter! That's the gravity I like!"

We were in a similar mountain region. The sun that was straight above felt burning hot on my face. The vegetation was in it's full lush early summer growth. There was an explosion of colors and fragrances all around us, together with the buzzing of insects and the calls of birds. The place was intensely alive.

"I'd love to go to your pace in Mu'ad." I said.

"I had the same thought," she said," let's go and make it ours!"

"Yes, our place on Ke'a!" I exclaimed and kissed her warm lips.

Michael, who had joined us in the hot sunshine, said, "For now, we'll go different paths. I have to see people from the planetary council, to discuss the situation in Paris. I'm sure we'll meet soon again."

"I'm sure about that," I said, smiling, "Ke'a feels like a

real village, where everybody is nearby."

After our goodbyes, there was no more hiking, nor taxis, nor rentals. We stepped on the nearby translocation anchor and instantly were in Ary'a, Ke'a's version of India. We appeared at the same spot on the outer edge of Mu'ad, and it was already getting dark. The lights of the small city were crowned by the huge diamond-shaped temple that was radiating it's light all over the area.

"It's really like coming home. I know this place!" I happily stretched my arms out, embracing the whole area, before throwing them around Alma. She laughed, her eyes beaming.

"Let's stay here for a while!"

"Yes! Whatever a while turns out to be!"

It was more than three weeks, where Alma and I lived the highly evolved, but yet very simple life of a Ke'alian couple. The use of the holo info technology for creating rooms, items, even food had rapidly become second nature to me. It felt totally natural to visualize something in my mind and see it instantly appear. I soon did not give a second thought to making occasional jumps to any point on the planet. But having dinner while watching a sunset on Mars was a real stunner.

We met people, visited friends of Alma's, joined in public group events and attended incredible live performances.

The most amazing events took place at the temple, in the big hall. The one that touched me most was about the connection to the Spirit Realm that Ke'alians considered being the source for themselves and of everything in the material universe.

There were hundreds of people attending, standing in a big circle. A huge light ball was hovering above us all, and it started to shoot very tight and bright beams of light, straight to the heart of individuals. Each time a person was touched she said three things for which she felt grateful. It was very heart opening and personal, and I could feel that this praxis of gratitude was central to the harmony and peace of Ke'alian society.

All the Ke'alians I've come in touch with feel connected to a source, an energy that flows directly from the Spirit Realm. They also link that energy to the info particles and the holographic nature of the universe. In that way, spirit and science are connected, not separated as on Earth.

But I kept having a nagging dissatisfaction with all being so free of problems and negativity. I asked to see the head shaman Gahala'o. During our last meeting, he had blown my mind, and given me a deeper understanding that was beyond words.

I had a sense that my intellect, my inquiring mind was in the way and needed to get one more blast.

That time, I met him in another room that was smaller and darker. Only one single octagonal facet of the diamond-shaped wall was transparent to bright daylight. It shone a large tight beam of light to the center of the room, leaving the rest in relative darkness.

I could feel Gahala'o's presence before I heard him coming, clad in his long blue kaftan.

"Welcome, Luke, new child of Ke'a."

Without waiting for an answer that my lips had begun to form, he continued in his deep warm voice, "You have questions, and hope to get answers from me."

I was already swept by Gahala'o's powerful energy and could only nod.

He opened his arms and gave me quick embrace.

"You know, Luke, having a question means that the answer is already somewhere inside you."

"What are you talking about?" I asked, his eyes reminded me of the burning energy of the sadhu's eyes in India. My head felt suddenly hollow, and all my stories about my question popped like soap bubbles in the wind. It all came down to one essential question.

"Where is the shadow on Ke'a? I see only light, and it worries me."

I felt a warm flow of energy emanating from Gahala'o who was standing very close to me.

"Why does that worry you?"

"I have suffered from depression for a long time. My therapist used to talk about the danger to suppress your own shadow, and the necessity to confront it."

"Why is that necessary, Luke?" Gahala'o voice had become very soft.

"A shadow that is denied and not expressed remains unconscious and can then sneak unchecked into your life and create a lot of pain and negativity."

"Do you think Ke'alians are suppressing their shadow?"

"I don't know. I often have the weird feeling that it's all too good to be true."

"Have you sensed anything on Ke'a that has confirmed your worries?"

"Not really, but sometimes I'm afraid that all this info particles stuff in our brains creates some control, taking away our free will."

"Do you believe there is something that you call free will?"

"I know what you're getting at, Gahala'o, that an average human has minimal free and original thinking, and what he thinks to be his choices are in reality deeper impulses that he's barely aware of, but…"

"Why is there a "but" Luke, do you have the impression Ke'alians are more or less conscious and free in their thinking than Earth people?"

"My impression is that they have much more clarity. Maybe it's that clarity that I'm still lacking?"

"Your questions are bringing clarity, Luke. Ke'alians have had much more time to confront their collective and individual shadows. Maybe you'll study our history, and you'll understand the long winding path Ke'alian civilization has gone to reach the place where it is right now."

"But, what is the key to that inner peace and clarity? I am not as evolved as Ke'alians. I feel my brain needs to be completely rewired."

Gahala'o laughed, "Your mind has been doing just that, and is entirely apt to make that leap. The keys are very simple, first the direct knowing and connection to the Spirit World, and simple practices such as gratitude and forgiveness."

"Is that enough to eradicate fear, hatred, and all the negativity in the human mind?"

"Yes, Luke, it is, when you practice gratitude, you can relax, as you are not the center of the universe any longer. You need no longer to defend. Forgiveness of yourself and others heals a lot of wounds and negativity. We have practiced that as a society for nearly a millennium. We support each other to find and express the uniqueness of our abilities and talents, knowing our inner self that has many ways to reveal itself. That has been a major focus of our culture. We are now harvesting the fruits."

"But, can I just jump in from Earth and enjoy these fruits?"

"Are you asking yourself if you deserve to be here in what feels for you to be paradise?"

I felt my eyes tearing up. "Yes, that's it." I managed to say.

Gahala'o put a warm hand over my heart and said, "Luke, you are a good man, and deserve it all. You have a Ke'alian body, allow your Earth mind to catch up. It will gradually happen if you relax and practice gratitude and forgiveness."

"There are many things I need to forgive myself," I said, tears running from my eyes, then a sudden realization struck me. "More than ten years ago I was on a paradise beach on Earth, but then that paradise transformed into the horror of a tsunami that killed my wife and my children. I also need to forgive Gaia, the living Earth."

"A living planet's consciousness is on a very different scale, Luke. The tsunami was one of the ways Gaia has to maintain her balance. Forgive her, and yourself. You know where to start," he said, opening his arms and briefly touching my shoulders. He turned and without another word left the room.

I stood there a long time, in the beam of light pouring from the ceiling, on the edge of the darker part of the room, wondering what the enlightenment had been.

As I was on my way out of the room, a young shaman came straight towards me, greeting me with a touch on my shoulders.

"I'm shaman Ho'apo. Gahala'o asked me to invite you to attend a forgiveness ritual that will take place tomorrow. It will show you how we practice forgiveness. We can meet tomorrow morning here on the six's morning hour. I'll accompany you if you want to do it."

I bowed to the shaman. "Yes, Ho'apo, I'd love to attend that ritual. I'll be here tomorrow."

I was very excited about the invitation, as this was a missing link for me, to understand how a complex society could be so harmonious and devoid of major problems and conflicts.

The next day as I met Ho'apo, he took me to a small circular meeting room where we sat down in comfortable seats. All around the room were flowers, green as well as orange leafy plants. The walls were transparent to the exterior, giving the impression that we were outside in nature.

Without preamble Ho'apo said, "Luke, I would like to give you a quick introduction to our ways of dealing with human conflicts and intended crimes."

"What do you mean by intended crimes?" I interrupted, not understanding.

"That is part of which I'm going to explain, as it will probably be unusual and even shocking for you."

He made a broad opening gesture and continued. "On Ke'a, we don't have crimes any longer, as intentions to commit a criminal act are detected by the info-particles which will prevent the person from acting on it. As you may know, part of what the info-particles do inside our mind-body system is to monitor our mental and physical well-being. Mental and physical states are totally connected."

"Wait a minute, are you saying that we are always being controlled by the info-particles?" I felt my blood pressure rise.

Ho'apo put a hand on my shoulder. "Luke, try to take in the whole information I'm giving you before you jump to conclusions. This is very important."

I took a deep breath. "Ok, I'll try." A few deeper breaths helped me get a grip on my rising unease.

"Thank you, Luke. As I was saying, the info-particles monitor your mind-body system without having any influence over it. They respect your personal integrity and do not consider you as a biological machine that could be controlled and predicted by complex algorithms.

Your thoughts and actions are much more influenced by your hormones than by the info-particles. In fact, the info-particles help us humans, to free ourselves from the automatic, unconscious instinctual influences that have guided human behavior in the past."

Ho'apo paused for a moment, giving me time to assimilate what he had said.

"That is why we only have intentional crimes on Ke'a. The person is prevented from acting out her destructive impulses. Subsequently, she is taken care of by a population focalizer who tries to understand her motives, and what actions or inactions of other people have contributed to the build-up of the criminal intention. The next step involves all the connected people, who are interviewed. Thus the forgiveness ritual you are going to attend is being prepared with everybody involved."

"How often does something like that happen?" I asked, starting to understand.

"Right now around ten times a week. It used to be only once a month a decade ago."

"Is that a number concerning the whole Ke'alian population?"

"Yes. Unfortunately, the numbers have been on a slow rise since the negative vibratory leakage from Earth has gathered momentum."

"But that number is incredibly low for a population of several billion people!"

"Yes, compared to the reality on Earth it's insignificant, but for us, it's unusually high."

Ho'apo stood up. "You now have enough preparation.

I think we can go to the forgiveness ritual. The location is on a small island in the equivalent of Earth's Pacific Ocean. That island is only used for that purpose."

We went to an adjacent translocation alcove. As soon as Ho'apo touched my hand, I was surrounded by a warm scented breeze. We had appeared on a narrow strip of land surrounded by turquoise water. I immediately recognized the atoll formation with its ring-shaped coral reef encircling a lagoon.

Ho'apo guided me towards a group of around a dozen people sitting in the sand near the lagoon. Their circle still had an opening into which we sat.

A white-haired shaman was sitting opposite to us. He opened his arms in a wide gesture.

"Welcome, Luke and Ho'apo. Thank you for joining your energy to our forgiveness circle. I acknowledge the ever present Spirit Realm that is our true essential home. I acknowledge and give thanks for the presence and wisdom of Ke'a who is our living planetary home of which our bodies are a part. I honor this place of beauty that gives us the water from the ocean, the earth from the sand and the rocks, the air we breathe and feel on our skin, and the fire that moves deep inside the old volcano that has become this lagoon.

We are here to take responsibility and forgive ourselves for what happened to Oka'ina here on my right. Oka'ina had the intention to kill Mirussa here on my left. The motive was passion and love for her former partner Sedral here present at the right of Mirussa. Oka'ina had a great challenge when Sedral ended their relationship in order to be with Mirussa. Mirussa was her friend as well as an important partner in the creation of a music opera, which is a vital life project for her. All Oka'ina could think of was killing Mirussa or ending her own life. For that, we all present in this circle are sorry and are here to forgive ourselves and take responsibility for what happened."

He then took the hands of Oka'ina and Mirussa sitting next to him, imitated by the whole circle. I instantly felt the powerful energy of the group moving through my body. I was aware of the air, the smell of the water, the ground under me, and the power of the planet's fire not far beyond. I could feel that something was blocked in the group energy. I also sensed a caring willingness, the loving intention of all the people present to take care of what was blocked.

This led me to sense something very particular in the group energy as if there was an additional separate entity formed by the group intention. It was a strong presence, like an angelic presence caring for the whole group and its purpose.

When we let go of each other's hands, the shaman made an opening gesture towards Oka'ina whose face was wet with tears. She started to speak.

"I could not continue feeling the pain, the betrayal, the loss, and the jealousy any longer. It hurt too much. Anything was better than having that pain."

As it was clear that she would say no more, Mirussa, on the shaman's left started to speak.

"I'm deeply sorry for the pain I caused you, Oka'ina, I regret that I was so taken by my personal bliss and was so unaware of your distress and pain. I'm sorry, please forgive me."

Then next to her, Oka'ina's ex-partner continued.

"I'm sorry that our separation caused you so much pain. I stand to my decision, but I see that I could have been more sensitive and aware of what was going on with you. I could have found opportunities for us to talk. I'm very sorry, please forgive me."

Everybody in the circle took turns to share their experience, or how they felt about certain past situations connected to what happened to Oka'ina. Her parents were there, some of her closest friends and colleagues working on the opera project. They all expressed their regrets that they had not been more aware of what was happening to Oka'ina and that they had not given as much support as they could have.

A friend said that she had been aware, but it had touched an old wound that she still had from a former relationship, and so had been unable to help. But now she felt very much connected to what happened to Oka'ina and wanted to forgive herself and heal her own wound.

The sharing continued for a long time, going around the circle several times. Some people remained silent, but their faces and tears showed that much was going on inside.

I was not a mere observer, as I felt that everything that had happened, and was being processed, was also part of myself. I felt I was part of the healing and forgiveness that was happening.

Nobody blamed anyone or shared with angry emotions. I could feel that something powerful was happening. Each person took responsibility for herself, and for the reality that had been created. Everybody forgave and received forgiveness, thus releasing and loosening the negative energies, the pain, the hurt, the blame, and self-blame.

During the whole process, I had been in touch with my own gnawing feelings of guilt and self-blame. It had been my idea to travel to India, and I had been unable to protect and save my family. Each time somebody in the group expressed regrets and forgave others or herself, I felt that I was going deeper into my own forgiveness. I felt we were all connected.

In the end, the old shaman made a closing gesture, and we held hands again.

"We have sought and found resolution. Together we have stopped the suffering circle and brought peace. Everything has been set right again, in harmony with our true nature. We will remain aware of this precious experience in our lives."

I could feel and see the transformation in the whole group. All the faces were shining and smiling. Everybody got up, talking, hugging, laughing. It was an extraordinary transformation. I saw Oka'ina, Mirussa and the man, Sedral stand together, speak to each other and finally have a big threesome hug.

The ritual ended with everybody jumping like kids into the ocean, releasing the remaining tension with a playful time in the delicious water.

Later we all sat together again and shared a meal.

When I returned to the temple with Ho'apo, I was

filled with the beauty and power of the forgiveness ritual. I felt lighter and purified. Something very powerful had happened in me. A genuine healing had taken place that went much deeper than the particular circumstances that had been addressed.

Chapter Twenty-Two

One morning, several days later, as I woke up, Alma sat next to me, grinning broadly, her eyes beaming with joyful anticipation.

"Good morning!"

"Good morning, you look like you've been given the key to Santa's storehouse! What is it?"

"Ah, what could make me so happy?"

"I don't know, and you can't have won the lottery, as there's no money on Ke'a. What does that leave? Let me think… I recognize the expression on your face. There's mischief in it!"

She laughed, "You could be on the right track, but this is huge!"

"I've heard those words before! Yes, now I get it! It's in the category of 'you've seen nothing yet!'"

She giggled, "You're burning!"

"Wow!" I suddenly understood. It was something that had gone out of my mind.

"We're going to travel to the other star!"

"Yes! I just got the clearance for us to go. They expect us; we can go anytime within the next few hours. Do you need to prepare yourself mentally?"

She still smiled, but I could sense a small degree of earnestness in her voice.

"I guess I should try and wrap my poor mind around the fact that we are going to travel nearly four and a half light years in a heartbeat."

She was right. Just the thought threw my mind on a speedy merry-go-round of all I had ever read, heard and thought to know about light speed and cosmic distances.

After a while, I said, "Well, you're right! My mind cannot cope with it, just as well I turn it off. Do you have any idea where the off switch is?" I tried to joke, but my smile felt tense.

She hugged me and said, "Let's go walk to the sea, fresh air is a good off switch."

That morning, as we walked through Mu'ad, it was like being in a big garden. What was visible were trees, plants, and flowers. The houses, holographic or constructed were either transparent or hidden in small clearings that were encircled by dense vegetation. There were none of the noises I have always associated with towns and cities. No engines, no vehicles, no massive constructions. Only the very occasional silent hover carts, like the one I had first seen on Mars. There were lots of people and children walking in the avenues, looking relaxed and happy.

"This is like the garden of Eden. Are we in paradise?" I asked, as we approached an area that was particularly vibrant with life energy and colors of the vegetable kingdom.

Alma stopped and put her arms around me, "I guess we are, but we cannot take it for granted, it's something we all care for each moment of our life. That is why it is as it is."

"I feel sorry for people on Earth who still are so far away from this."

"The time will probably come when it will be possible to bridge, or at least ease that gap. Our agents on Earth are doing all they can to help accelerate the process."

We continued our walk.

"But in many ways, Earth's universe is quite different, as it is in a denser dimension. Now that governments have seen their suspicions justified, it's going to be even harder," I said.

"Don't be so pessimistic, Luke, this is our present moment in paradise. Our life is here, and I trust life's intelligence to work things out"

"Yes, you're right, feeling bad has never helped anybody!"

We had just passed a mound, and the view had opened to a gorgeous bay roaring with high tide waves. The sea was the same intense blue as the sky.

Alma ran down the slope. "Catch me if you can!"

I laughed, kicking all the crappy thoughts out of my mind, and started to chase a naked woman that had already reached the water's edge.

Swimming had become joyful for me again. The warm sea, tumbling in the waves with the woman I love, managed to clear my mind. We finally stretched on the hot sand. Just being, with a spacious quiet mind.

We walked back silently, content with each other's presence.

When we arrived home, we sat for a while on the cushions in the middle of the room.

"You know, even for a Ke'alian, going to Kai'ila is something very special."

"Yes, Alpha Centauri, our neighboring star, what are we waiting for, let's go! Do we need anything?"

"No, our info particles are fully operational on Kai'ila."

We went to the temple, as it had the only local translocation anchor that could link to Kai'ila. As usual, much was going on in the hall. We entered a smaller adjacent octagonal room. The walls were active windows showing live images received from the main Ke'alian orbital telescope.

"Look here! This wall shows the twin stars of Alpha Centauri," said Alma, pointing to a panel between feeds from Mars and the Moon.

I could see two big points of light standing out from a sea of stars in the background. Alma pointed to a green dot a short distance away from one of the stars.

"This is a simulation of the location of Kai'ila. It cannot be seen, even with our most powerful telescopes."

I felt my heart beat faster with my growing excitement. "What are we waiting for?"

"Are you ready?"

"As ready as I'll ever be!"

Alma took my hand, and the room disappeared.

The first thing that hit me was the smell. The air had a bizarre stink. I could taste it in my mouth, feel it down my throat into my lungs. The sky was low with grey clouds. We were outside on a vast rocky plateau. A hundred meters from the translocation anchor, were half a dozen dome-shaped constructions arranged in a circle around a bigger one.

"It smells bad," I said.

Alma punched me playfully in the belly, "Are these the historical words you pronounce after your first journey to another star?"

"The air smells and feels weird," I stubbornly continued, a bit disappointed by the location.

"Are we really on Kai'ila?"

"Yes, we are on Kai'ila, the second planet of the biggest star."

I looked into the sky but could not see anything beyond the clouds. It was windy, and a few drops of water had fallen on my face. It was cold, and I instantly changed my clothes to a warmer outfit. I could not sense any noticeable difference in my body weight.

"Is somebody going to meet us?" I asked, feeling a bit lost.

"No, let's go to the main building," she pointed to the tallest dome at the center of what looked more like a camp than a village. I could see nobody outside.

As we passed through the wall, I nearly fell over my feet. I had not expected the huge underground space. We were standing at the apex of an enormous cave.

"Holy cow! You could have warned me! That is a bad habit you have!"

Alma smiled sheepishly, "Forgive me, I like so much seeing surprise on your face. Here's the underground village of Sa'a."

A deep melodious voice behind us continued, "Underground to minimize our impact on Kai'ila's biosphere."

I turned to see a tall black woman. Her eyes and teeth were white jewels in a jet black face on a perfectly black body. Her long black curly hair was flowing widely over her shoulders. Whichever black holo-clothes she had, perfectly matched the outlines of her powerfully built body. In my time on Ke'a I had seen an infinite variety of holo outfits, but her total blackness topped everything I had seen before.

The surprise of the cave and the appearance of the woman had left me speechless.

The woman made an embracing gesture and touched our shoulders. "Welcome, Alma and Luke, I'm Zuinoa, I'm part of the science team and your guide while you're on Kai'ila."

"Thank you Zuinoa for being our guide," Alma said.

"Come, let's go down to the circle center," Zuinoa

took our hands. We were instantly at the bottom of the cave, surrounded by what looked like a Ke'alian village in a temperate zone. There were spherical holo constructions of various colors and sizes. Plants, flowers and bizarre trees were growing in areas covered with fresh soil. The light emanating from the cave top and part of its sides was bright and felt warm. The air had the same bizarre rotten potatoes smell as outside.

A group of a dozen people was holding hands in a circle around a tree, whose crown looked like an upturned octopus.

On one side of the cave, that must have been at least three or four hundred meters wide, towered a diamond-shaped building, that looked like a smaller version of the temple we had departed from barely minutes ago. Its numerous facets reflected the light and produced a spectrum of vivid colors.

Zuinoa saw my gaze. "That's where the shamans do their particular work and research. As you probably know, the exploration and connecting we do on Kai'ila are exclusively done by a scientific team and shamans. We are slowly finishing the initial phase of getting to know and understand Kai'ila's biosphere. We also have been connecting with her Spirit energy field."

"What can we do as visitors?" I asked, eager to see something more exciting than a cave village.

"As we still limit the visiting time to six hours, I can show you the main geographical areas and some of Kai'ila's very particular fauna. Then, if you like, you can have a meeting with Viyla, our head shaman who has recently opened up a new angle on stellar research that could pave the way to the whole galaxy."

"Wow!" I exclaimed, "that's the stuff of my dreams, of course I'd love that!" I looked at Alma, and she was smiling, probably getting a glimpse of my inner child jumping up and down.

"But before we go, let's sit down and have a cup of Kai'ila's herb tea, and cookies made from seeds and fruits growing in the valley below our rock. It's a way to welcome Kai'ila into your body and become part of her."

As I tasted the round cookies and smelled the fragrant steam rising from the cup, something more in me landed to the fact that I was in another solar system. Maybe it was suggested by Zuinoa's words, but I felt a unique energy entering my body as I drank the tea.

"We can go when you're ready." The melodious voice of our black guide tore me from my inner experience.

We went to a flat stone platform, took Zuinoa's hands, and in the blink of an eye we were outside, somewhere on the planet.

"Yeah! That's more like it! I cried out. We were on a mountain ledge overlooking a plain that stretched to the horizon. The sky was an intense blue, and the amazing part was that there were two suns in the sky, one similar in size and intensity to our sun, the other much smaller, but showing a tiny, fiery disk. That majestic view was topped by an enormous moon slowly rising from the horizon. Its milky color was tainted with red, and on its surface, I could see huge craters and big darker patches and lines.

"Now, this is the real sci-fi!"

Alma smiled, and gently pushed my mouth shut, that I had forgotten to close.

The plain below us was a dark shade of yellow, with patches of brown. Tall trees were scattered throughout the landscape. In the distance I could see a moving white spot. As I strained my eyes, I saw it was a big herd of animals, so packed together that only their small heads on long necks were visible, like worms sticking out of the soil.

After a while, Zuinoa took us to another location. We were again on a high mound. This time it overlooked a bizarre forest. The trees had grown in a regular pattern, like in a pine tree farm on Earth.

"Have these trees grown naturally like that?" I asked, puzzled.

"Yes, they seem to optimize the amount of sunshine they are getting. But these trees have the particularity that they are hybrid beings, in a way they are vegetal animals. Look now!"

The sun had just disappeared behind a big cloud, and suddenly there was motion in the strange forest. It looked like all the trees had started to move towards a patch of land that was still illuminated.

"Wow! How can they coordinate their movements? They march like a Roman army!"

"As much as we understand, they have a hive mind that connects all the trees in a particular forest."

"Is this the kind of animals that are a whole new category?"

"Yes, and there are many more. What's so different in

this ecosystem is that there are lots of species that bridge the usual categories of land, aquatic and air animals, including the plants that can move like animals. We have many creatures in the ocean that are able to run on land and even fly. They have developed truly polyvalent, multipurpose bodies that function in practically all environments."

To demonstrate it, she took us to the edge of a vast ocean. We observed sea creatures, walking and crawling out of the water, as well as the opposite. Many of the animals that had come out of the water would also fly off into the sky. I saw that many of these animals had scales, like reptiles.

On another shore, there were massive round towers placed at regular intervals. As we approached, I saw creatures that resembled enormous crabs in their hard-shelled bodies, but these bodies were on multiple long spider-like legs. They were crawling all over the stony beach, in and out of the sea. They were the builders, inhabitants of the towers. It was a nightmarish sight, and I was glad when we translocated away.

The tour showed us a planet that has as much in common with Earth and Ke'a's biosphere as well as incredible deviations from it. The continental mass is bigger with a smaller ratio for oceans. This affects the climate, that is drier and cooler. There is a vast desert continent that has a fauna and flora that lives mostly underground under a sea of sand.

As we came back to the base, my inner exoplanet explorer was satiated. This planet had everything humans needed to thrive on. It looked familiar, with its rivers, mountains, plains, and seas. But there was always something that said, 'this is not home'. Part of the fauna and much of the flora looked and behaved in ways that were uncomfortably alien. I was starting to get used to the smell and taste of the air, but Earth with all her pollution smelled better to my human nose.

Zuinoa invited us to have a meal together with the group of scientists she was working with. Most of them had been on the planet for several years without going back to Ke'a. Part of the research was also to observe the long-term effects the world and its solar system had on humans.

The man who sat next to me said, "Everything we use here, are holo constructions and devices created locally. The food we eat is indigenous or recreated using patterns from this world. Material imports from Ke'a have been restricted to the absolute necessity and are soon going to be reduced to nothing."

"When are Ke'alians going to be allowed to colonize Kai'ila?" I asked, thinking it was a fundamental question.

The man looked at me quizzically.

"I guess you have not spent enough time on Ke'a to know that colonization has never been our prime motivation when we came here. It is a possibility that we explore, but which is only going to be considered if there is a real need for it. For now, we are gentle explorers."

"I admit, I had assumed it was planned for a near future," I said, impressed by what the man had said.

"Zuinoa told me you were going to see our head shaman. He has been at the forefront of solar and stellar research. In the same way, as shamans have been connecting with the living being that is Ke'a, Viyla has been trying to connect with the solar entity. It has been his life's work. As he had successfully established that contact was possible with our solar entity, it was a great opportunity for him to continue his exploration in a different solar system. He has recently had very promising breakthroughs that he has shared with us. You are lucky to be here at this time!"

The man's eyes were beaming the same happy anticipation that I was feeling. It was now time to meet Viyla.

We walked to the temple and entered the main hall. The inner walls were alive with aerial and satellite pictures of Kai'ila. The ceiling glittered with a sea of millions of dots of light, stars from our galaxy.

There was a big group of shamans at the center of the hall. They were holding hands and had created a live spiral that was slowly moving inward. At the core of the spiral was a tall man. He had snow white hair cascading to his shoulders.

"Gandalf the White!" I thought to myself, finally meeting the big wizard. I was mesmerized by the shaman's slow motion at the centre of the spiral. The blue dresses of the shamans were shimmering in the starlight. It's the closest thing I've ever seen that looked like a magic ritual. I thought I was seeing little shimmering fairies doing their wild dances above the group.

The hall was totally silent, bathed in the light of the stars and planets that were all around us. It was a sight I will never forget. Alma and I took each other's hands. We were part of the mysterious ritual that was unfolding. I felt my thoughts drain away into the energy vortex that had built up in the room. On impulse, I slowly walked with Alma to the blue spiral and took the last shaman's free hand.

Instantly I felt a torrent of energy that flowed from my right hand into my body, then I felt the stream pouring into the ground before rushing upwards through my spine and head and finally flowing into Alma's hand. Sparkling energy instantly filled me with light. That light filled all the space around me with the warmth and the love of life. Then it expanded outwards to the planet's surface, before diving into the vastness of interstellar space. I became a bodiless entity floating among the living light of the stars. I could sense the galaxy pulsating around me, a fiery brain, alive and conscious. The light was everything. Space and time were gone.

When I regained my sense of self, Alma was still holding my hand, but the shamans of the spiral were gone. Only one stood next to us. I knew who he was before he spoke.

"Welcome, Alma and Luke, children of Ke'a. I am Viyla."

His face radiated kindness as well as strength. I thought I could see in his eyes the light of the galaxy I had just experienced.

I saw that Alma, like me had not yet recovered her mind. We both had big wide eyes and a mouth that could not speak.

Viyla gave a warm chuckle and touched our shoulders. "I know the effect these visions have, come let's sit here." He guided us to a round of comfortable seats in a corner that was ringed by alien looking Kai'ilan flowers and leafy plants.

We sat silently for a while, then Viyla said, "What you have seen and felt is the living galaxy."

Alma said, "Yes, alive like a planet, but so incredibly bigger."

"Yes," said Viyla, "we cannot compare a planet's consciousness to a human consciousness. In the Spirit Realm, a planet's inner being is fundamentally similar to the inner being of a human, on its own path of evolution."

Viyla bent down and gently touched the ground, as he continued.

"She chose her role as this planet, that takes part in the overall evolution of this universe. She began just as you and I did, with an awareness of herself as light. Over the eons she, like we humans has evolved within that light. Here, in the manifested cosmos, her body is vast, and her inner world of perceptions, awareness and consciousness are extremely different. The speed and the nature of thoughts are literally universes apart. That's why shamans dedicate much of their lives to connect to that planetary consciousness that has a very special wisdom. Not wisdom for the immediate, but a deep wisdom for the long times."

"So stars, like planets also are sentient beings?" I asked, my mind finally getting online.

"Yes, and again, they have their conscious being and awareness with all the inner thoughts and perception on yet an entirely different level and scale."

I saw that Alma was as excited as I felt, "Viyla, from

what you said before, their inner being that is in the Spirit World is our sister-brother, equal to our inner being."

"Yes, Alma. They have just chosen a very different path, and are on a different plane of evolution. They inhabit a much bigger body and live on a vastly larger timescale. Time and space are creations in the manifest cosmos, and do not have the same importance seen from the Spirit Realm."

"And such a life is nearly unfathomable for us," I said pensively, trying to imagine life as a solar being. I thought, what would I do, all these eons? Just beaming light?

I voiced my thoughts to Viyla, and his face brightened even more.

"Great reflection, Luke. That same thought led me to interesting insights."

"Which insights?" I asked, getting excited.

"I asked myself, what kind of life I would have as a star. Even with my insights into the planetary consciousness, it is hard to imagine what such a being would do in its immense radiating body. I was radiating, giving light to my planets. I was beaming light that was traveling throughout the universe."

All of a sudden I saw it, "Light carries information!" I exclaimed, "like fiber optics!"

Viyla looked at me questioningly, "You have a quick mind, my young friend, but I'm not familiar with fiber optics."

"It's a special cable used on Earth that carries enormous amounts of information through a light beam."

"Yes, that's an excellent analogy! Live connection, communication, and information carried by light, that's how stars live their existence on a cosmic scale. Everything that they are and everything that is present in their awareness of their particular solar system is contained in the light they beam to the Universe."

Viyla made an encircling gesture and continued, "That's how they communicate with each other. That's how the whole Universe is connected on the physical plane. It is connected by its holographic nature where all particles are linked, but on a level that even we humans can potentially perceive, everything is also contained in the light."

I got goosebumps and hair standing on end from what Viyla had just said.

"And there could be a way to connect to that flow of information?" I asked.

"Yes," said Viyla, "that's exactly what we are exploring at the moment. The communication between the solar beings is extremely removed from what we humans can comprehend, but the light of these great beings contains the full spectrum of all the information of their solar system. That includes the planets and all the beings that live on them."

Alma looked at me, her eyes full of excitement. "That means, there could be a way to connect with these beings and access information about their planet."

"Yes, that is where we are, finding the key to the Universe. My scientist friends tell me that this could give us enough information to travel to the next stars without having to travel there by spaceships to establish anchor points."

Viyla stood up. "I must take my leave now, Alma and Luke, children of Ke'a. Great times are ahead of us." He opened his arms and gave us a quick embrace before he left.

We were standing there, in the temple, lit by the galactic light on the ceiling. My perception of the billions of light dots had completely changed. They were no longer cold abstractions of a reality that my mind could not comprehend, but the whole galaxy had become tangible and alive.

Alma took my hands and kissed me, then started to laugh, as if she just heard a good joke.

"What's so funny?" I asked.

"And you have seen nothing yet!" she said.

We both laughed, holding each other, feeling the magic of the moment and of the things to come.

End of book one

Your thoughts and inspirations: